# Katie Kincaid Candidate

Andrew van Aardvark

# Table of Contents

| | |
|---|---|
| Prologue | 5 |
| 1: Katie Fights | 7 |
| 2: Katie Dines | 21 |
| 3: Katie Commits | 37 |
| 4: Katie Gets Schooled | 51 |
| 5: Kate Goes to Work | 61 |
| 6: Katie Copes | 73 |
| 7: Katie's Close Call | 83 |
| 8: Katie's New Mission | 99 |
| 9: Katie's Grand Adventure | 115 |
| 10: Katie on the Carpet | 127 |
| 11: Katie in the Dumps | 141 |
| 12: Katie's Desperate | 153 |
| 13: Katie All In | 171 |
| 14: Katie Outnumbered | 181 |
| 15: Katie Endorsed | 193 |
| 16: Bon Voyage Katie | 203 |
| Appendix A: | 215 |
| Scout Courier Operations | 215 |
| Appendix B: | 217 |
| The Sand Piper, a Bird Class Scout Courier | 217 |

Copyright © 2020 NapoleonSims Publishing

www.NapoleonSims.com/publishing

All rights reserved.

Cover image credits:

Asteroids near planet | 114855385 | Sdecoret | dreamstime.com

Girl with braids | 80240505 | RimmaZaytseva | dreamstime.com

Space ship | 2693698 | Gerhard Janson | pixabay.com

Starry background | Brandon Siu | Unsplash.com

ISBN-13: 979-8-55783-303-5

# Prologue

*"Hello my heavily encrypted diary. And if any rat bastard is reading this who shouldn't be, know you're already cursed and should desist before your fate worsens.*
*The safest thing would be to not keep this diary at all.*
*Anyone who reads this before I'm gone after being duly deified is going to think I'm batshit crazy. Crazy, megalomaniacal, and not to be trusted with any important responsibility.*
*That would nip my plan in the bud.*
*I finally realized today what I want to do in life.*
*I want to be a hero.*
*Not just any old hero, a hero of at least the stature of Nelson.*
*Unlike Nelson, I don't plan to die on the day of my greatest triumph.*
*Unlike Nelson I don't want to be just a military success, I want to be one of the Great Captains, like Alexander, Caesar or Napoleon. Only I don't plan to die on the verge of my final success or have my empire disintegrate in short order.*
*Unlike Frederick the Great, Wellington or Grant, I don't intend to ride my military success to the leadership of my country only to be thwarted in my political goals, my reputation diminished, and most of the fruits of my success squandered.*
*No, I don't intend to be just any old hero, or Great Captain, I intend to be the greatest hero humanity has ever seen.*
*It's not going to be easy.*
*I'm a young girl, the daughter of asteroid miners, without great wealth or connections.*
*The Space Force is the closest thing to a military force humanity currently has. We don't yet realize as a species how badly we're going to need it, and it's quite small. The only path to its limited number of officer slots is through the Space Force Academy. Positions there are eagerly sought after.*
*It's going to take a lot of work to get one of them.*
*But I'm smart and ambitious, and I'm going to get one of those positions.*
*Do or die.*
*I'm going to be a hero.*
*The greatest ever."*

## 1: Katie Fights

Ceres wasn't Katie Kincaid's favorite place. Within Ceres, the tunnels between the Kid's Home Base's gravity rings were one of her least favorite locations.

Too bad like every Rock Rat minor she was required to spend time on Ceres enjoying Earth level gravity. Necessary to proper development, they said.

Too bad that for every kid not lucky enough to have rich parents, or at least ones with good connections, this meant long trips through the tunnels. Trips between the different gravity rings devoted to exercise, education, and living quarters as the case might be.

Too bad that budgets and official indifference meant a high ratio of children to adults. A ratio that left the older children largely unsupervised. Uncontrolled they ran riot almost to the point of being feral. Gangs and bullying were just par for the course. The tunnels were a favorite spot for ambushes and the consequent shake downs.

Katie, as she bunny hopped down the tunnels that only had Ceres' weak natural gravity, was careful to stay alert to trouble. Trouble being anyone else practically speaking.

She heard voices. Loud, hard voices for the most part. "So what do we have here?" "Jumped up Rock Rat from a nice family."

"Brown nosing wimp." "Well teacher isn't here now are they?" Mocking voices. Eager voices. Not hard to imagine what was going down.

Katie was very bright. She knew the smart thing was to back off and take another route. Whatever sort of trouble was going to take place, it'd be better if she wasn't involved.

Another different voice spoke. "Rocks to rations, you're a brave one Billy. How come it takes a half dozen of you to pick on me?"

She recognized that voice. Calvin Cromwell, a skinny young man like a lot of spacers, kept too busy with chores to do the hours of exercise needed to have an Earth normal physique. One she'd half accidentally broken the nose of when they were just toddlers starting school here. She'd felt she'd owed him ever since. Felt responsible for him.

She wasn't going to let Billy Boucher and this cronies bully him.

Too bad Billy was big and strong, and that although a likely three to one odds was better than six to one, it still wasn't good.

Worse, she'd just messed up and inadvertently qualified to apply to the Space Force Academy. She did want to go, but it was too soon. She was too young, fifteen going on sixteen soon, and the local Space Force commander's recommendation was a requirement for a successful application. Commander Tretyak was not overly fond of Katie's family or Katie herself. Getting his approval was going to be difficult. Burnishing her reputation as a troublemaker by getting into a fight wouldn't help.

Katie didn't hesitate. She pushed off hard and flew down the tunnel to trouble. Being smart was good. Having the courage to do the right thing was even more important. She'd decided she was going to be a certain sort of person. The sort with courage. Courage enough to do the right thing if need be.

She found Billy and Calvin facing off in a wider, brighter section of the tunnels, an intersection of sorts.

Billy's boys didn't see her coming. Their first hint of her approach was when she slapped tagged one of them to lose momentum before sliding feet first into a stop. She ended up beside Calvin and in front of Billy. "Hey!" the young man she'd used to slow down yelled.

Otherwise, they all just stared at her in surprise for some tens of seconds. Calvin threw her a look of apologetic thanks. Katie couldn't help thinking that might be premature.

Finally, Billy realized he needed to say something. "Well,

lookee here," he said. "If it isn't the red headed bee-atch princess of attitude and snottiness herself."

"Hi Billy, see you're being your normal suave and charming self," Katie replied.

"I was minding my own business," Billy replied to a chorus of snickers. "You should try it sometime."

"I'll remember to start tomorrow," Katie said. "Right now, me and Calvin will be on our ways. Leave you in peace."

Billy looked around at his followers and grinned. "You think so?" he asked. More snickering from his followers. It really was getting tiresome. One spoke up. Marvin Minakowski another long time acquaintance. The remora fish to the shark that Billy was.

Marvin was even skinner than Calvin, and shorter. He looked for all the varied worlds like a human rat. Pinched features, furtive body language, and even a pair of large buck teeth. In exchange for freedom from too much bullying, Marvin acted as the brains Billy didn't have. Kept him from doing anything too stupid and likely to backfire and egged him on when it was safe.

"We have business with Calvin," Marvin squeaked.

"You can leave," Billy said to Katie. "The sooner the better. We're, uumm, like knights, in shining armor," he said, looking at Marvin.

"Chivalrous," Marvin supplied.

"Yeah, that," Billy said. "No rep in beating up girls. Not even nasty skinny ones that were spawned by a pair of dirt huggers."

"You're the expert on nasty," Katie replied. "You want to hang around and trade insults or can we leave?"

"You can leave," Billy said with an ugly smile. "If you do it quickly. Like in the next ten seconds. Calvin's going to stay here and talk to us."

A chorus of half muttered "yeah"s from his followers. A couple in addition to Marvin behind him, Katie noted, and another couple behind and to the side of Katie and Calvin. Even if she'd wanted to, she couldn't grab Calvin and run.

"You're getting to be an adult, Billy," Katie said. She'd at least try sweet reason. Billy wasn't really helping himself here. Maybe he'd realize that if it was pointed out. Or at least maybe Marvin would realize it for him. "The authorities aren't going to overlook muggings and extortion the way they did bullying the other kids and stealing their lunch money. Bad boy rep isn't going to help you get a good job."

Billy laughed out loud. Most of the rest of his guys followed suit. Marvin's face pinched up some more. Katie would have sworn that was impossible.

"You really believe that shit they tried to fill us with, don't you?" he asked. "All lies, at least for anyone's not a loser. Anyone clever that has the right contacts."

"Look around, there's six of us to the two of you," Billy said. "Sure that means we can rough you up and you can't stop us, but even better it means you go running to the cops and there's six witnesses against two. And you know we're the well behaved offspring of reputable citizens, not the get of hard scrabble Rock Rats. Just guess who they're going to believe."

"You've got a bad reputation that's not getting better," Katie said. "I wouldn't be too sure of that."

"Just shows you're not as smart as you think you are," Billy said. "Brains aren't what they're cracked up to be anyways. Look, my dad is head of logistics for this heap of rock. I've got a job as soon as I want it. The other people running this place are all his friends. Even if they think his kid isn't perfect, they're not going to piss him off by hurting me. Not unless you can prove one hundred percent I've done something really bad. Guess what? That's not going to happen."

"You sure of that?" Katie said. Billy might not be a genius, but he wasn't wrong either. All she could do was hope to seed some reasonable doubt.

"Yeah, I'm sure," Billy said with an evil grin. "You know you're good at getting the right answers on exams and sucking up to the teacher. You know what you can do to someone if you've two or three helpers to hold them down?"

"Feel bad about needing so much help?" Katie ventured. She thought back to strange changes in attitudes some of the girls had developed towards Billy. Eager to avoid him if they could, but eager to please him if they couldn't. Was he a rapist too and not just a bully? A chill ran down her back that she fought to control.

Billy smirked at her. "A lot of things," he said. "Including hurting them in ways that don't show. Not much anyways."

Katie shook her head with as much sadness as she could feign. "You're a piece of work, Billy Boucher. You really don't have the guts to take on a skinny girl by yourself, do you?"

"You think you're smart and I'm stupid, don't you?" Billy asked. "You think I'm that dumb? I know your dirt eating parents run that fancy rig their rich family paid for at full Gee constantly. I know you get real milk and meat. A little bit of luck and you could break some of my bones. Leave a few bruises on me at least. Still wouldn't work out for you, but we'd all be in trouble. Not going to happen, little girl."

Katie didn't know what to say to that. Billy seemed as impervious to reason as he was to common decency. Time for action. Grabbing Calvin and using him as an anchor, she lashed out with a full body kick at where she thought the closest of Billy's bullies behind her was. She didn't hit him straight on. She clipped an arm, and he stumbled back with an oath.

Unfortunately, Calvin stumbled too and Katie lost her balance also and valuable seconds with it. The second boy to the rear moved to block their way out as the first scrambled to his feet. They weren't getting out that way.

So Katie went into a crouch and then launched herself the other way right at Billy who'd been playing spectator.

Caught him by surprise.

Right under the chin with the palm of her hand snapping his head back and knocking him right off of his feet.

She grabbed him by that head and put him in an arm lock.

She stuck the tip of one thumb right in an eye. Billy started to struggle and complain. "Stay still or you lose the eye," she hissed. Only Marvin had been close enough to maybe intervene and Calvin getting his balance had fended Marvin's half-hearted efforts off.

The rest of the gang stared, uncertain what to do.

"Any of you move and I take his eyes. Want to think what his high and mighty dad will do to any of you that cause that?" she asked.

To a boy they shook their heads and muttered no. Marvin spoke up, his high pitched warbling not doing anything for anyone's nerves. "She's crazy. Better leave her alone. We'll get her later," he said.

"Mighty Mouse is right," Katie said. "Better bugger off. Now."

One of the ones she'd tagged earlier was the first to break. Once he'd run for it, the rest followed. Marvin remained. Katie had to give him a hard glare before he scampered off too.

Once they were out of sight, she choked Billy unconscious and then bounced his head off of the tunnel floor. She was running the risk of suffocating him to death or giving him brain damage as well as a concussion. She had a hard time caring.

Calvin looked on, aghast. "We're going to prison," he said.

"No, we're not," she answered. "You really think he's going to tell the police he got beat up by a girl while trying to mug you?"

"You heard him; it'd be our word against his."

"Yeah, and if it was handled informally between his dad and the Police Chief that might be a problem," Katie admitted. "Something this serious there'd have to be a full formal investigation. Bet you all of those rats would crack. It'd only take one though."

"Guess so," Calvin agreed half heartedly helping her to her feet. "Story is going to get around just the same. Not going to help you get that recommendation from the Commander."

Katie sighed. "No it's not," she had to agree. Her application to the Academy might have just have died. "We'd better get going."

"Yeah. Thanks, Katie."

\* \* \*

Katie was exhausted, edgy, and worried.

She couldn't have just left Calvin to fend for himself, but it was trouble she hadn't needed right now.

Gravity, really centrifugal force, grabbed her as she rode the lift down to the floor her quarters were on. As usual with when pulling full Gees in a medium or short radius ring secondary forces played hob with her inner ear. Katie had seen tourists recently up from Earth or Mars puke in lifts like this one.

Katie herself was an old hand, having literally learned to deal with this sort of transition since before she could walk.

She just wished it was as easy to adjust to being a misfit girl. One who was constantly in trouble simply for standing up for herself. She'd thought when she was a kid that she'd learn to live with Ceres' bullies and bureaucrats. Her parents had assured her of as much. Sadly, as with so much of what her parents liked to think, it hadn't turned out that way.

Practically speaking as she entered her small cabin she realized she had a decision to make.

It'd be so easy to just ignore what had happened. Do nothing and hope it all passed unnoticed. Hope that the trouble went away on its own.

What she'd told Calvin was true.

Billy, Marvin, and the rest of the boys weren't going to make a formal complaint about the damage she'd done to Billy. Heavens knew what story he'd give to the medics. They weren't going to get into official trouble because of what had happened. None of them.

That didn't mean that the medics and Billy's father wouldn't realize something fishy had gone down. It'd didn't mean that Billy wouldn't be unofficially plotting his revenge. Beans to blasting caps, whatever moonshine confection Billy sold his Dad and the authorities it wasn't going to make Katie look good.

Katie thought the smartest thing for Billy would be to just leave her out of his excuse and forget the whole thing. Fat chance. She'd made him look too bad. He might omit her name with the medics and the authorities they represented, with his father his desire for to get back at her would be too strong.

He'd be putting out some story that made her look bad. A story she couldn't afford to have drifting about blackening her reputation right now.

Normally a Space Force regional commander would be happy to sponsor an Academy candidate from their area. Made them look good by association somehow. Only Katie suspected Commander Tretyak was just looking for an excuse to not sign off on Katie's application. A smear on Katie's reputation right now could destroy any chance she had of a Space Force career. Suck her life's plan right into the crapper and compost it down to its constituent components. Go straight to Jail, do not pass Go, like in that silly Monopoly game her parents so liked.

On the other hand, trying to be proactive and get out in front of the problem might backfire.

The minute she discussed what had happened with anyone, she was confessing to what she had done. You'd think defending a friend from bullies was a good thing. Authorities probably wouldn't see it that way. She'd intervened in a dispute that wasn't hers. She'd hurt Billy. She'd threatened to do much worse. However bad the whole thing made Billy and his friends look, it didn't make her look good either. Not from the point of view of officialdom. Commander Tretyak was certainly a paid-up member of officialdom.

Tretyak took the rules and himself very seriously. The joke was he must have imported a stick straight from Earth to shove up his butt. Which was all well and fine, but no joke under the circumstances.

She needed help figuring out what to do.

Sam Williamson, her friend, ex-marine, and the machinist who Katie inevitably used to make parts for her family's ship, the *Dawn*

*Threader*, was the obvious person to talk to.

As soon as she did so, she'd be putting him on the spot.

She pulled open her cleaned clothes bin as she thought about it. It was always soothing to keep her hands busy on a routine task when thinking hard about something. She folded and stored clothing as she mulled the matter.

If at some point there was a formal inquiry into the fight with Billy, they were still technically minors, but it was Ceres, and, hey, she had likely given him a concussion, anything she'd shared with Sam he'd have to share with the investigators. Couldn't plead self-incrimination or whatever like Katie and Calvin. Also, they'd take him to task for not reporting it immediately. She was sure he'd not do that.

Sam wasn't a fan of confusing the authorities with information they didn't need.

So yeah, she'd be putting him on the spot.

Only she knew he'd want her to.

So she would.

She'd tell Sam and ask him for advice.

\* \* \*

Calvin Cromwell was embarrassed. Worried and lovesick, too.

It made him immensely glad that nobody was home in the family's suite of apartments to greet him.

He loved his family. Treasured them as they treasured him.

When he thought of Billy's family, just his harsh busy father, or even Katie's, her two parents lost in each other to the exclusion of the rest of the world, he felt very lucky.

Just the same, he was glad none of them were home to greet him and ask him what had happened. He was glad he'd not been beaten to an inch of his life by Billy and his hangers on. Wh wouldn't be?

He was even more embarrassed at being rescued by Katie of all people. He wasn't sure he'd rather not have been beaten black and blue.

Stars help him if one of his older sisters cottoned on to how he felt about Katie. He'd never hear the end of it.

He'd known Katie since they were pre-school kids.

They weren't kids anymore. He'd become acutely aware of that. Katie, not so much.

As far as Calvin could tell growing older for Katie meant thinking about advanced education options. Specifically, what school she planned to go away to. Though in truth, she'd seemed to set her sights on the Space Force Academy back on Earth. Calvin desperately wanted to tell her she didn't need to think about going away at all, but he hadn't figured out how to do that.

Katie bubbled with plans. Most of them didn't seem very realistic to Calvin, but that didn't mean he wanted to bust her bubble. No, he didn't want to do anything to hurt her feelings.

He'd been hoping his crush on her was a passing phase.

He'd been thinking that maybe they could be merely the friends she thought they were.

That didn't seem to be working. A fact the incident with Billy as problematic as it was in its own right had brought home to him.

Regards Billy and his bully boys, Katie seemed to think it wasn't an issue. So carry on, and act like it had never happened. He could do that.

Carry on ignoring his feelings for the girl. He couldn't do that.

Should he tell straight up how he felt and ask her indulgence?

Or should he maybe prepare the ground some before forcing her to make a decision? Stars knew she could make decisions. Unfortunately, she had a ruthlessly pragmatic streak and could be harsh as well as decisive.

Maybe he should fess up and show some guts, but he'd rather take the indirect approach.

He'd start to woo her.

With luck, she'd notice and approve at some point.

\* \* \*

Commander Yuri Tretyak, Space Force commander of Ceres and district, was a happy, if not chipper man. Not as much as usual right now.

Usually, he knew what to do and had no qualms or doubts about doing it.

He looked around his spartan office. He liked it that way; free of distractions and clutter. Usually. Right now, some object capable of inspiring a start on a thought about how to solve his current dilemma would have been nice.

Usually, he didn't feel any great need of inspiration. Usually, he had rules for what to do. Usually, if those rules should clash, which the heavens around knew they sometimes did, he knew which ones to prioritize.

He could almost wish that the Academy didn't insist on having field commanders involved in their recruitment process. Only that would have been an abdication of responsibility. Yuri Tretyak did not dodge his responsibilities.

Sitting on his desk, his virtual desk, not the scarred heavy metal object propping up the screen holding it, he had a file. A file that had just been forwarded by the SFHQ Induction and Training section. A regional commander wore a variety of hats, and one of those hats was regional head of recruitment.

For the bulk of recruitment in the district, this was not a heavy burden. Most of it was of enlisted spacers and the Commander delegated the day-to-day responsibility to a senior NCO. Said NCO who supervised a small team of more junior NCOs.

Occasionally Yuri would check recruiting reports for anomalies and trends or do the rounds to see morale was fine. At regular intervals, he'd preside at small signing in ceremonies. He say a few solemn words. Look on as recruits pledged themselves to their new lives. Give a few more grave words of optimistic welcome. He took these responsibilities seriously, but they weren't arduous or problematic.

He had direct responsibility for the recruitment of officer candidates from the district, too. In practice, that wasn't much of a problem either. There were almost never any viable candidates. Only a tiny fraction of humanity's billions ever became Space Force officers. There were barely a thousand of them. The Academy only needed to have a very small intake of candidates. At most a couple of dozen candidates a year. That even though most of the graduates of the Space Force Academy returned to civilian life after their obligatory four years of service.

It meant brutally high academic standards. In most years, no one from the district qualified.

In most years, he'd have been happy someone had. Not in this case.

In this case, he knew the young lady in question altogether too well. Worse, he knew her family too well. They were a continuing blot on his existence as far as he was concerned. Katherine Anne Kincaid herself was a loose cannon. Energetic, dangerous, and out of control. Not somebody he wanted in the Space Force. Not somebody he wanted to be on record as having recommended for the Academy.

He did feel bad about it. As irritating and worrisome as the girl was, he couldn't blame her for being who she was. He didn't doubt if her parents had stayed on Earth where they belonged and fulfilled the social obligations they'd fled that it'd be different. She'd have a bright future in front of her. Perhaps even one at the Academy.

Only they hadn't and she didn't. She was largely unsocialized, and the little socialization she'd had was all the wrong sort.

He couldn't refuse to endorse her candidacy without reason. The Academy had been under heavy political fire about its narrow source of recruitment. A few very powerful and rich families on Earth dominated the annual intake. Worse, there was a definite gender unbalance. The Admissions Board would jump all over the chance to add a Belter girl to the mix.

It'd be highly irregular if he failed to endorse Kincaid girl, but she was admitted anyways. It wasn't beyond possible. Not if he didn't give convincing reasons for not endorsing her. They might put his lack of endorsement down to personal animus. In any event, it could be career limiting. He was already a little over due for his next promotion.

He needed good, solid reasons he could put into writing. That he thought she'd be a bad fit wasn't good enough.

It was true. She was too young, only fifteen. Most of the other cadets would be eighteen. Three years was a lot at that age.

She tested very well on technical knowledge. Only she didn't have the networking or social skills most candidates did. So she'd be a bad fit. It didn't matter.

The Admissions Board couldn't, for political reasons, admit that fit mattered. The Academy was in good part a chance for the children of a small elite to build their personal networks while still young. It wasn't something they were eager to tell the voters. It wasn't something they could admit. Usually, that wasn't a problem.

Most Belters would have failed on the physical criteria. Most of them could handle light duties under one Gee for a short time. The sort of hard competitive physical training the cadets were subjected to on the Earth surface part of the campus was not something they could be expected to succeed at. Unfortunately, the Commander knew Kincaid was an exception. With a large expensive survey ship, one bigger than most Rock Rat mining rigs, they had a large full Gee gravity ring and being from Earth originally they used it. The Commander had also heard informally that ex-Chief Williamson, who the girl apparently had some sort of crush on, was including her in the Gee-plus marine training regime he still maintained. Once a marine always a marine. The Kincaid girl was fit as well as smart.

Perhaps she was smart enough to see with a little encouragement that the Academy wasn't for her. If she failed to accept the invitation, the Academy had sent her to apply, then his problem would go away. Only he knew the girl was stubborn as well as fit and smart. She came by it honestly, he had to admit. Her parents were the same way. Why a young Rock Rat girl had set her heart ongoing to the Academy, he didn't know. Probably her idolization of Williamson had something to do with it. In any event, she had. It was a widely known fact. He'd try talking to her, but he didn't hold out much hope she'd change her mind.

It was intensely frustrating. You'd think a fit, smart, and determined candidate would be exactly what the Space Force wanted. Only he knew in his heart and guts it wasn't true. She'd be a disaster. A worse disaster if she made it into the Academy and somehow graduated to become a Space Force officer.

Her aggressive character coupled with her almost complete lack of socialization to large groups and teams made her a dangerously poor fit for the real Space Force. The real Space Force wasn't the daring fighting force of stalwart heroes that one saw in the vids.

The real Space Force was in the main a stodgy bureaucracy that existed to enforce safety rules. Its main tool was the stifling degree of paperwork it required before allowing anyone to do anything in space.

Its enforcement arm was basically a collection of auditors, custom officers, and traffic cops.

The traffic cops in particular would bridle to hear themselves called that, but that was what they in truth were.

The only things that kept a different image in being were speculative fiction works. They leveraged off the existence of actual aliens in the solar system. Also the fact that the aliens wouldn't reveal any significant details about the wider galaxy. In particular they were mum about its political geography. Left the fiction writers free to speculate it was a version of the seventeenth century Spanish Main. Pirates, men of war, and plenty of colorful action. It made for great fiction.

The Commander doubted it had much relation to reality.

He suspected humanity was more like Pacific islanders on a small island in the nineteenth century. Only the Star Rats had assured humanity they didn't need to worry about being decimated by epidemic disease. Which was a relief. But in any case he suspected any aliens out there would look on the ships of the Space Force much as the nineteenth century Europeans had looked upon the war canoes of the Polynesians. If they thought of them at all, it wouldn't be to factor them into the naval balance of power. Once true galactic contact was made, it was going to be careful diplomacy that was needed, not derring-do.

He suspected very strongly that displays of aggressiveness would be throughly punished.

Not at all the right setting for the aggressive, but not very diplomatic Katie Kincaid.

So he'd work hard to reveal these facts to both the Admissions Board and Kincaid herself, and then hopefully once he refused his endorsement it'd be clear it was the correct decision.

## 2: Katie Dines


Sam sometimes regretted not having kids of his own.

Sometimes he didn't.

Sometimes he thought it was just as well he hadn't. Even the best kids could be a handful. You tried to teach them. You tried to keep them safe and watch out for them. Still they'd get into trouble. You couldn't protect them. Not from themselves, and not from the world.

Katie Kincaid was the daughter Sam had never had. He loved her as much as he could of any daughter he was the actual father of.

Right now she was seated on a stool next to his workbench while he refurbished a fuel injector off of a mining rig. He could tell she was working up the nerve to tell him about the latest trouble she'd gotten herself into.

"Out with it," he said.

"Coming back from class in the tunnels found Billy Boucher and his gang picking on Calvin."

"And?"

"There were six of them."

Sam gave Katie a hard look she knew when she was making excuses.

She returned a lop-sided grin. She also knew Sam didn't have the heart to be truly angry at her. He'd told her himself in the course of multiple stories that hesitating and holding back when threatened and out numbered was the worst thing to do. That the predators would surround you, edge in, and finally take you down.

"You hurt some of them?"

"Knocked Billy out. Probably gave him a concussion."

"He'll be seeing a medic then."

"Have to."

"So no pretending it didn't happen. It's not over," Sam summarized.

"I guess not," Katie admitted. "Sam, I got an invitation to the Academy today. I think I aced some of the standard tests. I didn't expect this. Those tests were hard."

Sam was an ex-Chief in the marines. He had hard, implacable, and impassive down to an art. On the other hand, Katie wasn't one of his jarheads. Too bad maybe it'd be easier to knock some sense into her if she was. He allowed himself a small sigh. "Billy's not likely to make a formal complaint," he said. "He will tell his father something. His dad's pals with Commander Tretyak. You're worried that whatever Billy's story is, it won't incline the Commander to endorsing your application. Correct?"

"That's right," Katie replied. "What do I do?"

"First off, we do a post mortem," Sam said. "Figure out where you went wrong."

Katie frowned at that. She quite obviously didn't accept she'd done anything wrong at all. The girl's moral certitude was disconcerting at times. It also made for a lot of trouble.

"You understand they likely wouldn't have done Calvin any visible let alone permanent harm, right?" Sam asked.

"They're snakes who don't want to be caught," Katie replied, practically spitting.

"Yes, and somebody should rein them in sometime," Sam said. "But it didn't have to be you right then. Your intentions may have been good, but it's results that count."

"So, I should have let them bully Calvin?"

"By intervening you upped the ante," Sam replied. "You increased the odds Calvin was going to get seriously hurt and added in the chance you'd get seriously hurt yourself."

"Well, we didn't," Katie replied. "Proof's in the pudding," she added defiantly. Sam knew he should knock that attitude down, that it was doing her no good. Only he couldn't. She reminded him of a lion cub he'd seen on a nature show whacking his father, King of all he surveyed, on the nose. The cub had no clue of the risks it was running. It'd been insufferably cute, and somehow admirable, for all of that. The girl probably had no idea what the saying meant. Pudding was likely just another label for a type of goop that came out of ration tubes for her.

"But somebody did get hurt, didn't he?" Sam said.

"Billy deserved it."

"Really? Who appointed you judge, jury, and executioner?"

She crossed her arms and glared back at him. "My own conscience," she said.

Sam did suppress his sigh this time. She was quoting him back to himself. "What works in the jungle, or the savanna, or, the good Lord help us, the streets of the inner cities back on Earth doesn't necessarily work on Ceres," he said. "People here live in each other's pockets. They try to be civilized, or at least to maintain the appearance of it."

"So we abandon all principle for the sake of appearances?"

"That's politics. Sometimes it goes too far, but if large numbers of different people want to get along they have to make compromises."

"Bottom line; no way I'm ever abandoning a friend," Katie declared.

"I'm not knocking the sentiment," Sam said. "Sometimes you have to think of the longer-term consequences of your actions though. You haven't stopped Billy's bullying, just made him look like a victim and maybe killed your chances of ever getting into the Academy. People problems aren't like engineering problems they're a lot less clear, much messier and less certain. You have to consider the optics of what you do as well as the immediate results."

Katie visibly struggled with herself. Arms crossed, hunched over, head down but a scowl still visible. Sam figured she'd have to learn to hide her feelings better than that, but that was a lesson for another day. The girl had enough on her plate for today. "Yo really think so?" she finally said.

"I do."

"I threatened to gouge his eye out if they didn't back off," she said.

"Which I imagine was effective at the time," Sam said. "Suppose Billy mightn't mention that to his Dad, and his Dad might not pass it on to Tretyak, but I wouldn't bet on it. I imagine they'll mention it and use it to suggest you're an untamed animal. A vicious animal that's good at math, but an animal all the same. Not a person fit for civilized society, let alone one that should be allowed any power. You see the problem."

"Damned mudballers think that of all of us Rock Rats," Katie said with heat. "They don't think we're really human."

"It's neither here, nor there. Where ever you go you're going to find prejudice," Sam said. "People aren't really meant to live in anything bigger than small groups. It takes imagination and civilization both to get them to treat people they don't know the same as those they do, as other people rather than threatening alien animals that look a little similar."

"You're exaggerating," Katie said. Arms still crossed, but with skepticism in her eyes, and not defensive anger on her face any longer.

"I'm afraid not," Sam said. "It's not something people like to admit to, but did you know that on parts of Earth there's people that would consider me a dangerous sub-human just because my skin is a lot darker than theirs?"

"Didn't they solve that with the American Civil War?" Katie asked.

"Not exactly," Sam said smiling. The extent of racism and its persistence were apparently a complete mystery to Katie, and in a way he supposed that was progress.

"Anyhow they had us outnumbered, and they were talking about how they could hurt us both in ways that wouldn't show," Katie said. "They said it'd be our word against theirs and no one would believe us."

"I wasn't there," Sam admitted. "Perhaps it was the best you could do, but think on it. Could you have done better? Twisted his arm rather than slamming him in the head and threatening to gouge his eye out?"

"I'm not sure," Katie said. "Didn't have much time to think then, but even now I'm not sure."

"That's fair," Sam said. "Sometimes there's no way of knowing. Not for sure, if you're honest. Only, try to think as much as you can afford about these things. Fights have consequences. Maybe limited time right at the moment, but before if you can."

"Not planning, is planning to fail," Katie interjected. Quoting himself at himself again.

"And 'Prior Planning Prevents Piss Poor Performance'", Sam elaborated. "Nice that you listen sometimes. As I was about to say, and afterwards too if you can. Don't agonize, but do try and learn. Please, Katie."

Katie's expression softened at his plead. "I'll try. I promise," she said.

"It's all I can ask," Sam said. "Let's move on. Billy and his boys are going to be spreading rumors. His Dad too, though Guy will be a lot more subtle about it."

"Mr. Boucher is a friend of the Commander's," Katie said in a desolate tone.

"Yeah, but one thing you can say about Yuri Tretyak, he might have too much starch in his uniform, but he genuinely tries to stay on the straight and narrow," Sam said. "He's not going to give credence to unsubstantiated innuendo even from someone he thinks of as a friend."

"He's not?"

"No, he'll consciously try to be fair," Sam said. "Not saying it won't influence him especially if you don't have a different better version of events to put out yourself."

"Thing is," Katie said, perhaps blushing a little. She was so fair it seemed she was always blushing. "Is that I don't know what story they're going to put out, and the full blunt truth doesn't really look that good for me."

Sam didn't answer. He'd let her figure it out for herself.

"I horned in on a dispute that wasn't mine, then I injured Billy, and badly, and I threatened to do much worse," Katie said. "That doesn't look good. Sure, they had us outnumbered, and were set up to lay a beating on us. Only I attacked first and won. People'll have to think it wasn't that one sided."

Sam just nodded. "Not much to be done for it," he said. "Anyone asks questions answer honestly without trying to shade it or elaborate. If you can't make it better at least don't make it worse."

"Still isn't going to look good, is it?" Katie said. "Was already a stretch expecting the Commander's endorsement. He hates me, and he hates my family. Don't know why, this place wouldn't be half so profitable without us, but he does. Hoped if I kept my nose clean and didn't provoke him he'd go along just to avoid a fuss. Not a man that likes fuss much."

"Which answers your question," Sam said. "Neat, tidy, and no fuss is not how I'd describe Dave and Allie."

"No, Murphy knows, Mom and Dad aren't naturally neat and tidy," Katie said. "They worry me sick at times."

"I'm sure you've never forgotten to properly stow a tool," Sam said, "but I don't think you can claim you never create a fuss."

Katie frowned. "If people would simply do things right, I'd never say anything."

"But they don't and you do, and it ruffles feathers," Sam said.

"So what do I do?" Katie asked again.

"You deal with the problem straight on," Sam said.

"I march into the Commander's office and tell him he's going to endorse me?" Katie asked.

"I think it'd work better to be a little more circumspect than that," Sam answered. "Ask him what his objections are and what you can do to alleviate them."

"Just like that."

"Just so."

"It's not going to be easy."

"No. He'll go through the motions but he'll ask you to do things you won't like and aren't good at. Which are plain hard. You'll have to suck it up, girl."

"I'll think of it as a test of courage," she answered.

*  *  *

Katie had always found sitting still for the regular family meals excruciatingly painful. She liked to be moving. Always.

This was as true for remote virtual family meals as much as it was for the in person we're all sitting around the same table ones. More so even as when getting together remotely to eat at the same time her parents felt obligated to pay her more direct attention.

Her parents were lovable and caring. They wanted her to be happy. They were always pleasant and courteous and infinitely patient. They were also completely clueless goofballs. In the nicest possible way, she didn't agree with them about much of anything. Being her parents, they of course got their way whenever that disagreement came to a head. Hence her current presence on Ceres. Hence her discomfort with their attention.

She had to tell them about the invitation to the Academy. She needed to convince them to let her go. For the next couple of years at least she'd need their permission to do so. Unfortunately they weren't fans of Earth or the Academy.

She'd hoped to slip it into the conversation in a careful

controlled way and leave them on a back foot. They didn't like to be negative, sometimes she could use that. It'd be harder if they were actively engaged and paying attention.

She placed her meal on her desk in front of her screen and made the connection to the *Dawn Threader*.

"Hi, Mom. Hi, Dad," she said when her parents and the food in front of them appeared on the screen. She hoped they were being careful about not generating too many crumbs when she wasn't there to clean up after them.

"Hi, dear," her mother said. "How are your studies going?"

Her father looked on expectantly. Katie had really hoped they'd open by telling her how their day had been going. Time to bite the bullet. "Wonderful news!" she exclaimed with all the chipper, buoyant charm she could muster. "I've got an invitation to apply to the Space Force Academy. I must have done really well on the standardized tests. Isn't it great?"

Her mother's smile became forced. Her father failed to manage that much. He looked despondent. "You're still only fifteen, dear," her mother said. "Most of the new cadets start at the Academy when they're eighteen. It's only a few years, but that's a lot at your age. I think it might be better to wait."

"Mom, the Academy rarely issues multiple invitations to the same candidate," Katie replied. She'd been dreading this conversation. Hadn't stopped her thinking it through. "Almost wish hadn't done so well on the exams, but this might be my last and only chance. We can't risk missing it."

"I see, dear," her mother replied.

"You know, Katie," her father said. "We had friends and family go to the Academy. It's not free form like school on Ceres or home schooling here on the *Dawn Threader*. It's very regimented. Apparently, they schedule every minute of your day and try to control every aspect of your life. Very rigid and militaristic about it from what I've heard."

"Yes, dear," her mother said taking up the point. "You know that at heart you're a free spirit like us. You wouldn't fit in there at all."

"I can be very disciplined when I want to," Katie insisted. "Anyhow it's not because I think it'll be easy that want to go there, it's exactly because I think it'll be hard. I want the challenge."

"Well, that's admirable, dear," her mother said. Katie tried not to be annoyed at what seemed a condescending tone to her. "But," her mother continued, "you might feel differently after you've been there a while. In any case, we need you here. You're so good at maintenance and engineering. Besides, this one in two watch schedule leaves us no time for ourselves or even each other. As a temporary thing that's acceptable, but not permanently."

Katie completely agreed with her mother that running the *Dawn Threader* with only two watchkeepers wasn't sustainable. She also didn't doubt a back list of maintenance tasks were building up. Only she didn't plan to spend her whole life babysitting her parents, no matter how adorable and needy they were. "You should have hired outside crew years ago, Mom," she said.

"We don't want crew," her mother replied. "We came out her to get away from other people. To be practical it'd cut into our profits. Make it hard to profit at all."

"Mom, however much you might want it, I can't stay in the nest forever," Katie retorted. "You need outside crew. Always have. Commander Tretyak was always right about that. We've been running short handed and at a much slower operational pace than we could. A faster survey pace would mean more revenue and more than pay for the extra crew. Besides, the *Dawn Threader* isn't brand new any more, you need a dedicated engineer. Older ships require more tender loving care."

"Well, we've tried to give you room to do your own thing," her mother said. Her father nodded in agreement beside her. "But we've always hoped you'd find a nice boy like Calvin, say, and stay in the Belt with us. Inherit the ship when we're too old to work. Hoped you'd have kids of your own to take up the slack by then."

Katie took a breath, and tried not to let her feelings show on her face. Her mother's dream was Katie's worst nightmare. Katie had nothing against Calvin, but that didn't mean she wanted to settle down and have kids with him. All the while living in close quarters with her parents. She could see doing it. She most certainly did not want to. She didn't think it was fair of her parents to try and make her do it. "Not going to happen, Mother," she said. Much colder and more determined than she'd intended.

Her mother looked shocked.

"I'm sorry, Mom," Katie said. "I want a chance to decide my own life. I'll keep what you've said in mind, but I want this chance to go to the Academy. You have the legal right to prevent me from going now, and probably ever. You do that and I'll leave in a couple of years anyways."

"You can't mean that, dear," her mother said. Her father laid a hand on her mother's shoulder and looked at Katie with a distressed expression, but said nothing out loud.

"I'm sorry, Mom," Katie replied. "I really am, but I do mean that. You can accept this in good grace, or we can have the sort of break you and Dad made with your own parents. I don't think any of us want that."

"No, dear. Your father and I don't want that." She sighed. "Being stubborn must run in the family. Both families. I can't see Commander Tretyak endorsing your application anyways. Never thought I'd agree with Tretyak on something. We've got no need to fight and generate hard feelings."

"Please, Mom," Katie asked. "Don't do anything to make this harder."

"Katie, me and your mom will give you your head," her father said finally speaking up. "We won't pressure you. We won't do anything to further antagonize Tretyak. If he endorses your application and it's accepted we'll give permission for you to go to the Academy. Promise. Okay?"

"Thanks, Dad."

"Good, let's forget all this for the time being and try to enjoy the rest of our meal," he replied.

Which they did. Eating and talking pleasantly about things none of them really cared about much. They all ignored the gloomy elephant sharing their video session.

Katie wondered if things would ever be the same again.

\* \* \*

Katie had little trouble finding Commander Tretyak's office, though it didn't stand out in any way.

Say whatever you wanted about the man, he didn't give himself airs. She'd heard it said he used his bare bones approach to everything as a kind of intimidation. That he set out to present himself as a distillation of duty and self sacrifice without weakness or anything in the way of self interest, only duty. The man was intimidating. Katie was willing to believe it wasn't deliberate, that it was simply who he was.

He was too consistent and too lacking in ostentatious flair for her to think otherwise. Katie had set herself on a course to embody a few simple, but difficult to follow, principles. She was willing to sacrifice everything to her goals. She thought she could understand someone who'd chosen to do the same.

So Tretyak not having a fancy receptionist in a fancy waiting room, or anything that made his place of work stand out from anyone else's didn't surprise her. She went down the corridor of the block of offices for the local Space Force HQ the directory outside on the main concourse had indicated and had no trouble finding the office labeled with the Commander's name.

She was impressed with the lack of pretense. She was even more impressed with the speed with which the Commander had made time for her when she'd called that morning. He'd answered the call himself, listened to her, and asked if first thing after lunch was good. No fuss, no muss, right to the point. She liked that. Her parents had never been impressed with Commander Tretyak. She was having doubts about their judgment in that regard.

Anyhow enough wool gathering. No getting cold feet now. She knocked on the door.

"Come in," came a man's voice.

She opened the door and marched in.

Commander Tretyak was seated at his desk, scribbling away at a pad with a stylus. He didn't look up or otherwise acknowledge her.

Katie wondered what she was supposed to do. This smelled like a test.

She looked about. There were no plants or paintings on the wall. Nothing on the walls, in fact. All the officers in the vids had what Sam called "I-love-me" walls. Not Tretyak. Interesting. Also interesting was an empty chair in front of Tretyak's desk. Another two chairs sat by a small table and a refreshments cart. Otherwise, the office was barren of anything not related to work. Was she supposed to choose a chair to sit in?

Was that the test? No, this was a test of patience and self discipline. She waited just standing calmly and quietly.

After a few minutes that seemed longer, the Commander looked up and smiled slightly. Maybe she'd passed. "Would you like coffee, tea, juice?" he asked.

"Tea would be fine," Katie replied. Her mother was a tea drinker and Katie preferred it, as she suspected the Commander did.

Commander Tretyak stood up and gestured towards the chairs and small table. "Take a seat," he said. "You don't prefer coffee or cola? Most native Belters seem to."

"No, Mom likes tea and I learned it from her," Katie replied as she moved to sit herself down. "Coffee is a kick in the brain cells, but tea is more relaxing. More civilized."

His lips twitched as he sat down. "That's one thing we agree on then," he said. "I'm somewhat surprised."

"You're very different people, I think. Though I don't know you well that much is apparent," Katie said.

"Yes," the Commander agreed, "there's a lot we don't agree on. But we're not here to talk about your parents, are we? We're here to talk about you and your invitation to the Academy, yes?"

"That's right," Katie said. "I suspect given the friction between you and my parents and what you've likely heard about me that you might be reluctant to endorse my application. Is that right?"

The Commander reaching over to the refreshments cart assembled plain, but fine, china on the little table and finally poured them both some steaming hot tea. "Milk, Sugar?" he asked.

"Just milk," Katie answered.

He added it and answered her question as she took a sip. "You're not mistaken."

"I'm curious as to why," Katie said, trying for a detached tone. "Mostly, I'd like to know what I can do to assuage your concerns."

"Right to the point. I like that," he replied. "I don't think you've got the background to fit in at the Academy and succeed there. If by some miracle you were able to scrape through, I think you'd be a poor fit to the Space Force. I don't think your candidacy is in the interests of the Space Force. I don't think it's in yours either if I may presume."

"For clarity's sake may I presume that the problem's not with my academics, or whether I'm physically up to it, or my individual competence?" Katie asked.

"Formally speaking you're academically outstanding," the Commander replied. "You greatly exceed the standard, the already high standard, set by the Admissions Board. I think you've focused far too narrowly on scientific and technical subjects. Unlike most Belters, I think you're up to the physical demands of the Academy, and as an individual you seem quite competent, especially at solving purely technical problems."

"Thank you," Katie said. "So you think my education has been too narrowly technical and you doubt my ability to work in groups." Katie knew he thought her parents were irresponsible and disrespectful of authority, and she suspected he thought she was the same. He doubtless had doubts about her character too, but she didn't want to be the one to open that can of worms.

The Commander pursed his lips and paused for a few seconds. He seemed to be suppressing a sigh. "Correct on both counts," he said slowly, "but it's not quite that simple. The fact that you were brought up practically alone except for your parents with very limited time dealing with other people except during the mandatory time here on Ceres is a major issue. It means you just don't have the experience dealing with other people almost every other person your age has had."

"And when I have dealt them I've been a little rough around the edges, right?"

The Commander coughed. It seemed she'd amused him. Once again she was surprised how much she liked the man even though he was standing between her and what she wanted. "Miss Kincaid," he said. "I've been in this post far too long. It doesn't suggest good things about my career. I've been on Ceres for most of your life, and everybody here always knew when you were in residence."

"Oh," Katie said. She hadn't realized that.

"You always got into trouble or clashed with someone in ways that entertained the whole base. Generally harmless and you always had the best excuses for your behavior, but if you were here there was fuss and controversy. You were the terror of your teachers. Nobody likes being made to look like an idiot by one of their students."

"I never meant to cause trouble," Katie said. If she was honest, she'd have to admit she never went out of her way to avoid it either, but she wasn't actually setting out to cause it.

"And yet it always found you," the Commander said. "Am I wrong?"

"No, sir," she said. "I know I'm stronger at tech than at soft skills, but I am determined to make that up."

"That's good," the Commander said, "it will serve you well later in life. Right now no matter how intelligent and determined you are I don't think you can fake it. I think you'd need to internalize a whole different set of beliefs about the world and I'm not sure you can do that."

"Sir, it's not my fault I've always been an outsider and don't know all the unwritten and unspoken rules everyone else knows," she said. "Where the rules are clear, I've always been very careful to follow them to the letter."

"I know I've reviewed your file carefully," the Commander said. He sighed. "You could be a fine lawyer if you wanted to be."

Katie shivered. "My parents have never spoken well of lawyers," she said. "They've always said one of the best things about the Belt is that there are so few lawyers."

The Commander's lips quirked. "Yet something else we agree on," he said. "This has been an educational talk, if nothing else."

"Yes, sir."

"Miss Kincaid," the Commander said, "I do feel bad about not believing I should endorse your candidacy. Whatever your personal imperfections, it's mostly not your fault. Your upbringing was in your parents' hands. I know you're smarter and more knowledgeable than many adults but you lacked, and still lack, the experience to know what's important to learn. It was your parents' job to provide you guidance. For someone who was going to spend the rest of their life on a ship in the Belt, maybe you got an adequate education."

"Belters are better at math than any other group in the Solar System," Katie said. It was a matter of local civic pride.

"They're good at solving technical problems, navigating, and doing accounting," the Commander said.

Katie wasn't sure if that was agreement or not.

"I shouldn't be so blunt about airing the Space Force's dirty laundry," the Commander said, "but I think we owe you. The Space Force Academy's formal admissions requirements have been heavily distorted by political forces."

"Meaning what, sir?" Katie asked. She hoped she wasn't being curt. She did need more of those social skills he was talking about.

"Meaning that they're formulated to be fair and open to everyone and are based solely on tests that can be objectively scored."

"That's good, isn't it?"

"The vast majority of the Solar System's voting population would like to think so," the Commander said dryly. "The Admissions Board wants the optics of being fair. Unfortunately, trust me on this, they don't match what's needed to succeed at the Academy. Even if you were a much better fit personally, you wouldn't get a fair shake there. You're not from one of the right Earth families. You haven't gone to the right schools."

"That's not fair," Katie protested.

"No, it's not," the Commander. "It's the truth, but I can't say it publicly, and it won't do you any good to protest it, either. Not your fault, but your inevitable failure at the Academy would be bad for you, and it'd also set back hopes of widening the diversity in the Space Force's officer body."

"Sir," Katie said, "this might all be true. I'm not qualified to know. I know that. I don't want to give up just because you've given me a discouraging talk."

"I see."

"Please, sir. Give me a chance to do something that will show I can learn to fit in better."

"I have something," the Commander said. "Your reputation for being determined matches that for being a trouble maker." He smiled grimly. "You won't like it. It won't be easy. It's really a softball pitch just the same."

"Yes, sir," Katie said. "Anything."

"Miss Ping," the Commander said.

Katie had heard of her. The dragon lady, the single most feared teacher on Ceres. Her classes mandatory for anyone taking the Earth Equivalency Baccalaureate. Katie had followed the Advanced Belter course of study with a bunch of Advanced Placement courses in math, the sciences, and engineering. She'd had Mr. Malik's history course on the settlement of the Solar System as both her single mandatory history course and her writing one to boot. He was a dear. Everyone's favorite teacher. His stories made his subject matter come to life, even if they did tend to drift a little off topic from time to time. He was everything Ping was not.

"Yes, sir."

"She's been convinced to do a special condensed version of her regular course that starts soon," the Commander said. "Rather like what we called a summer course back on Earth. All day every day for six weeks. Mostly for students who need it, but have already failed it once or twice."

Katie blinked. Miss Ping was not noted for compromising and her full length course was already infamous for the dense amount of detail she required her students to master. "Convinced, sir?" Katie asked. "Not much in the way seasons out here," she added for no good reason. She realized she wasn't fully parsing what he was trying to say.

"She was bitterly opposed to the idea," the Commander said. "Again not a point for public consumption. She believes her course is already too short. There are, however, important people whose children won't be able to go to university on Earth this Fall without passing it. Earth still runs by the seasons in its northern hemisphere. My suspicion is she'll happily flunk the whole class. Lady is an institution and has the letter of the law on her side.

"You want me to take this course?"

"Yes, and to get good marks and a favorable report from Miss Ping herself," the Commander said. "If you manage that, I'll review my position on endorsing your application to the Academy in the light of it."

"I'll sign up immediately, sir."

"Very well. I think we're done here. Good Luck, Miss Kincaid."

## 3: Katie Commits

Commander Yuri Tretyak hit the punching bag with every ounce of strength he could muster. He was frustrated and unhappy. Better to take that out on a punching bag preserving his upper body strength than some other way. So as soon as the Kincaid girl had left, he'd scheduled an extra exercise session in at the end of his afternoon.

You had to set priorities. You had to take care of yourself. You had to keep your saw sharp as the adage went.

Also, he thought better when his blood was up and moving.

Katie Kincaid had been something of a surprise. He'd seen her around and he'd thought he knew her through her reputation and records. They hadn't done her justice. The girl wasn't a mere savant. She wasn't just book and exam smart. She had a sharp aware intelligence that shone through her every word. He could see how many people might be intimidated by that and resent the fact of it. Also gave every indication of being pragmatic and determined both. He'd rather liked her. Which was unfortunate.

He was tempted to give her a minimal pro forma endorsement and let events take their course.

It'd be a mischievous and irresponsible course of action.

He grabbed the wildly swinging punching bag and held it still. He punched it again. Quick, hard jabs in fast succession. It helped some.

For all that his personal sympathy for the young woman had increased, he'd also substantially increased his perception that she'd be a disruptive influence both at the Academy and later in the Space Force.

He'd been very impressed by her indeed.

He'd thought she'd likely embarrass both herself and him at the Academy given the chance.

He now thought she had a lot more potential than that.

He now thought she had it in her to do genuine damage.

He suspected she might actually have it in her to fake being the epitome of what a Space Force officer ought to be. That she might be able to fill the gaps in her education. That despite being a social misfit, she might be able to finesse that somehow. He couldn't imagine how. That didn't mean a capable young woman intensely focused on the issue wouldn't find some workaround. Belters were nothing if not adaptively innovative.

Sadly, that'd likely only reinforce an internal conviction that she knew best. At some point in an important crisis, what the Space Force thought was right and what Katie Kincaid thought was right wasn't going to be the same. She'd do what she thought was right.

Given her inexperienced arrogance who knew what damage that'd do.

It couldn't be risked.

Not much immediate action was required. He'd talk to Miss Ping tell her to keep an eye out. He obviously needed to dig into the history of her and her family more deeply.

Fortunately, the young woman's candidacy allowed him to do so without all the privacy constraints such research would normally face.

He'd been blinded by his dislike of her family to a degree. He didn't think that altered the basic facts of the matter.

Eventually it'd be obvious to everyone it wasn't right she should go to the Academy.

That she should never be allowed to exercise command in the Space Force.

\* \* \*

Calvin looked around the best restaurant on Ceres he could almost afford to buy dinner at. It was a cozy imitation of a twentieth century diner back on Earth. It had burgers, fries, milkshakes, and pizzas that were outright addictive. Katie should be arriving soon.

There she was. Practically bouncing into the diner even though it was at close to full gravity. She waved at him with a big grin.

It pierced his heart with affection. An affection he hoped to tell her about this evening. As part of explaining she didn't have to leave the Belt, or even Ceres, to have a good life. Maybe he'd even hint that that good life could be with him. Might be too much too soon.

Before he could finish the thought she was sitting down. "It's nice of you to be buying me dinner like this tonight," she said. "Mom and Dad aren't hurting for extra funds, but I try to be responsible, and eating at a fancy place like might seem profligate."

"I owe you for helping me out with Billy," Calvin replied. "Besides it doesn't hurt to indulge on the rare occasion."

"You're my friend, Calvin, I had to," Katie answered. "This is almost overdoing it. I mean the pizza is famous, and I hear they import real milk concentrate and reconstitute it for the milkshakes. Authentic is great, but that's crazy, there's nothing wrong with synthetic milk."

"Well, we're here," Calvin said. "Try to enjoy it. How'd your day go?"

"Wow, Commander Tretyak is not at all what I expected," Katie said starting into a long discussion of her meeting with the Space Force District Commander. It took them all the way through ordering a meat lovers pizza and a strawberry milkshake to share. Katie did cease her long relation along enough scoff most of both the pizza and the milkshake. She didn't seem to notice that fact, and Calvin didn't bother to point it out. He'd wonder where she put it all, but it was obvious she burned it all to provide her the constant energy she exhibited. It was something he'd gotten used to long ago.

Finally as Katie ate the last piece of pizza Calvin got in a word. "So despite hitting it off well, he's still determined not to endorse your application?" he asked.

"Yeah, it's odd," she said, "but he's convinced I wouldn't be a good fit."

"It could be you really do belong in the Belt here," Calvin suggested.

"I don't know," Katie replied. "Being a tough independent Belter far from the maddening crowd that was my parent's dream.

I've never fit in well. I don't have that many friends here."

"You've got me, and Sam, and a lot of people probably be willing to be better friends if you slowed down a bit and spent more of your time actually socializing here on Ceres," Calvin suggested.

"I'm sorry," Katie said. "Didn't mean to suggest you and Sam aren't great. Maybe I could try harder. No, I definitely could. Time is so short and there's so much to do. Mainly I want to go somewhere I can be someone who makes a difference."

"You could make a difference here."

Katie looked at Calvin like an inquisitive bird. Like he was a shiny object that she'd noticed. Calvin had wanted her to pay more attention to him. Maybe not like this, though. "The Belt is a resource outpost," Katie said. "We exist for the convenience of the industries that serve the populations on Mars and Earth. We're important in that regard, but the big decisions, the future course of humanity is being determined elsewhere. Mainly on Earth still, no matter how stodgy they are."

"So we're just not important enough for you here in the Belt," Calvin said. He couldn't help feeling annoyed.

"Everybody is important as an individual human being," Katie said. "Only a few people are to make decisions and act in ways that will critically affect everybody's future. They're mostly at the top of big organizations headquartered on and around Earth. Organizations like the Space Force. It's simply the way it is. I'm not apologizing for telling it the way it is."

Calvin wondered how the evening had gone so far sidewards. Time to change the topic. "So he wants you to take the Dragon Lady's course, a short version," he asked.

"Yeah, I think he means me to do the labors of Hercules thing," Katie replied. "Not exactly a short version either, more an intensely compressed version. I got the impression he doesn't expect Ping to take it easy on us."

"My parents made me take that course," Calvin said. "It was tough. They let me out of my chores so I could concentrate on it. I sweated that course and let everything else slide for an entire semester, and I still barely passed."

"Maybe you could help me study?" Katie asked.

It was the last thing Calvin wanted to do. Still, it'd mean spending more time with her. "Sure," he said.

"Thanks," she said.

It might have been what earned him a hug when they left after he'd paid the bill.

She made her own way home, though. Had studying to do. They agreed to meet the next day. He was going to bring his notes.

He wasn't sure if he'd made progress at all.

Somehow it didn't feel like it.

*  *  *

Sam was working with a door mechanism that'd been beat to crap. It was the first job of his morning. He liked to front load his least favorite tasks for the day. Might not help his overall mood, but it did see that the necessary chores got done.

It was a sad and annoying fact that people often abused the gear they needed. Usually through indifference and neglect, but also sometimes it was apparent somebody had taken out their frustrations with other people on their poor inanimate helpers.

It bothered Sam on one level. In a world that already had enough problems, why create more? On the other hand, it provided him at least half his business.

"Hi, Sam," came Katie's voice.

He hadn't noticed her coming in. He was getting soft in his old age. Or maybe his unconscious had just registered her as a friend. Wasn't sure which was more worrisome. Good to see her, though. Always nice to have other peoples' problems to solve. "So what brings you again here so soon?" he asked.

"What a friend can't just visit a friend?" Katie retorted. "What are you working on?"

Sam noted the transparent attempt to indicate interest in whatever he was doing, though he had no doubt she'd get to the problem she'd come to ask him about soon enough. The girl did have to work on her social skills. "Door lock," he said. "Been beat to crap by people slamming it closed day after day."

Katie came over and eyed the large square hunk of metal. Locks weren't something you saw much of on a family operated ship. "Awfully thick plate metal. Must be a centimeter thick. You'd think that thing could survive Armageddon," she said.

"It looks that way true," Sam replied. "The whole point really. Plate's mostly for show. Sure it makes it real hard for anyone to get directly at the lock mechanism, but the thing is vulnerable in other places. It's a common flaw in security systems. An old instructor of mine used to call it 'the steel door to the grass hut syndrome'".

Katie blinked. It was obviously not a clear analogy to her. "Because an attacker doesn't need to go through the door, they can just go through the hut walls?" she half asked, half stated.

"Exactly," Sam confirmed. "People get so focused on one part of the problem they miss the wider picture."

"That's a neat way of thinking about it. Thanks."

"So why are you here? Billy spreading rumors? You see Tretyak yet?" Sam asked.

"Haven't heard any rumors or even a peep from Billy and his Dad," Katie replied. "I went and saw the Commander yesterday afternoon. He's not such an ogre. He's set me a task. I've got to take a condensed version of Miss Ping's class, pass and get a good report from her. Calvin's going to help, but I thought you might have some insights."

"Miss Ping?" he asked. "She's still around? Never much for school myself, and don't have kids, but customers and some of my buddies have mentioned her."

"And?"

"And apparently she's the single biggest obstacle to the future happiness of Ceres' young people there is," Sam replied. "Kid wants to go to higher Ed on Mars or Earth, they've got to pass her course and she doesn't make it easy. How is it you don't know this?"

"My parents never wanted me to go away to college," Katie said. "I figured I'd have another couple of years to take all the needed courses. Only I went and accidentally tested out on the standard exams. I didn't know that was possible."

"I'm sure it's rare," Sam said dryly. He stared through her for a second. "I hate to suggest anyone ever do less than their absolute best at anything, you know that?"

"Yep, it's one of the things I really like about you. Everybody else is always telling me to dial it back," Katie replied.

Sam sighed. "You do seem to have a tendency to break systems designed for more, ah, standard people," he said. "It might be an idea to learn to anticipate that problem. Go around it or manage to color within the lines, even if it otherwise doesn't make sense. I mean if you have a badly written computer program you don't insist on feeding it input it's going to blow up on do you?"

"I find another program," Katie said. "Write a new one myself if I have to."

"Sometimes that may not be an option," Sam said. "Anyhow I do have advice regards Miss Ping and her course. Most of her students have a problem with the sheer volume of information she gives them to memorize. That's not going to be your problem. Make sure you memorize all the facts she wants you to, but don't stop there. You need to make a point of understanding her interpretation of those facts and working within that interpretation."

"Okay, huge amount to commit to memory," Katie said. "I'm sure Calvin will help though. I love to play with the different interpretations you can place on the same facts."

Sam stifled another sigh. He'd never been a mopey emo kid, he didn't plan to morph into one in his old age. "It'd be better if you didn't indulge that love in Miss Ping's class, I think," he said. "A lot of people get very attached to their particular interpretation of facts. To the point of ignoring new facts that don't fit. They don't like it when you bring those interpretations into doubt. Not even if it's only by suggesting alternative interpretations in a playful way."

Katie looked at Sam skeptically. "Seriously?"

"Yes, surely you've noticed how some of your bright ideas have disturbed your teachers in the past?"

"They never said anything. I thought maybe I was just getting ahead of the rest of the students and confusing them."

"Maybe that too, but although people don't like having their ideas challenged they also don't like admitting they're not more open minded."

"Wow."

"Nobody expects, or even wants, fifteen-year-olds to be worldly, but you have to start paying attention, Katie," Sam said. "You can't keep treating people as momentary distractions or easily bemused and buffaloed like your parents. Some people you're going to have to learn to live with. Take the time to understand them."

"Yes, sir."

"Look, it's like this lock here," Sam said resorting to an impromptu metaphor. "The thick plate is all the facts you need to know. Not unimportant, but don't get distracted by it. The theories you need to understand are like how the mechanism is delicate and needs some respect. The fact you oughtn't antagonize Miss Ping is like the fact that you can open the lock by just cutting the power to it. The power supply is almost never adequately protected. That's the most important yet least obvious fact. Understand?"

"I think so," Katie said, frowning. Her tone wasn't entirely convincing.

"Learn what Miss Ping wants you to," Sam said. "Learn the facts. Learn her theories about them. Don't challenge them. Don't invent a bunch of your own. Be respectful. Make her happy. Understood."

"Yes, sir. Not going to be easy."

"Suck it up, buttercup."

\* \* \*

"Thanks a lot, Calvin," Katie said. "You've been a great help. mostly read old classics my parents got on sale. Miss Ping's reading list is way different. Thanks."

Calvin stood awkwardly in the door, seeming uncertain about something. Poor boy probably wasn't used to being praised. "That's great," he said, his tone less certain than the words. "Miss Ping is tough enough normally I can't imagine what the condensed version of her course is going to be like."

"Yeah, even Commander Tretyak didn't pretend it was going to be easy," Katie replied. "I'd better get some sleep while I can."

"Yeah right, see ya," Calvin said, giving her a limp hand wave and finally moving off.

Katie closed the door to her room after him, observing the click of the lock mechanism as she did so. It was designed to lock from the inside. It was intended to keep people out rather than in. Most of the locks she seen so far were designed that way. She'd been inspecting every lock she came across since her talk with Sam earlier in the day.

She'd never paid them much attention before. Now she was and noticing things that had never occurred to her to pay attention to before.

For instance, although her door was designed to lock from the inside giving her privacy and some protection from intruders she'd learned by inspecting the part of the mechanism in the door frame that it could be unlocked remotely.

In fact, it had turned out to be easily dismantled given the right tools. Ones she carried with her as a matter of habit because she was constantly doing maintenance while on the *Dawn Threader*. Looked like it was a fail safe mechanism too. The door would automatically cease to be locked if it lost power. Suggested the designer was more worried about a first responder being unable to give assistance in an emergency than stopping intruders in such a case. It fitted with Belters being more worried about threats from accidents than deliberate attacks by other people.

During the period she'd be studying, the nineteenth through twenty-second centuries mainly on Earth, it seemed like the biggest threat to people had been other people. One of the many pictures she'd flipped through with Calvin had been of a door to the domicile of a late twentieth century urban dweller. The edge of the door had been lined with a whole array of large locks, deadbolts, and chains.

It'd been fear of intruders incarnate.

It'd also been silly theater to some extent. A flimsy pair of hinges secured the other side of the door. The door itself looked like wood.

Yesterday it'd not have registered on her. This was what she loved about new ideas. They made familiar things new.

At the same time, she could understand the other thing Sam had been trying to tell her. That wasn't true for most people. For a lot of people she realized now thinking about seeing old familiar things in a new light wasn't delightful it was threatening and eerie. Finally she understood some of those horror movies Calvin and other friends were always telling her were so great.

Thinking in broad historical terms. She was going to have to get used to doing so. Thinking in those terms, life had been on a knife's edge for most people for most of history. In those circumstances, it made sense that any change would be interpreted as a potential threat. An indication of something that needed to be treated with caution and the utmost suspicion.

It was an odd and disconcerting idea. Still, she could see the logic.

She needed to understand people better. If this was the way most people thought, even if they didn't like to admit it, then she needed to understand and allow for that.

Particularly when dealing with Miss Ping.

It wasn't going to be easy to restrain herself. She did love novel ideas and challenging received fact.

She'd rein it in all the same.

\* \* \*

So Katie was studying with Calvin in her room again. It'd been less than a week since the fight with Billy. Only five days by the calendar. It felt much longer. It felt like centuries. They'd started with the end of the Napoleonic Wars in the early nineteenth century and worked all the way up to the founding of the first settlements on Mars and Ceres in the middle of the twenty-first.

Katie intended to do everything she could to prepare before the actual start of Miss Ping's course. Calvin had pledged to help her. He hadn't said as much, but Katie could tell he didn't think she understood the enormity of the task she was taking on. He underestimated just how much energy Katie had. As witness his current bleary eyed state of stunned wiped out exhaustion from the long day of study they'd put in. In contrast, Katie had plenty of energy left.

She also thought he underestimated her ability to memorize large amounts of material other people found too dry to be digestible.

Katie had cut her teeth on books of safety regulations and technical manuals as a pre-schooler.

Her parents, her mother in particular, had been delighted when she'd learned to read not too long after learning to walk and being potty trained. Katie had been a happy kid and had been delighted in turn to please her mother. At first safety and technical manuals had been all there'd been to read besides her mother's romances. Katie hadn't been planned, and they'd not thought to pack kid's books when they'd emigrated from Earth. Katie hadn't understood what the romances were about and her mother had been at pains to direct her to other reading matter. Later they'd picked up all sorts of old classics in the public domain and therefore cheap. Most of the history Katie knew came from books written in the late nineteenth century or early twentieth.

Katie had learned early on that most people weren't interested in how voracious a reader she was and from what an early age. Katie was even less inclined to bother them with two other facts about her pertinent to the current problem.

Her mother had also been delighted to let her young child to "play" at maintenance tasks like cleaning all the various filters for air, water, fuel, hydraulic fluid, and every other gas or fluid you could think of. Katie now realized that this amounted to criminal negligence on the part of her parents, but at the time she'd been happy to play at anything that pleased her mother. When a couple of years later she'd realized to her horror just how wide the gap was between the maintenance and upkeep recommended in the manuals and what her parents were prepared to understand and do she'd resolved to fill the gap herself.

She'd started by resolving to memorize all the manuals in question. She'd been too young to know how insane that was.

The first step, of course, had been to read books on memorizing. She'd learned to her surprise that reading wasn't natural and memorizing facts as standalone individual printed items was not something the human mind was designed for or good at.

No, the human mind craved the concrete that could be seen, smelled, felt and touched. Ideally, heard too. And not just any old things that could be seen, heard, touched and maybe tasted too, but ones that stood out for some reason. People naturally loved, or at least paid attention, to the unusual, the exaggerated and surprising. They also remembered what they associated with other things, the more things and the more those things invoked strong emotions, the more likely they'd be remembered.

Turned out people had only recently been born on space ships, where doing tasks outlined in printed manuals were what they did to stay alive.

For most of people's existence, the books explained, people had lived in the wilderness threatened by wild animals and competing with both them and other people for the resources, both food and water, to stay alive.

The key to memorizing things in books, the books explained, was quickly imagining concrete things that were colorful and surprising. Then associating the words or numbers in the books with them. Then situating them within concrete structures like a landscape or a building. They'd given many specific examples of how to do this.

Katie had mastered them all.

When most people thought of safety manuals, they thought of dry tomes full of musty boring words it was hard to focus on.

When Katie thought of safety manuals, she thought of a vast collection of graveyards full of tombstones under each of which lay an undead creature that had to be placated in the name of the great God Murphy if they were not to rise and threaten your very continued existence.

The graveyards were each body of safety regulations. The tombstone each regulation. Each one, as the preface to one manual had said, related to some problem that taken lives or threatened them in the past. Each tombstone was engraved with a regulation aimed at keeping the problem, the undead monster, lying below in its grave where it belonged.

Thought of that way safety regulations were much easier to remember.

So Katie had a great memory based on exercising a set of techniques she'd spent her whole life refining.

When in classes teachers insisted on repeating a set of facts over and over again so that other students by some chance might manage to absorb them long enough to pass the mid-terms or finals, Katie was bored out of her tree. Something she'd learned to try to hide from both her teachers and fellow students.

Including Calvin.

"I'd forgotten how crazy this was," he was saying. Katie knew she'd missed something more he'd been saying while she'd been lost in her own thoughts. She felt too guilty about that to ask him to repeat it.

"How so?" she said, pretending she'd been listening.

"To start with she wants you to remember every person, she deems important for three centuries," he said. "Every major state's leader for every year of that period. Half the time she wants you to remember who their foreign minister and finance minister was. Then she throws in a few generals, economists, scientists, and special cases like this Kissinger guy. That's only the people. Then you're supposed to remember a bunch of important dates and why. Then a bunch of places. And you're supposed to be able to connect them all together. It's like some game show you can't win. I don't know how any of us ever managed to pass this."

"I find making connections helps," Katie ventured.

"More facts to remember," Calvin said. "Wait until you get into class and she starts talking about them as long-lost friends. Expects you to know them too. Like it was today's gossip. These guys are all dead and gone. I bet even their grand children don't remember who half of them were."

Katie remembered a quote. *"The past isn't dead. It isn't even past."* She didn't say it aloud. No point confusing things. She wondered who was right, who'd ever said that, Faulkner maybe, or Calvin. She also noted that connections didn't place facts in context for Calvin, that they instead multiplied the individual things to memorize for him. She wondered how common that was. "You think so?" she said. "There must be a point to this course, right?"

"It's a hoop to jump through in order to get into a good school," Calvin said. "Something easier for rich kids with plenty of time and whose parents can afford tutors for them. Then when they get to their fancy school, they can trade quotes to show who really belongs."

"Well, I guess I'm their performing dog then," Katie said. "I intend to jump through all the hoops I need to. Anyhow, we've covered almost up to the present day."

"Yeah, we looked at it all once," Calvin said. "My head hurts."

"It'll help," Katie said. "I'm good at memorizing facts. Sam said I need to do more than that. Said Ping not only wants you to memorize a bunch of stuff but to interpret it in a particular way."

Calvin looked around at the piles of books, papers, print outs, and several screens filled with data. "I'd forgotten what a nightmare this was," he said. "Yeah, there was a ton of economics and stuff on tech advances too. Ping has this fascination with class divisions based on economics. She claims tech and finance let them kick the can down the road. Fancy way of saying putting stuff off. Anyhow she'd start ranting about bread and circuses, and Rome, which is not even in the period, and how space exploration has delayed the revolution. I'd put it all out of mind. It was one long bad dream."

"Okay, so it's going to be tough," Katie said. "Any hints how I can absorb all these ideas and make Ping happy?"

"I don't know, Katie," Calvin said, running his hands through his hair in distress at the memories. "I just studied, and studied, until I was dreaming about the stuff when ever I could get some sleep. I wrote the essays she wanted in a daze. I regurgitated everything I could remember on the final. I barely passed. I'd forgotten all of it until you asked."

"I guess we're both tired," she said. "Maybe you should go home and get some sleep. Thanks for doing this. I'm sorry to work you so hard, but I really want to pass this thing and get into the Academy."

"You sure it's worth it?" Calvin asked. "You sure you wouldn't be happier staying here?"

"I'm sure," Katie answered.

She thought about that after she'd ushered him out.

Yes, she was sure she wanted to do it.

She wasn't sure how she'd manage to please Miss Ping. She could memorize facts. She could avoid contradicting the woman or spit balling ideas on her. It wasn't a wholly satisfactory plan. It'd have to do.

## 4: Katie Gets Schooled

The last week had passed in a daze of dates.
　Katie didn't know how the rest of her classmates were managing it. She was having trouble keeping up. With no false modesty, that must mean the rest of them were drowning.
　She barely had time to eat and sleep. The rest was all study. If she hadn't already committed a strong basic framework of facts to memory, she'd have been lost.
　Miss Ping lived up to and exceeded her reputation. She really wasn't that old. She was early, late middle age, maybe. She must have started teaching on Ceres very young. Katie knew there had to be a story there. She couldn't bring herself to care currently.
　Physically, Ping wasn't that imposing either. She was a slight woman of barely middle height. Shorter like most originally from Earth and much less stout and muscled than most of them. She was fined boned, almost fragile in fact.
　But the will that radiated from the woman was fierce. She felt like an implacable force of nature. Something that you couldn't argue with only get out of the way of.
　It was Monday and the day's class was over and Katie had been called in to have a one-to-one talk with that force of nature that Miss Ping was.
　She didn't know why.

She was too tired to care much.

They'd all been required to submit their first essay of the course this morning.

Something on the basis of the economic underpinnings of the ancien regime. Farming and trade not to put a fine point on it. Landowners and merchants battled it out and the peasants hardly mattered. Might be rather interesting if she'd had the energy for it. She didn't. She also wasn't sure what the application to a modern technological society was. Didn't matter.

Miss Ping wanted an essay, Miss Ping got her essay.

Katie had a rule about getting enough sleep. Lack of sleep was bad for your health, and tired people make mistakes. She'd had to break that rule to get the essay done for Miss Ping. She'd been up most of last night.

Katie knew she could be impetuous. She didn't think she lost her temper much, if ever. Right now she was feeling grouchy and short tempered.

They'd finished their class for the day and the rest of the students had stumbled out of the classroom.

Not Katie.

"Miss Kincaid, could you remain behind for a few minutes, please," Miss Ping had announced. She'd gathered a few glances of sympathy from some classmates as they fled.

Ping hadn't had much to say, not then. She'd had a "request". "Miss Kincaid, would you mind coming back after an hour for supper?" she'd asked. "I have some additional tests I'd like to give you. When you're done, we'll need to discuss them and your progress so far." She'd looked at Katie expectantly, as if there was more than one answer Katie could give.

Of course, Katie minded. The homework Miss Ping had assigned them along with time for a meal and some quick toiletries would bring her right to bedtime. Any extra time spent in discussions with Miss Ping would come right out of her sleep time leaving her short for the second day in a row.

She couldn't say that. She had to please Miss Ping, so she'd help convince the Commander to give her a break. "No, ma'am, not at all," she'd lied. "Can we do it now maybe though?"

Miss Ping had shook her head. "No, I need time to prepare," she'd said. "You should get your blood sugar levels up. I don't know how long this will take."

Like that didn't sound ominous. Katie had helped herself to an extra dessert in case Miss Ping was being literal.

Now dinner over, she was back in front of the classroom door wondering what was up. She'd know soon.

She took a deep breath and opening the door went in.

Miss Ping was standing still, and ever so erect, with a tablet held in both hands in front of her. That erect posture and stillness were quite imposing Katie noted, something she'd have to remember for herself in the future.

Katie marched up to Miss Ping. "I'm here, ma'am," she announced.

"I see," Miss Ping said. Had she just made a joke? Didn't seem possible. "Here, there are a set of tests on this tablet. Do them here now, take as long as you need. I'll be here the whole time if you have questions. I trust you used the facilities before coming."

"Of course, ma'am," Katie said taking the tablet.

She then lost herself in the tests.

There were no essay questions. There were hundreds of multiple choice ones. They gave way to short answer ones. Not only did Katie have to recall all the people and places Ping had wanted memorized, she had to remember how to spell them too. Mostly she thought she managed it.

Those gave way to worse questions. Questions that could have used essay answers, but came with the instruction to answer the question in a single sentence. Katie felt the need to indulge in some long runaway run-on sentences. She couldn't help it.

Worse, some of the questions seemed like trick ones. Like "What was the most important event of 2001?".

Katie answered, "The attack of 9-11 leading to the retardation of the American pivot from its Cold War strategic posture.".

She wasn't sure Miss Ping would agree, or that she wanted the elaboration of why it was important, but it was the best she could manage.

Finally there were no more questions.

Katie checked the time, it'd been well over two hours. If she'd answered the exam questions like any normal person or agonized over even one of them, they could have easily been here all night.

She looked up at Miss Ping. "Done, ma'am," she said.

"Very well, Miss Kincaid," Miss Ping said. "Just another minute or two while I check over your answers."

Katie blinked. Normally it'd take a few days for a test like the one she'd just done to be marked. Miss Ping must have been following her answers in real time and marking them as she went. Rather scary. At least it meant this would be over soon. She hoped Ping wasn't planning on flunking her out already. She'd thought she'd done pretty well. Only it wasn't like Miss Ping was going to be reasonable, or even fair. This could be the end of her plans for her future. Finished before they'd even really got started.

The next couple of minutes, more like five really, seemed like an eternity spent in a hell of anticipation.

Finally Miss Ping looked up. "You prepared carefully for the course, Miss Kincaid," she said.

Katie wasn't sure if it was a statement or a question. "Yes, ma'am," she answered. "I'd heard the full length course was challenging. I assumed the condensed course would be more so. This course is very important to me and my future, and I didn't want to take any chances."

"Yes, well congratulations your command of the material exceeds that of any student I've had to date," Miss Ping said. "Including all the ones who actually completed my course. In fact, I'd say your command of the facts in the topic equals or exceeds that of most graduate students and Ph.Ds."

"That's good isn't it, ma'am?" Katie asked. It sounded like it should be. "Are you sure?" Too late, she realized that sounded like a challenge to Miss Ping's credentials.

Miss Ping simply smiled at her. It was a shocking expression. Worse was it seemed like a sad smile.

"I was an outstanding student myself," she said. "I'm fully qualified to be a professor of history at one of Earth's more prestigious universities. Yet here I am teaching secondary school in the Belt. You're not the only talented person, Miss Kincaid, that has managed to upset the powers that be."

"I try not to, ma'am," Katie said with heartfelt sincerity. "Does this mean I'm going to pass the course? I have to prove to Commander Tretyak that I can handle the Academy. Your recommendation is critical, ma'am." Katie really hoped this didn't sound like begging.

"As far as I'm concerned, you've tested out of the course," Miss Ping said. "It isn't that you haven't got more to learn, but that's true of everything. Your command of the material is excellent. You know as much about late modern history as all but a fraction of humanity. Again congratulations. It's an amazing achievement, especially from a fifteen year girl from the Belt. Finishing the course would be a waste of our time. It'd also distract me from trying to drill something into the heads of the rest of these numbskulls. I'm passing you."

"Ah, thank you, ma'am," Katie replied. "What are you going to tell Commander Tretyak?"

"I'm going to write Commander Tretyak a nice formal letter saying that your command of the material is exceptional," Miss Ping said. "I'm going to say I'm passing you based on a rigorous testing of your knowledge. I'm going to write that I believe more classroom time along with slower students is not the best use of my time or yours." She paused at looked at Katie expectantly.

"What aren't you saying, ma'am?"

"I'm not saying I don't think you'll be a good fit in the Space Force," Miss Ping said. "I'm not going to express an opinion on that at all. Not formally."

"I see," Katie said. She didn't know how the Commander would react to that. Was just passing the course enough? Or was she supposed to have passed it in a certain way? What was Miss Ping going to say to the Commander informally?

"I doubt it," Miss Ping said. "You're mature for your age, but you're a young girl from out in the sticks."

"The sticks?"

"Not the metropolitan area where the sophisticated and powerful congregate along with their spawn," Miss Ping said. "You're not plugged into the informal networks of the people who run things."

"Is that an insurmountable handicap if you're talented enough and work hard enough, ma'am?"

"That depends on what you're trying to achieve," Miss Ping said. "You've impressed me, Miss Kincaid. I believe that you're capable and determined enough not only to have passed my course here, but to act like, and appear to be, the very epitome of a good Space Force officer."

Katie wasn't sure what Miss Ping meant. She was tempted to let sleeping dogs lie, but of course she couldn't. "You think I'd b faking it?"

"I think you're capable of it," Miss Ping replied. "I think you're capable of parroting back to me anything I want to hear, and I think you're capable of doing that to Commander Tretyak, and to whatever instructors and superiors you might encounter at the Academy and in the Space Force. I think we both know this."

"Ma'am," Katie said. She didn't want to say nothing, but neither could she think of a sensible reply. Miss Ping had as much as said she didn't believe anything Katie might say to her. If she said as much to the Commander Katie could kiss her prospective career good bye.

"Cheer up, Miss Kincaid," Miss Ping said with a twisted little smile. "What I'll report to the Commander is that I think you're capable of performing as an outstanding officer in the Space Force. That despite a formally deficient education that your capacity for self study more than compensates. That you were diligent and well behaved in your studies."

"Thank you, ma'am," Katie said.

"It may not be enough for Tretyak, but it's as far as I'm willing to go," Miss Ping said. "Also I'm not at all sure this is the best course for you. I think you should rethink it. You're an outsider, as am I. If you're outstandingly capable and don't rock the boat the powers to be will be willing to use you. They'll treat you like a valuable tool. That doesn't mean they'll ever fully trust you. If you cease to be useful or you look like you're a possible threat, they'll discard you. Is that really what you want?"

"Ma'am, I want to make a difference," Katie said. "I know I can't change everything. I want to make the world a better place, but I know I have to pick my battles. Fight the ones I can win. Avoid the ones I can't. Please give me a chance to try."

"Very well," Miss Ping said. "I'll do what I can in good conscience."

"Thank you, ma'am."

"Come back in twenty years and say that."

\* \* \*

Katie's guts were in turmoil as she made her way home through the tunnels. The extra study to prepare, the first week of the course, those crazy exams that'd eaten most of the evening, and finally that weird talk with Miss Ping. It was too much, too fast. Her head was ringing.

Bunny hoping along the dark deserted tunnels she knew she needed to be paying more attention. There were worse things than Billy and his buddies in the dark corners here. The Commander and Miss Ping might think Ceres was a staid little place that nothing ever happened in. Katie knew it had a dark underside they never saw.

She focused in the moment for the remainder of the trip. She didn't encounter any trouble, but if she had she would have seen it first. In time to avoid it this time. She hoped. She hoped she was capable of learning.

It was a relief when she reached the lifts that led into the gravity ring her rooms were in. You'd think this would be a chokepoint, a natural point for ambushes. In fact, the area was well lit with multiple security cameras. Everyone knew anything out of the normal would bring the patrol out and quickly. Whatever you might say about the vermin on Ceres, they tried to stay out of sight. Out of the light.

She'd seen the news casts and documentaries about the no-go zones in some of Earth's large cities and knew that wasn't true everywhere.

She got back to her room on automatic.

Once there she sat down on the edge of her bed. She had to clear off a bunch of hardcopy papers she'd been studying first. Papers she didn't need anymore.

She let the feelings come.

They were confusing.

There was relief. Miss Ping might not be quite the monster her students thought she was, but her course was a trial all the same. After all the preparation, Katie was a little disappointed to not be doing the whole course. She wasn't going to miss another five weeks of stress, exhaustion, and confusion.

There was bafflement. She really didn't understand where Miss Ping was coming from. She knew she was missing something. Maybe multiple somethings. She didn't know what.

There was apprehension. Sure she hadn't failed the course. Sure Miss Ping wasn't going to denounce her to the Commander, whatever she thought privately. On the other hand, it didn't appear she was going to give Katie a ringing endorsement either. Who knew how the Commander was going to react to that?

Finally there was determination. Miss Ping had added herself to the long list of people who believed Katie ought to rethink her goals. Reminded Katie she had no intention what so ever of doing so.

So what to do?

She could accept what had happened and steam straight on as she was. Full speed ahead and damn the torpedoes, as one famous American Civil War hero was supposed to have said. That would have been her favored approach. Just march into the Commander's office, assuming she'd done what he'd asked and daring him to break his word.

Alternatively, she could back off a little and study the situation. Maybe there were new tactics she could try. She would like to have a better idea of what was going on. She'd always tried to be as prepared as possible in the past. At the very least, she could ask for advice. She knew Calvin would volunteer something. Seemed like he worried more about her than she did about herself.

Her parents she feared were secretly hoping her whole quixotic quest failed, and she'd return home to the *Dawn Threader* and life would go on as before. No help there.

Sam now. Sam would be willing to help. He sometimes expressed reservations about her ideas, he never discouraged her from trying them. He'd once said, "Failure might not be an option in some circumstances, but generally if you're not willing to fail, you're not really trying and won't get much done." She'd had the feeling she was missing some context there, but the gist was clear.

She'd get a good night's sleep.

She'd go talk to Sam.

\* \* \*

Ceres had been founded by people with no time for caste distinctions. In particular, everybody ate together. Executives and managers didn't get their own better places to eat.

So Commander Tretyak was eating his lunch in the same cafeteria dining room that everybody in the administration offices section did. In the senior's corner. It wasn't a formal designation. Everybody simply understood that that was where the Commander and other top officials of Ceres liked to sit and eat.

Other top officials included Yuri Tretyak's colleague Guy Boucher, who headed up Ceres' logistics department.

Normally, Yuri enjoyed sharing his lunch with Guy, who was an easy going pragmatic kind of guy.

Only Guy had just added to Yuri's growing headache. The one labeled Katie Kincaid.

One of the first things that'd gone across his desk this morning had been a notice from Miss Ping. She was testing the Kincaid girl out of her modern history course. Said the girl was the most academically gifted student she'd ever seen. She'd written that she had no doubt that despite a formally deficient academic foundation the young lady could not only handle the academic work at the Academy, but excel at it.

If he'd not been so surprised the Commander might have shrugged and appended his endorsement to Kincaid's application then and there. Case closed. Problem solved. But he had been surprised. He'd expected another several weeks at least to let the issue percolate in the back of his mind.

To be completely honest with himself, he'd expected the Kincaid girl, who however smart she was an arrogant trouble magnet, to either quit the course or to so annoy Miss Ping as to be expelled.

Still, he'd given his word and technically Kincaid had done the task he'd set her. As a concession to his gut uncertainty, he'd delayed the decision until after lunch. He'd been fully expecting to return to office after he was done with his soup, crackers, and assorted bits of vegetable and sign off on the girl's documentation.

That had been before he talked to Guy Boucher.

"That Kincaid girl up to go to the Academy," Guy had asked.

Yuri had hesitated before answering. Technically, the process was an open one. On the other hand, it wasn't exactly any of Guy's business and personnel decisions were tricky. Yuri liked to avoid gossip and any possible suggestion of favoritism. He had a policy of not talking about personnel issues if at all possible with anyone not directly involved. Still, it was Guy and he couldn't see the harm in the question. "Yes," he answered.

"You know I had to take my boy Billy into the medics for a concussion about a week ago?" Guy asked.

"No, I didn't," Yuri answered. "Sorry. Is he okay? What happened?"

"Not sure," Guy said, "but I think Kincaid was involved. Billy won't come clean. I think he's covering for her because she's a girl. I think she gets away with a lot because of that and being cute."

"Smart too," Commander Yuri Tretyak said. If there was one thing that stood out in this mess that was it.

"Maybe not as smart as she thinks she is," Guy replied.

"You're free to make a formal presentation if you wish, Guy," the Commander said. His friend was placing him in a bad situation.

"Nah, can't prove anything, and I bet she'd find some way to make Billy look bad."

The Commander didn't have the heart to tell Guy Billy was managing to do that on his own. A single father with one son couldn't be expected to be completely objective. "I do have some doubt about her ability to work with others," he admitted.

"Bet she wouldn't last a day down on the processing line," Guy said.

"Maybe not," the Commander said, "but let's talk about more pleasant things."

As it turned out Guy had some interesting, if unlikely, theories about what the Star Rats were up to in the system.

Commander Tretyak managed to mostly forget about the Kincaid girl until he was back in his office looking at her file once again.

After what Guy had said, he couldn't bring himself to endorse her application. On the other hand he owed her a fair chance. Maybe Guy had supplied the answer to the problem he'd created. It was a good question; could Kincaid last a day or a couple of weeks on the processing line? Being good with academics wouldn't help her there. If she couldn't could she actually be expected to succeed at the Academy? It'd show a lack of commitment or inability to get along with others.

Kincaid's original task should have lasted six weeks. Arguably, she still owed him five weeks.

He was going to have to have another talk with her.

One way or the other, he was going to find out what she was made of.

# 5: Kate Goes to Work

Calvin had gotten to the fast-food outlet early. Bob's Burgers wasn't one of the chains, but rather a generic rip-off. Katie had called him this morning and offered to buy him lunch. Said it wasn't much, but she owed him still for all his help preparing for Miss Ping's Modern History course.

Katie had said she'd been allowed to test out of the course entirely. Calvin was astonished by that. He'd known Katie was extraordinarily smart. Also that she had an almost superhuman memory. She'd once claimed it was a bunch of tricks anyone could learn. Calvin thought that was rather optimistic.

Beyond simple astonishment, his feelings were very mixed.

Anything that made Katie happy made him happy too. At least to some extent.

Things that increased the chance she'd be going away in a couple of months, they didn't make him happy.

Of course, Ping passing her ticked off both boxes. Hence the mixed feelings.

"Hey gloomy, why the sad face?" the object of his confusion said while dropping into the seat opposite him. "Order yet?"

"Your going away is starting to seem real," Calvin answered. Honesty is the best policy. "I'm going to miss you."

Katie frowned slightly. "I'll miss you too," she said. "Not that

55

I'm sure it's going to happen yet. I was hoping to hear from Commander Tretyak this morning. Miss Ping said she was sending over the file last night and it should have been on his desk this morning. If he was going to endorse me for certain I think I would have heard by now."

Calvin tried not to grin in relief. He rubbed a hand over his face to hide any traitorous expression it might be showing. "That must be disappointing," he said. It couldn't hurt to be sympathetic.

"It is," Katie said. "Doesn't change the fact you helped me a lot, and I wanted to say thanks. I was so buried in work I don't think I took the time to do that properly earlier. Also, I'm kind of baffled how it all went and I could use a sounding board. You're always willing to listen. I appreciate that."

"Anytime," Calvin said, "though I'm not sure how much help I can be. Honestly, I'm not even sure going to the Academy is a good idea for you."

"Well, the Commander has his doubts that's for sure," Katie said. "Miss Ping says she thinks I'm capable of handling it but she didn't seem to think it was the best thing I could do with my life either."

It was a day full of surprises. Calvin had never expected to find himself grateful to Miss Ping. "Did you ever think the Commander and Miss Ping might be right?" he asked.

"Well, Commander Tretyak seems to have gotten the idea somewhere I'm some sort of monstrous about to explode loose cannon," Katie said.

"Both loose and about to explode?" Calvin asked, bemused. His emotional turmoil lost in amusement over this exaggerated concern.

"Yeah, crazy, eh?" Katie said. "I think I'm bringing him around to a less paranoid point of view."

"So what's the problem?"

"Both Miss Ping and the Commander used this word 'fit' ," Katie said. "They seemed to think I wouldn't fit in with the people in the Space Force and the Academy. That even if I jumped through all the formal hurdles, I wouldn't be happy. Though what my happiness has to do with anything I don't know."

"You don't think happiness is something important when planning your life?" Calvin asked. "I mean you don't want to be unhappy do you?"

"I suppose it'd be nice," Katie replied. She seemed genuinely baffled by the discussion. "I mean if I was too unhappy and depressed I'd be less effective, wouldn't I?"

"I think maybe if you're not happy you have to think you've made bad life choices," Calvin said. "And if you're to be happy, a familiar culture where you understand people and they understand you, and you have family and friends is important. I think Ping and the Commander have a point."

"You do?"

"Yeah, I mean the Space Force is a bunch of bureaucrats mostly from rich Earth families, right?" he said. "That's not you."

"Maybe but I think it's obvious that being happy is not the point of life no matter what you or anybody else including the old American constitution says."

"Wow, way to take on the world, Katie," Calvin said trying to diffuse her obvious annoyance.

"If having a happy life was the only important thing, why not cut to the chase and just take an overdose of some happy juice," Katie said. "Game over, you're deliriously happy for the rest of your life. Makes no sense."

"Okay what is the point of life? What do you want to do with your life?" he asked, fearing the answer.

"I want to make a difference," Katie said. "Maybe getting filthy rich, or inventing something, or making a scientific breakthrough might do that, but they're not what I want to do. They're not what I think will be important. We're going to the stars sometime in our lifetimes, Calvin, and the Space Force is going to be in the forefront of that effort. What they do or don't do will seal the fate of our species. I want to be there."

Calvin was sure Katie was sane. Her ideas he wasn't so sure of. Wouldn't help his case to say so.

"Not sure I agree that makes sense," he said, "but not going to argue with it. Let's order."

"Cheeseburgers and fries make everything better," Katie agreed.

\* \* \*

Sam had already planned a couple of hours this afternoon in the military exercise facility before Katie had called him out of the blue. He hadn't seen anything of her for over a week. That was unusual, but he knew it was because of the history course Tretyak had her taking as some sort of trial.

It exasperated Sam. He hadn't been patient as a young man,

but thought he'd learned it in middle age. Maybe not so much. Sam understood the Commander's reservations about Katie. He also thought it was clear that whatever her flaws, she was a superior candidate and Tretyak ought to bite the bullet. He should stop delaying and simply endorse the girl's application.

Sam had figured that after Katie had passed the course in a few weeks, the Commander would break down and do just that. Only somehow Katie had managed to break the system, and the Commander wasn't comfortable with that.

He'd been looking forward to his time in the exercise facility. Sam followed a physically tough and challenging regime. Mentally, it was restful. The tasks might be hard, but they were mostly straightforward. What complications there were, were narrowly technical. Usually, it was emotionally and intellectually restful. A great way to work off stress, in fact. Usually.

Only today he found himself counseling an uncharacteristically angst ridden young woman. Trying to tell her how to deal with an unreasonable and obstructive bureaucracy. He was being forced to give advice to someone without the experience to understand or accept it. Advice about how to deal rationally with a fundamentally irrational reality. Great. Sam wondered what sins he'd committed in an earlier life to deserve it.

At least, he'd had no problems getting Katie to meet him in the gym. He'd sponsored her membership in the training facility years ago. He'd learned a long time ago that the way to keep young people with excess energy and drive out of trouble was to keep them busy with physically challenging tasks. Tasks that kept them too tired to go looking for it.

"You're doing great, Katie," he yelled up at the young woman. Katie was tackling the gym's most difficult climbing wall. Its handholds were limited in number and not the easiest to use. The gravity was also somewhat greater than a standard Gee. This facility was designed to support a much larger military contingent than was currently stationed on Ceres. Sam and Katie had the place to themselves.

"I wish it was as easy to figure out what the Commander wanted," she yelled back. Sam almost smiled. The girl was single minded. Hanging on for dear life and she still wasn't going to forget why she was here.

"Remember three point hold," he yelled back. "Safety gear is good, but you still don't want to fall."

"I'm not a beginner," she returned.

"Maybe you're not focused either," Sam yelled back.

Katie found and stretched for a new hand hold. Shifted her weight to it. "I'm not going to be distracted," she hollered down.

"Different strokes for different people," he yelled back.

"What's that mean?"

"Something from an old sitcom," he yelled. "Means different things work for different people. With them, too. You're not taking this climbing wall like it was a zero Gee access on a ship or in microgravity outside the rings here on Ceres, are you?"

"Of course not," she yelled, taking a breath. Even just resting on the climbing holds took constant physical exertion. "That'd be silly."

"Well, so is always taking the same approach with different people," Sam answered.

Katie didn't answer immediately. She moved several holds closer to the top of the wall. "That's clear, but people make no sense," she eventually yelled back down to him. "Moving under different accelerations has different rules, but they're fixed for each one. They make sense. There's no fixed rules for people."

It was Sam's turn to take his time answering. Katie moved a couple more times and a little higher as well as a little sidewards. "People are too complicated for fixed rules," he yelled. "You've got to figure them out case by case."

Katie finished her climb and repelled back down to the deck beside Sam. She took a deep breath and wiped the sweat off her forehead with the back of one hand. "How so?" she asked.

"You've heard the joke about the physicist postulating a spherical cow in a frictionless vacuum?" Sam asked. "What do you think it means?"

"That some people are lazy about getting all the facts and including them in their calculations?" Katie suggested.

Sam gave her a hard look. They both knew she was being difficult. "You want advice?"

"Okay," Katie conceded. "Means sometimes even in the hard sciences that including every factor into a calculation is too complicated. As a first cut, to save time, or because the full calculation is error prone or outright impossible to do with full accuracy, it's necessary to simplify."

"See, that wasn't that hard was it?"

Katie grimaced. "I'm not sure how useful the observation is.

People are always telling me I'm over simplifying."

"Sometimes people don't want to admit what's obviously true," Sam said. "They often have reasons."

"Ones that make sense?"

"Sometimes," Sam said. "You're used to dealing with your parents and technical problems, mostly. Other people mostly deal with other people."

"It's like you were telling me about poker versus chess," Katie said. "They're not going to put all their cards on the table."

"Exactly," Sam said. Katie was a hard sell, but it wasn't impossible to get through to her. "You know how it is with the pop up target range here?"

"Never can be quite sure what it's going to do," Katie said. "Sometimes it falls into a pattern, but never for long."

"Because it's trying to fool you," Sam said. "It doesn't want to be predictable. Real world people and groups of them are like that. You can't really be sure what will happen. You simply have to try and see what patterns you can, but be ready for anything."

Katie frowned as she removed and stored her climbing gear. Sam followed her, waiting for her reply. It was almost plaintive when it came. "Aren't we all rational creatures trying to work together?" she said.

"Ideally perhaps," Sam agreed after a pause. "But there's a lot of detail and a lot of history, it's not so simple. In fact, smarter people than me say it's complex. I've read they've even worked out math for it."

"I'd like to see that math," Katie said.

"Be nice if there was a couple more hours in the day, too," Sam said.

Katie grinned. This was something she understood. "Yeah," she agreed.

"Look, young Miss Kincaid, me dear," Sam said in an exaggerated Irish accent. He wanted to lighten the mood. Sam also wanted her to pay attention. "You have to think of societies as heavy things in zero Gee with a lot of momentum."

"That's redundant," Katie observed.

"Indeed," Sam agreed. Not to be deflected, he continued. "Lot of momentum. Hard to get started moving. Hard to stop. Sometimes it's best not to try too hard and build up too much momentum. Can't stop thing. Thing crushes other things. You follow, me dear?"

Sam could tell Katie didn't like the medicine, despite all the sugar he'd put on it. "Maybe," she said, "but I've got some heavy stuff I want to move and I want to move it some distance."

"Best you be careful doing it then, Katie," Sam said solemnly.

\* \* \*

Morning of the second day after she'd tested out of Miss Ping's course and Katie found herself outside of Commander Yuri Tretyak's office once again.

Katie sure hoped she wasn't going to be making a habit of this.

It was better than the Commander refusing outright to endorse her Academy application. She didn't know for a fact that wasn't why he'd called her in again.

The purpose of this meeting might only be to explain why he couldn't bring himself to endorse her. That despite her having passed Miss Ping's course. And despite what she was sure was a fairly positive covering letter from Miss Ping.

Katie didn't think so.

Katie was also darned sure he wasn't going to explain how he was endorsing her despite some reservations. Only thing more unlikely than that was a profuse apology for not seeing what a wonderful candidate she was from the start. That wasn't going to happen. She wasn't good at reading people, but she wasn't that bad at it.

So she figured the Commander was going to try to thread the needle again. Have his cake and eat it too. Meant her fate was on a knife's edge again.

Well, she was trying to learn courage and how to handle stress. Perhaps in her heart, not to his face to be certain, she ought to thank the Commander for providing the practice.

Thing to do was have a clear goal. Not to be distracted. To push on as best as she could and not get discouraged.

Katie wanted to convince the Commander to give her his endorsement.

She'd jump through any hoops he asked her to. She'd do it cheerfully. Katie would do it in the way he wanted, with the form he wanted.

Katie took a breath and knocked.

This time there were no delays, but no tea either.

The Commander motioned at her to sit in the chair in front of his desk.

"So, Miss Kincaid," he said as soon as she was seated. "You appear to have impressed Miss Ping. I didn't know that was possible."

"Does that mean you'll endorse my application to the Academy, sir?" Katie asked.

The Commander leaned back, took a deep breath, puffed out his cheeks, and blew out a long sigh of air. Quite the production for such a normally staid man. "Not automatically," he said.

"I did as you asked, sir," she said. "Excelled at it according to Miss Ping. Wouldn't it be only fair to keep your word?"

The Commander looked at her with narrowed eyes. "Perhaps," he said, "but honestly you didn't exactly finish the task I gave you. I wanted to see how you'd behave over a six-week period under stress. In particular, how you'd interact with your classmates and Miss Ping. Not your fault maybe, but that's not what I got is it?"

"No, sir," Katie agreed. "But Miss Ping told me what she planned to say in her letter to you. She said she thought I could handle the Academy, didn't she?"

"She did," the Commander admitted. "That has caused me to reassess my opinion of your social skills in fact. I was afraid you'd be socially inept due to insufficient experience with people. You're apparently a quicker study than I'd have thought."

"That's good isn't it, sir?"

"Maybe, maybe not," the Commander answered. "It's possible that you've learned to manipulate your teachers effectively during your stays here on Ceres. I'm curious if that extends to getting along with peers in a non-academic setting."

"Isn't that moving the goalposts, sir?"

"Perhaps I could have been clearer about what I was looking for," the Commander allowed. "On the other hand I don't believe you've been entirely open with me either. Do you know anything about how Billy Boucher ended up in med bay a couple of weeks ago?"

Katie colored. This was bad. Somehow even worse it was embarrassing. "I do, sir," she said reluctantly. "Only, sir, I don't think Billy will be willing to tell the truth about it and it'd be my word and that of a friend against his and that of even more of his friends. If you insist, I'll waive my rights as a juvenile and submit to a biometrically monitored interrogation. And, sir, I won't look great, but it'll destroy Billy and his Dad. It'll be a everybody loses thing. Please, don't insist on pursuing this."

The Commander stared at her hard. "If either of you was a year or two older, I'd insist," he said. "As it is, it's hard to tell the difference between schoolyard squabbles and junior criminality. I have heard the rumors about Billy's bullying. I suspect you overreacted to it. I don't like letting it go, but you do have more to lose than he does. I'll accede to your wishes against my bette judgment. You do understand how it casts a shadow over you and your suitability as an Academy candidate, don't you?"

"Yes, sir," Kate said. "I regret what happened."

The Commander sighed. "Though I suspect you don't feel responsible, despite having the sense not to say so."

"Sir."

"Miss Kincaid, you've either read too many old war memoirs or spent too much time with Chief Williamson," the Commander said. "What you haven't done is proven you can color within the lines. Work as part of a team without being disruptive. Are you game to try to fix that?"

"Yes, sir."

"Very well," the Commander said. "I believe you owe me five weeks. You can spend them working on the processing line as a bottom level intern. If you can manage to do so without creating some sort of fuss, I'll grant you your endorsement."

"Thank you, sir."

\* \* \*

Not so very long ago, his daily lunches in the admin cafeteria with Guy and the other administrative heads had been one of Commander Tretyak's favorite parts of an established and comfortable routine.

Not since Katie Kincaid had forced her way into his life.

The Commander was reconsidering his conversation with Kincaid this morning.

Superficially, he thought it had gone well. On reflection he was worried he'd might have made a fundamental error based on a misperception.

"A penny for your thoughts," Guy, who was sitting across the lunch table, asked.

"Not sure they're worth that," Yuri said. "Not sure it's entirely appropriate to discuss them either."

"You can trust me," Guy said. "Nothing you don't want to will go any further."

Yuri wondered for a moment if he should broach Kincaid's

implication Billy was a bully with his friend. Her suggestion that Billy's bullying had gotten out of hand. He wished he could. He couldn't see it would do any good. He didn't see any chance that given the source, his friend would lend the accusation any credence. Especially given the unwillingness of any of those involved to admit to the facts of the matter. His own unwillingness to press Kincaid on the matter would be a problem. Best let sleeping dogs lie. "I think I may have mishandled the Kincaid girl," he said.

"Not hard," Guy said, "that girl's a tricky piece of trouble."

"And you see, Guy," Yuri said, "that's why I'm concerned about talking to you even though I value your advice. I trust you, but other people might think that sort of talk indicates clear bias."

"I call them the way I see them," Guy replied.

"Okay," Yuri said. He needed to move on. "The way I see the problem is that Miss Kincaid never learned the deference to adults from her parents that most kids do. It extends to her attitude to authority in general. It not only gets her into trouble, but it's led me into forgetting she is, in fact, only a young girl."

"Yeah, that sounds right," Guy replied. "Can even admit it's not her fault. Not your fault either, though. You have to admit it's not like it won't get her into trouble at your Academy. It's a problem she needs to fix. Makes sense you want to see if she's capable of it before signing off on her."

"That's reassuring," Yuri said. "Nice to know someone thinks I'm not totally off course here. Only I've arranged for her to spend time on the processing line. On reflection, I'm not sure she isn't too young for it. It can be a rough place. Dangerous too, if you're not careful."

"Not fond of the girl," Guy said, "but do have to admit she can take care of herself."

"No kids of my own," Yuri said, "but they can be hard to peg at that age, can't they? They're like young adults some of the time, and still only kids other times."

"Yeah, tell me about it," Guy said. "You have to start letting go, but it's hard. No guarantees it'll work out."

"I feel a certain responsibility for her now," Yuri said. "I also feel it'd be getting a little out of my lane, but that I ought to be careful and make a point of monitoring her progress personally. Just in case. I've heard rumors about processing line personnel getting rough with outsiders."

"They don't send the best people down there, true," Guy said, "but I figure those rumors are exaggerated."

"Still maybe I should haul her back in," Yuri replied. "Give her a better briefing. Make sure she understands she can call me if problem comes up. That I'll abort the trial without prejudice if her safety seems threatened."

"Kind of undermines the whole purpose of the exercise, doesn't it?" Guy asked.

"Guess it does," Yuri admitted, "but I can't in conscience leave things as is."

"Tell you what, Yuri," Guy replied. "I've got friends on the line there. I can call in favors. Ask them to keep a special eye on her. Is that good enough?"

"Hate delegating responsibility like that," Yuri said. "Guess it's probably the best solution. I know the Kincaid girl is not your favorite person. I'm glad you're the sort of responsible adult who can be trusted to do the right thing in a situation like this."

"What are friends for?" Guy asked.

## 6: Katie Copes

Katie gripped a handrail and looked around. The stars overhead she ignored. Fascinating as they were she had no time for "lollygagging" as Hanna would call it. The spidery metal framework of the ore docking facility she paid a bit more attention to. Some parts could move in order to adjust to different ships or other needs. Mostly she kept an eye on Hanna, the line worker who'd been assigned to mentor her.

Hanna Rhinehart was less than pleased by the assignment. She'd already remarked to Katie that she didn't have time for babysitting, that she had a job to do.

If Katie hadn't already had doubts about the task Commander Tretyak had given her, Hanna's attitude would have created them. As it was, Katie was convinced it was a sure sign that the Commander, despite the years he'd spent on Ceres, was completely clueless about its social structure. In particular, what life was like for those at the bottom of that structure.

Being on the processing line was the lowest rung of gainful employment on Ceres. Any lower and you were subject to deportation to a Mars, or for those fit enough Earth, based habitat for the delinquent or unproductive. Just keeping a person alive and out of trouble was much less expensive on the planets.

Basically, the processing line was manned by the desperate

dregs of Belter society.

The work was boring, largely unskilled, and dangerous. Supposedly, the only reason it was not automated was because it was not quite routine enough for standard procedures. One size fits all couldn't eke out the last few percent of needed profitability. Individual humans, their base salaries augmented by piecework bounties, were allegedly more adaptable.

In any case, it was no place to drop a fifteen year girl into for a few weeks. Not that Katie intended to let that stop her. No, she'd have the courage to tough it out and the sense and discipline not to annoy anyone or get hurt.

She'd start by trying to soften up Hanna.

The fact she'd known how to put a spacesuit on properly and then do the necessary safety checks both on herself and Hanna had started the process. Her ability to maneuver in vacuum and microgravity had helped further.

Hanna had gone from bitterly and coldly hostile to sullen and indifferent. Progress! Yeah!

Right now at least Hanna's constant anger wasn't directed at Katie.

The crew of the ship they were unloading containers of minerals from had somehow fallen behind in detaching them. As a consequence, Hanna, and Katie were waiting on them.

Katie's main goal for the next few weeks was just to keep her head down and not offend anyone. Still, this seemed like a chance to pry some information Hanna and maybe glean a sliver of sympathy. "Doesn't seem like it should be that hard," she said over their private channel on her suit's radio. "Do glitches like this happen often?"

"Often enough. Too often," Hanna all but grunted back.

Katie got the hint for the time being. She let the conversation lapse. A few minutes later there was a container ready to go. Together following Hanna's instructions they guided it down the large down shaft into Ceres' depths where the preliminary storage caverns were. Katie was impressed by Hanna's careful professionalism. She was all business. Didn't waste any time or energy. Didn't cut any corners either.

Once they had the container in its resting place and dogged down Katie ventured some further comments. "So that went okay, right?" she asked. "I imagine as long as I don't make a fuss and follow all the rules and directions it'll work out, right?" She was feeling unusually uncertain.

Hanna grunted and pointed across the cavern to something painted on its floor. Katie zoomed in with her suit's optics. It looked like a blobby rounded human silhouette. "That's where Jack got smeared," Hanna said. "Tripped, got trapped under a container. Once these things get going, there's nothing going to stop them short of solid rock. Got to keep your eyes open. Always pay attention and even then you can get unlucky."

"I guess this has got to be the most dangerous part of the processing line," Katie said. "Imagine it gets better later." She was scheduled to move down the line after a week in unloading. She didn't understand why if they were testing her ability to get along with people they were moving between teams every week. She hadn't figured it was a good idea to start off asking impertinent questions either.

Hanna barked. Took Katie a moment to realize it was a bark of laughter. "No, kid," Hanna said. "It does not get better."

Hanna hadn't sounded too sympathetic, but she hadn't sounded angry either. At least not at Katie. Katie decided to take advantage. "How's that?" she asked.

"It's dangerous here," Hanna said, "but it's routine. No competition. You do your job careful like and you're not too unlucky and you'll be okay. No way to make extra money except overtime, but you can get by on the base salary. Further on it gets less standard and more competitive. Still dangerous. Loose rock as well as moving containers. Conveyor belts to get caught in. Nothing is standard or routine, and you can't trust any of those rats."

"Sounds bad," Katie said. "Any advice?"

"Yeah, give it up," Hanna said. "You quit you don't get into your fancy school, but there're worse fates."

"I'm not a quitter."

"You get killed or maimed you're still not going to the Academy. Somebody's got it out for you, kid."

Katie didn't have an answer for that.

* * *

They were back at Bob's Burgers. There'd been a time when Calvin would have been thrilled to have been spending so much time with Katie. He'd always enjoyed the food at Bob's too. It was a treat.

Right now he could barely stomach it.

Katie was telling him about her first few days on the processing line. She was telling him about what the woman she'd been working with had told her. She was concerned.

Not half as concerned as Calvin was. Somehow he had to convince her to give up on this craziness.

Calvin figured he'd take the bull by the horns. "So it's not going well?" he said.

"That place is all messed up," Katie stated. "The people are even more messed up."

Calvin blinked. Despite a predilection for critical thought, Katie usually managed to be positive. To look on the bright side of things. To see the best in people when she bothered to pay attention to them. "Processing line isn't safe," he said. "They don't want to be there. Frankly, I wish you weren't there."

"It's only five weeks for me," Katie answered, "and I've done almost a week of it. It's been a couple of years since anyone was killed."

"But people do get killed," Calvin said, "and even more get injured. Maimed for life, some of them. It's not worth it, Katie. Give it up."

Katie gave Calvin a glare that made him want to crawl under the table. He didn't. He stared right back at her. "It isn't only your life," he said. "Some of us care about you. Do you really think the Commander is going to relent and endorse your application? Or more likely isn't he going to keep giving you harder and more dangerous tasks until you fail or get hurt?"

"I don't think the Commander or the authorities in general understand how bad it is on the processing line," Katie said. "I think if I can prove to him I can toe the line and get along on a team that'll he'll endorse me. He might be somewhat blinkered, but I believe he's an honest man."

Calvin sighed and decided to bite the bullet. "Bottom line, it's just not worth it," he said. "Going to the Academy is a dream for you because you want to prove you have what it takes. In reality, there's nothing there for you. It wouldn't be worth it, even if you weren't taking all these risks. You can have everything you want here. I'd be happy to spend the rest of my life here with you. This is where you belong. You won't find more happiness anywhere else."

"Calvin, you've been a good friend," Katie said. "Sorry, but never thought of you as anything more. Not you, not anybody. Wouldn't be fair, I've got plans that don't allow for that. A good friend ought to support me."

Calvin swallowed. His eyes felt sore. He hoped he wasn't tearing up. He spoke past a lump in his gut. "I'm sorry too. I want the best for you. This Academy quest of yours isn't it. I can't, I won't, help you dig your own grave."

"That's it then, isn't it?" Katie said.

"Yes, suppose so. I don't have anymore to say. Do you?"

"Nope," she said. And with that she got up and left.

As determined as ever.

\* \* \*

Guy was in his quarters. Drinking. He'd had just come from another lunch with Commander Tretyak. Not a bad guy, but completely clueless. He supposed he should be a little more forgiving. He'd missed the developing crisis with Billy right under his own eyes, after all.

It irked. He'd always prided himself on being hard headed. Not letting sentiment cloud his vision. Yet that's exactly what he'd done with his son.

It'd taken some work to winkle the truth out of Billy's friends and then Billy himself.

Billy and his gang had graduated from being bullies to outright criminal behavior. That wasn't what bothered Guy the most. It was the stupid short sighted and petty manner they'd gone about it. Worse, that sniveling little rat Marvin had probably kept Billy from being even dumber.

Guy turned and flung the glass he been drinking from at the wall. It bounced, scattering expensive liquor everywhere. Modern glasses didn't break easily. He'd have to clean the mess up himself. It wouldn't do to have anyone else realize he was losing his grip. That temper was what had driven Billy's mother away. He'd thought he'd long since conquered it.

Guess not. Billy's mother had been a fine woman. Very attractive and as sweet as can be. Not the sharpest knife in the drawer, though. Kind of dumb, in fact. Something a young man's hormones had led him to overlook at first. Later, it'd meant she'd not understood the business he was in. That she'd not understood what she was getting into when she'd married him. And so she'd left.

Leaving him with Billy, who'd had the luck to get his mother's brains and his dad's looks and character. Not a good combination.

Successful criminals had to be smart. Still, the boy was his son, and he'd do his best for him.

It'd turned out that the scrap with the Kincaid girl hadn't been the only incident he'd been in. If that'd been his son's only transgression, it could have been worked through with some awkwardness. Turned out Kincaid had been right to resist, otherwise it might have gone much worse for her. Like it had for others.

Problem was that if Kincaid was ever to provoke a proper investigation into Billy's doings it'd all come out.

If that happened, Billy was going away for a long time. Guy be lucky to keep his own job. His reputation would be in tatters. If his apparent weakness emboldened some of his less trustworthy associates, it might be worse than that. Guy might end up doing time himself.

He couldn't risk that.

Something decisive needed to be done about the Kincaid problem.

Fortunately, he had people in place on the processing line that could see to it.

\* \* \*

Katie had thought of Commander Tretyak's trials as meaningless in their own right. Jumping through some hoops to satisfy a man who'd spent too long behind a desk. Who'd forgotten how to make decisions.

She was feeling more stressed out than she'd ever been. She was revising that opinion. Two weeks into her stint on the processing line and she was having doubts. The place was a dog's breakfast.

She'd had to look up the meaning of the expression when she'd first encountered it. Space was no place for pets. A very few people on Ceres itself had cats, birds, or fish, and that was it. She'd been taken with how it epitomized the idea of a disgusting mess.

If that hadn't been enough the thing with Calvin was worse. It really wasn't pertinent to her current problems, and she wished she could stop thinking about it. It slammed home two points she'd rather not have acknowledged.

You'd have thought with her parents she'd have realized that simply because people wanted good things for you didn't mean they wanted what you did. Point one. Point two. She was bad at noticing things about the people around her. Calvin had a crush on her. How had she not noticed that?

It was depressing. She couldn't afford the time to moon over it.

Nobody on the processing line, on any part of it, could afford distractions.

Currently, she was working at a "second pick" station. First pick happened almost immediately after the initial unloading of the mineral containers.

Fact was, most asteroids were piles of rubble. You ran into the odd one, an "M-type", that was solid iron nickel and they were simple to process. Already reduced to reasonable sized chunks by the initial mining process, they could be sent directly to the steel foundries. Turned out despite the bad odds, the workers on the processing line still liked to pick them over. A single lucky find of a gold, platinum, or other precious nugget could set a worker up for life. Even a single small fragment of precious metal could mean a week off or some luxuries otherwise unaffordable.

If that was true for the M-types it was even more true for the other types of asteroids. Some of them were largely water, but even those had the odd surprise contained in them. And so a wasteful degree of effort of was expended on the first pick through the ore. Katie had seen hints of competition of politicking for positions there. She'd felt the resentment by the others that she took up one of those slots for several days. She'd not found anything. Had not expected to and would have gladly skipped the experience. Only someone had decided she was spending time at every station on the line.

After first pick, there was a further sorting and a grinding and crushing of the ore down to standard sized pieces. Some portion of the ore went directly from that stage directly to either water, organics, or metal processing, but most was more mixed and subjected to a second sorting.

It was all rather simple, but it involved moving a lot of rock around. Mostly routine, but if you got careless, got in the way, or flung some rock around too hard bad things could happen. Katie had thought she was strong minded, but it was trying. Mostly boring as hell, but with some slight chance of things going drastically wrong if you didn't pay attention. Maybe even if you did. Not much you could do about that. The stress built until it became a constant low grade headache.

So she had to pay more attention to the rocks in front of her and what they looked like. Very occasionally one was a little different and needed to be picked out and placed in a special bin. It might be a valuable organic or piece of metal. Mostly they were just rocks. Also, you had to be careful once you'd completed one pile of rock and another was incoming. Didn't want to be in the way. It'd be a crushing experience. Ha, ha.

"You need to focus, Kincaid," came a voice from behind her. It was Connie D'Souza her foreman. For some reason, most of the foremen on the line were women.

"Yes, ma'am," Katie replied. The woman was right, after all.

"You work on surveys on your family rig?" D'Souza asked.

"Yes, I did, ma'am," Katie replied wonder why if Connie wanted her to concentrate she was distracting Katie. Katie spotted an odd rock that might be worth special processing. She grabbed it and flipped it into the appropriate bin. "Mostly outer belt rocks. 'C-type' mostly. Lot of base material for the gardens."

"But bit of a mix, right?"

"That's right."

"Johnny," D'Souza called out to a man changing out bins, "come here." Johnny came over. He was skinny and gave the impression of never having been too bright. And having gone downhill from there. He was quiet and a hard worker. Connie didn't normally give him non-routine tasks that involved noticing things. "You take Kincaid's station for a bit, okay?"

"Sure, boss," Johnny replied.

"Kincaid, you come with me," D'Souza said, walking off towards a currently unused corner of the huge cavern they were in.

Katie followed the woman. They stopped by a large pile of variegated rubble. The color differences were subtle, but real. Connie D'Souza studied the pile with disgust. "This is just a sample batch," she said. "We've got a whole ship load of this crap coming through."

"Yes, ma'am," Katie said. Seemed the safest thing to say. Remaining completely silent might seem sullen.

"Can you make any sense of it?" D'Souza asked.

"Relatively recent accretion from an intersection between various groups, I'd guess," Katie said. "All sorts of pieces knocked off of first and second generation bodies mixed together. Mostly carbon and some water, but can be almost anything else mixed in."

"Yeah, mismatched junk. Knew that," D'Souza said. "Can you recognize the minerals when you see them?"

"Some," Katie said slowly. Who knew what would turn up in one of these things? Her father lived for finding rare never before seen minerals in asteroids. It was likely the reason that when he and her mother had decided to flee their families, they'd come out to the Belt. He'd spent hours talking about it to her. It was interesting, she had to admit, but she found a lot of other things more interesting. D'Souza doubtless wasn't interested in Katie's family history.

"More common minerals, sure," Katie said. "But I'm just a rock rat kid. Nothing special, not an astrogeologist or anything."

"You do the surveys. You know the science," D'Souza asserted.

"The basics sure, ma'am," Katie said. "Science is complicated and not settled yet, though. Lot we don't know yet. We often got surprises out there. It's why none of this is automated."

"So what are we likely to see when that load comes in?"

Woman wasn't taking "no" for an answer. Katie took a deep breath and did her best. "Odd pockets of high mineralization embedded in the watery crud. There'll be the occasional piece of rare mineral. They'll be worth looking for. Take a lot of patience and a sharp eye."

"Okay," D'Souza said. "Get a good night's sleep tonight. Think about it. You're coming in an hour early tomorrow to give the rest of us a talk on how to spot that stuff. It'll be worth a kind word in my report."

"Yes, ma'am. That all?" Katie said.

"Yep, back at it, girl."

They turned to go their ways when a whistling sound grew suddenly from a mere whisper to a loud screech. D'Souza looked up, fear on her face. Katie realized what it was. A load of rock was coming in way too fast and without warning.

"Johnny, run!" yelled D'Souza.

Johnny turned slowly at first, and then realization dawning started to move. He was too late.

The main load came roaring in and demolished the station Katie had been manning. That missed Johnny. The large fragments it sent flying all around, they didn't. In slow motion, Katie saw one piece catch him in the center of his back. Another piece clipped his head as he went down.

In seconds it was all over. A few loose pieces of rock still rolling slowly here and there on the cavern floor, but nothing dangerous anymore.

D'Souza rushed over to Johnny and inspected him. Half his head had been caved in. It lay in a large growing puddle of blood. It wasn't spurting, which Katie understood wasn't a good sign.

D'Souza laid some fingers on the wrist of an outstretched arm and leaned in close with an ear. "No pulse. Not breathing. Head smashed in. Don't think we can do anything for Johnny," she stated grimly. She spared Katie a quick glance before taking a deep breath and composing herself. "George," she yelled. George was the shift's safety officer. As far as Katie had noticed it meant he had a yellow hard helmet he could wear. "You call the medics?" "Yes, ma'am," George replied.

D'Souza stood and looked about. "Everybody else, okay?", she yelled. A chorus of "Yes, ma'ams" came back.

"Okay, line is halted. You're all to stay here. You don't talk to each other. Especially not about this," D'Souza announced loudly and clearly without any signs of the stress Katie had seen on her face just moments before.

"You don't think this was an accident?" Katie asked quietly.

"No, I don't," D'Souza replied, "and what did I say about talking?"

"Yes, ma'am," Katie said. She was starting to feel sick as what had happened started to sink in.

## 7: Katie's Close Call

Katie had never thought about it before, but the police must constantly monitor emergency calls.

They'd arrived close on the heels of the medical emergency team. Turned out they had a lot more to do and say.

The medics had dispassionately confirmed what everybody had already figured out. Johnny was gone and beyond any help. They'd remained only to answer questions for the police.

There were a lot of police. Katie figured most of the current shift must be here and then some. Chief Donald Dingle himself had just arrived. The police who were almost as numerous as the workers on shift had spaced everyone out in long lines. They'd reiterated D'Souza's instructions to not talk to each other.

Katie herself had been separated from D'Souza. She'd followed the instructions of the police officer who'd told her to stand there and not talk docilely. She was trying as hard as she could to be small and hard to see.

She couldn't help looking around some and observing what was going on. Her fellow workers were mostly standing about with glum, zoned out patience. Some looked half asleep. Sam had once told her one thing you learned in the marines was that you rested whenever you got the chance. You never knew when the next chance would come. Seemed processing line workers had a similar philosophy.

Katie just hoped the police would get through their interrogations quickly. That the line would go back to working and that she could finish out the rest of her stint on it without being in the vicinity of more accidents. She couldn't see how anyone could hold her responsible for what had happened, but somehow she had the sense the Commander would feel she was somehow guilty. She could only hope the balance of evidence and logic would outweigh those feelings. In the meantime, all she could do was wait and surreptitiously observe.

The regular policeman all had that bland intimidating look that even policemen in old pre-space age movies had. Must go with the job.

Most of them stood about making sure the workers, witnesses to the police she guessed, didn't take off or talk with each other.

A small group accompanied Chief Dingle as he moved from witness to witness asking questions. The Chief had a different vibe from the uniformed line officers. The traditional rumpled detective one. That he was wearing a fedora, likely the only one on Ceres, suggested this was no accident.

Eventually he reached Katie.

"Katie Kincaid," he said, looking up from a small tablet he'd been reading. Katie had the feeling he hadn't needed it to tell him who she was. "What are you doing here?"

"I'm working as a temporary intern on the line for a few weeks, sir," she answered. "Commander Tretyak arranged it. He wanted to see how well I could handle working at non-academic tasks in a team not composed of family members before endorsing an application to the Space Force Academy."

"I see," the Chief said, looking down at his tablet. He gave no hint if any of this was news to him or if he'd known it all along. "A dangerous place for a young woman."

"Sir. It's no more dangerous than working a watch on a mining rig," Katie replied. "People my age and younger routinely do that on family ships."

"Haven't had a shipboard accident like this in many years," the Chief said. "Did you know you have reputation as a trouble magnet?"

"I'm pretty much an outsider, sir," Katie said. "Not from Ceres itself and my family isn't one of the old mining ones that's been here for generations. We have a different business model and operating routine too. I guessing it's easier to blame things that happen anywhere near me on me rather than anyone else."

"So you do know you have a reputation," the Chief said. "You don't think it's a fair one?"

"I don't know, sir," Katie said. She didn't want to argue with the man or contradict him, but neither was she confessing to anything she didn't think was true. "It's not the sort of thing people tell you to your face, and I'm not sure how separate my individual reputation is from that of my family's."

"But you had an explanation?"

"Only a suggestion, sir," Katie replied. "For what you suggested." Yeah, we're all only making suggestions here.

"Any other suggestions, Miss Kincaid?" the Chief asked. "Maybe for an explanation of what happened here? A man died."

"Yes, sir, and I was an innocent bystander," Katie answered. "I was talking to Foreman D'Souza over there by that pile of congregate when it happened. As for being trouble, I'm only doing another three weeks here and then I'm gone."

The Chief smiled thinly. Almost indulgently. Katie didn't trust the expression for a minute. "You haven't addressed the fact it was your work station that was obliterated," he said. "You were lucky you didn't suffer Mr. Applebaum's fate."

Katie could only guess Applebaum had been Johnny's last name. "I've been told over and over again accidents can happen on the line, sir. I was picking through the rock. I've no control over the rock deliveries. They're supposed to come on a schedule. Warnings are supposed to sounded before each delivery. No way what happened was my fault."

"Yes, Foreman D'Souza was clear about the operating routine," the Chief said. "I wasn't suggesting you tried to kill yourself."

"Sir?"

"You know Mr. Applebaum well, Miss Kincaid?" the Chief asked next.

"Johnny was introduced to me along with the rest of the shift when I joined it," Katie answered. "We never talked any other time. He was a quiet guy and hard working. Almost part of the scenery."

"So no hard feelings?"

Katie wondered if they really thought she'd killed Johnny because she didn't like him or something. "Nope, we didn't interact at all, but I never sensed any dislike. He seemed like an okay guy."

Which was more than she could say about some of her co-workers, but the Chief didn't need to hear that.

"They're standard questions, Miss," the Chief said. "Most deaths that aren't accidental are the result of people who know each other and aren't getting along. So the standard procedure checks for that first."

It occurred to Katie that it was almost certainly not standard procedure to explain the procedure to witnesses or suspects. The Chief was indulging the curiosity she had a reputation for. Perhaps she should reciprocate the consideration. Perhaps that was the Chief's intent. Heavens, people gave her a headache.

A uniformed officer came up to them with a pair of clear plastic bags with what looked like lengths of chain in them. The Chief took them. "Thanks, Bob," he said before examining the metal within them. The officer remained, patiently waiting.

"Could have snapped after corroding naturally," the Chief said.

The officer leaned in and pointed at the end of one bit of metal. "See the flat bits through the pitting?" he asked.

"Yes, I see. It's more likely someone cut part way through with a saw and then applied acid to hide the fact and finish the job," the Chief said. "The Lab will have a better idea," he said, handing the evidence back to the officer who walked off.

The Chief turned to Katie. "You catch that?" he asked.

"You don't think it was an accident?" Katie asked.

"No, and you're not to share that insight," the Chief said. "You're a very lucky young woman."

"Unlike Johnny," a nearby officer muttered.

The Chief threw him a quelling glance. "That wasn't precision work. It could have snapped any time within several hours."

"Usually do an eight-hour shift with a few short breaks," Katie said. The Chief doubtless knew that. She was talking to fill air time. It was disconcerting. The Chief was right, the odds were she should be dead. Crushed beneath a load of rock.

"You know anyone who might want to kill you?" the Chief asked.

"No," Katie answered. She wasn't that annoying.

"Anyone on the line that you've annoyed or crossed paths with at all?"

Katie thought of Billy, but Billy wasn't on the line. "No," she said, "folks here mostly aren't really happy to see me, I'm afraid. They tolerate me, though. Some have been helpful. I've been careful to keep my head down and not irritate anyone. Haven't cheesed off anyone I know of."

"Glad to hear it," the Chief said. Katie couldn't tell if he was being sarcastic or not. "You do have a reputation for being smart and rather nosy. Is there anything you might have noticed that someone might have been worried you'd report?"

"Nothing worth killing someone over," Katie said.

One of the uniformed officers nearby snorted. They were quite the chorus, she couldn't help thinking.

"If you're thinking of supervisors getting little bribes in exchange for plum assignments, you're right," the Chief said. "It's not much more than office politics. Practically speaking there's not much we can do about it. So if you'd ratted someone specific out, or lodged a general complaint, there'd have been hard feelings. You didn't though. And nobody would want to up the ante by arranging a fatal accident even if you had."

Katie hesitated before speaking. "I'm surprised you're willing to be so explicit about that, sir," she said.

"Part of your reputation, Miss Kincaid," the Chief answered, "is that you don't take hints well. That you need things spelled out for you. I'm trying to elicit your co-operation here. Somebody tried to kill you. If you have any idea who or why you should share with me."

Katie thought of all the different people she'd encountered the last couple of weeks. They'd all seemed willing to live and let live in a grudging sort of way. She'd been careful not to upset anyone, and she believed she'd succeeded. She shook her head. "I can't think of anyone or any reason," she said.

The Chief grunted. "Anything comes to you don't hesitate to get a hold of me," he said, handing her a card. "Finally, you're going to be sixteen in less than a month, right?"

Was the Chief going to wish her Happy Birthday Katie wondered. "Yes, sir," she answered.

"After this I would have advised you to cease working on the processing line anyways," the Chief said.

"Sir, I have to complete my work here if I'm to satisfy Commander Tretyak and get my application to the Academy endorsed."

"Yes, I'm going to talk to the Commander about that," the Chief said. "He's often complained to me that shipping law allows family operated ships to use children in roles they're too young for. He doesn't seem to have realized that the processing line here on Ceres falls under UN Earth labor laws."

"Which means, sir?"

"Which means that even under direct parental supervision you'd have to be sixteen to work on the line legally. Unsupervised you need to be eighteen. I take it you're not being paid?"

"No sir, I'm an intern."

"First one ever on the line, I imagine," the Chief smirked. "If they'd tried to enter you on the payroll, the software would have flagged it automatically."

"And nobody realized this?" Katie asked. She was beginning to feel annoyed and indignant. They weren't wise emotions to indulge.

The Chief sighed and gave a small smile that seemed somewhat more sympathetic and genuine than some of his earlier ones. "Neither set of laws actually makes much sense," he said. "Though I'll deny saying that. One's too loose, the other too strict. Worse, they overlap. People like me and the Commander are stuck trying to apply them reasonably and the rule of the letter of law goes by the boards. If you succeed in becoming an officer in the Space Force, you'll face similar conundrums yourself."

"But now I'm stuck being unable to do the task the Commander asked me to," Katie said. "I'll have to go back to him and beg for another chance."

"With your presence here having been brought so forcibly to my attention, I have no choice but to apply the letter of law," the Chief said. "I'm going to be kind enough not to press charges against anyone."

He glanced over to where D'Souza was waiting patiently. "As I've already explained to your foreman, and will shortly explain to the Commander," he said. "I'll make it clear none of this is your fault. I think he'll give you another chance at the very least."

"Sir?"

"You're not our favorite daughter, Katie Kincaid," the Chief said, "but I think most of us here on Ceres would be proud to see you get into the Academy."

"Thank you, sir."

"You're welcome. You're dismissed. Turn in your gear and return directly to your quarters."

"Yes, sir."

"And try to stay out of trouble."

\*\*\*

Katie was feeling gutted.

She'd kept her head down and done what she was told.

She'd avoided doing things other than what she was told. She'd kept her mouth shut. She hadn't argued with people or pointed it out to them when she thought they were being irrational. She hadn't fought back or debated it with people when she felt they were being unreasonable.

When she'd noticed supervisors and their workers exchanging little favors, she'd kept her mouth shut. She'd not brought it up with anyone. She'd not reported it to the authorities. Which as they all seemed in on it was just as well.

She'd answered sullen hostility with unflagging patience. She'd never failed to be polite or respectful.

She'd been helpful when she could in as unassuming and non-intrusive way as she could.

She'd worked hard and done everything she'd been told.

She'd never complained.

It hadn't been enough. It was an understatement to say she was unhappy. She was devastated. What more could she have done?

The Chief hadn't said it explicitly, but he'd made an interesting point. He'd suggested that she didn't have to do anything to cause trouble. He'd suggested that given her reputation that all she had to do was exist and be around and someone might react with fearful hostility.

What the heck? How was she supposed to cope with that?

She found herself tearing up with the unfairness of it. She felt trapped. Escape seemed impossible. She sobbed.

She'd never done that before. She touched her face in wonder. She was crying.

She couldn't remember ever having done that before. Maybe that time when she was barely past being a toddler and whacked her knee on the edge of a hatch. There'd been actual blood. It'd taken weeks to heal. Still had a faint scar.

It'd hadn't been the pain that'd made her cry, though. It was the shock. The surprise that she could get hurt so easily out of the blue. Her father had kissed the knee better, and the fear had quickly faded. She'd learned to be careful though, and to always pay attention to safety. That had been the beginning of her obsession with safety rules.

Now that she thought about it, she realized it was the closest she'd ever come to hardship or any sort of setback before. Her parents, as fey and feckless as they might seem to her at times, had kept her safe. She'd never really suffered disappointment, let alone grief or loss.

The Commander was more than right. Not only was she inexperienced with people, she had no experience with failure or even disappointment. Her classmates on Ceres when she was here had left her alone after a few sharp lessons. She was not only smarter than all of them, she was stronger and faster too. She had no strong ties, so social shaming didn't work. She went her own way. She got her own way. Always.

She had no experience of failure or not getting what she wanted. She worked hard, true, but it'd always paid off for her before too.

Before the line, her closest experience with setbacks and failure had been in the old out of copyright books her parents had bought her. They depicted a different world, a century at least out of date, and predominantly planet bound. The trials and tribulations of the fictional characters in them hadn't seemed truly real to her. Also, they'd all eventually triumphed in the end.

Obviously reality wasn't like that, but it'd never really sunk in before.

No wonder she'd annoyed her fellow workers on the line. Their entire lives seemed to be a string of disappointments, of poor choices that they simply had to accept the consequences of. Her blithe assumption things would always work out for her had to be irksome.

Boy, she felt stupid.

And not nasty, but obnoxious maybe.

For the first time in her life, she didn't feel good about being who she was.

To be the cold and uncaring creature, she must look like to most people, it was a practical problem too.

The Commander was right. Made her want to gag to admit it, but he was.

She was practically ignorant about people. About the trials and tribulations they routinely faced most of all. It was something that had been bound to blow up in her face sooner or later. Particularly if she chose a career that meant dealing with people in crisis situations at times. She was profoundly ill suited to such a role.

And she'd had no clue it was so.

Maybe the Commander was right and she ought to give up the idea of joining the Space Force. Give up those other plans she didn't like to contemplate in the privacy of her own mind, even given their arguably insane degree of ambition. She might be mental, but damned if she was going to admit it to anyone. Or let it stop her.

There was a good reasonable argument for being practical and backing off. Of settling for a moderately successful career, doing something as a civilian business person in the Belt. The Commander, Calvin, and her parents all seemed to think it was a good idea.

Only Sam hadn't discouraged her, and he hadn't precisely encouraged her either. Let her have her head was all. He seemed to think if you wanted something, you ought to try to go for it. Didn't mean he thought it was necessarily a good idea, or that the chances of success were that good.

Well, okay, she could accept she'd been blind and that she needed to pay more attention. Specifically, it seemed that being a hero required being a good politician, of always thinking about how anything you did might affect your reputation. Who'd have thought it?

Didn't mean you could avoid taking chances or always do the most popular thing. Did mean when you took chances or did something unpopular, you recognized the fact and had good reasons for it.

She took a deep breath. She felt better now. Life made a sort of sense again. It was bleaker, more difficult, and not as nice as she'd thought, but it made sense again. She could do this. She could try, at least.

She'd go to the Commander and convince him to give her another chance. Maybe she'd talk it over with Sam first. She wished she could talk it over with Calvin too, but that didn't seem likely. But starting right now, she was paying more attention to people and how they felt.

She'd get her chance.
She'd learn from it.

*  *  *

When he was much younger Yuri Tretyak had had a strip torn off of him by marine drill instructors and more senior cadets at the Academy from time to time. He'd had them walk up one side of him and down the other as the saying went. He'd thought he'd had a good idea of what it meant to be verbally bawled out. To be motivated to never incur such wrath again.

He'd also thought he'd acquired a certain immunity to verbal abuse. An immunity he'd not needed for years and which he'd never expected to need again.

Turned out he'd been wrong.

He'd just come from a "discussion" with Police Chief Donald Dingle. Dingle had at no point raised his voice or employed profanity. The Commander still felt as if he'd been flayed and rolled in salt. Like he'd been shrunk, deflated, wrung out, and stomped all over.

Chief Dingle had been scathing.

Worse, he'd made it clear to Yuri that he thought he was letting him off easy. That he thought that Yuri had been stupid, not malicious. He'd been much more detailed in his lengthy and very clear exposition of that belief.

As the Commander sat in his office staring at his desktop, absorbing what had been explained to him he found he really couldn't disagree. It did nothing to make him feel better. It was going to be lunch soon. He had no appetite at all.

Unfortunately since he was a creature of routine, his absence in the cafeteria would be noted. It would send the wrong signal. As much as he'd like to sit in his office licking his wounds it wasn't behavior befitting of a Space Force officer.

Sometimes being merely human wasn't acceptable.

Neither was blaming other people for his failures. He hadn't mentioned Guy Boucher's offer to keep an eye on Kincaid to the Chief. He didn't intend to bring it up with Guy at lunch either. He did wonder what the hell had gone wrong.

Katie Kincaid might not be his cup of tea, but she'd done nothing remotely worth being murdered for that he knew of.

He didn't for a skinny second believe that she deserved it or had done anything to directly provoke it.

No, as unfair as it was the girl was likely the victim of her reputation for being smart and fearless. You'd think those be virtues and duly rewarded. Not if she'd noticed something somewhere someone wanted kept secret.

He felt a stab of resentment. He had no idea what or who that could be. Neither as far as he could tell did the Chief. Which was unfortunate because between the two of them it was certainly the job of one or the other of them to know that. Probably given the entanglement of affairs of Ceres with those of the wider Belt in its vicinity, both of them were responsible. Attempted murder was no joke.

Cold blooded attempted murder in such a small community was a huge risk and implied a commensurate fear of exposure. Someone somewhere had committed, maybe was still committing a crime that was so serious, that a risky attempt at murder seemed worth it. Worth it if it kept that crime from being revealed.

And he had no idea what crime or who could be responsible. It was infuriating.

Their best lead seemed to be the Kincaid girl herself. Only the Chief said she'd told him she had no idea who it could be or why. The Chief felt lying was one of the social skills she lacked and that she was telling the truth. Yuri had to agree.

For a brief moment he instantly felt ashamed of Commander Yuri Tretyak entertained the notion that their best chance of catching the criminal was if they made another attempt on the Kincaid girls' life. He didn't quite get to the point of deliberately planning to use her as bait.

But it would be wrong. He had to be frustrated to even have thought of it. He dearly wanted to wash his hands of the whole thing. Endorse the Kincaid girl's application to the Academy. Sit and do nothing until she departed. Hoped it all worked out.

That'd be irresponsible.

It still wasn't crystal clear the girl was capable of staying out of trouble. Also he was likely the one, however inadvertently, who had put her life in danger by having her work on the line. He owed her some protection.

If he could find a task for her that was under Space Force control where Space Force personnel could keep an eye on her that might kill two birds with one stone.

It was an idea. Seemed like a good one.

Lunch time now.

He was feeling better. Might be able to keep it down.

\* \* \*

Calvin sat in his room and agonized over wording. Who'd have ever thought writing a simple message could be so much work?

He'd been angry with Katie over her determination to pursue her quixotic quest to become a Space Force officer over settling down in the Belt like a reasonable woman.

That had all vanished when he'd heard about the attempt on

her life.

He'd realized that although they were both young, that Katie had never failed to get what she wanted, if only she worked hard enough for it. It wasn't that she was immature. She was simply inexperienced with having to compromise. He was sure that was something that would change with time. All he had to do was be patient.

In any event, he knew how to compromise. Several older sisters and a whole clan full of nosy relatives that all felt entitled to make decisions for one ensured that. Also in a case of life or death involving someone he cared about, it wasn't his feelings that counted.

With her parents off on a long survey tour with no way they could quickly return, Katie was alone on Ceres. Normally that wouldn't be a big deal, but if someone was trying to kill her for some reason something had to be done. He still couldn't imagine why, but if someone was trying to kill her, she needed to be somewhere safer than a school dormitory room. Anybody could access those with a little cunning. Automated systems provided some protection, but they weren't the same as living people keeping an eye out for you.

So he'd asked his parents and his sisters if they'd be willing to help. If one of his sisters would be willing to move in with one of the others and give her room to Katie. In the Cromwell family apartments surrounded in the gravity ring by the rest of the clan and other mining clans, no intruder would go unremarked. Katie would be safe in the Cromwell family home.

They'd agreed immediately. Nobody had ever felt entirely comfortable with the way her parents let Katie run free on Ceres with nobody around to watch out for her. However, she'd always seemed to manage on her own. Also, Sam Williamson and Calvin and his family had always kept something of an eye on her informally. That didn't cut it if someone was out to hurt or kill her.

It was hard to believe, but the facts spoke for themselves. There'd been at least a half dozen workers on shift when Johnny Applebaum got killed at Katie's station. The rumors had spread quick and wide.

And so Katie had a safe place available now. All he had to do was somehow convince her to take advantage of it, despite their having not parted on the best of terms the last time he'd seen her.

In the end, he decided to keep it simple.

"Katie," he wrote, "my family has a room here available for you. It'll be much safer with people around to watch out for bad guys if you take advantage of it. Whatever you or me think or feel, it's only sensible you take advantage of this offer. It's hard to believe, but it looks like somebody dangerous has targeted you. Please don't make it easy for them. Yours most sincerely, Calvin."

He pushed "send", hoping she'd listen to reason.

\* \* \*

Sam was feeling as alarmed as he'd ever had.

Sam had made entries into the lairs of armed criminals that'd worried him less than the news about the fatal accident on the processing line. The one that had apparently been intended for Katie.

Katie hadn't talked to him about her tiff with Calvin. Sam had heard about it all the same through round about channels. Ceres was a small, isolated and rather in bred community after all. News traveled fast. Gossip traveled faster.

He wasn't in general a fan of gossip. In this case, he was happy to have heard about it. He was happy someone cared about the girl other than him. Katie's parents did he was sure, but they weren't anywhere nearby and not all that effectual in their concern when they were. Nice people, but they had their heads stuck firmly up their butts.

Sam was also happy Katie had called to say she was coming by to talk. At least she had some inkling she was out of her depth and was open to advice to some degree. Speak of the devil.

Katie bounced into his machinist's shop with an approximation of her normal energy and verve. Sadly, he could tell she was faking it to some degree.

"Hey, Katie. How's it going?" he greeted her.

"Could be better," she admitted.

"Tell me about it," he said.

"You heard about the accident on the processing line?" she asked.

"I imagine all of Ceres has heard by now," Sam answered. "Way I heard it, someone tried to kill you and got Johnny Applebaum instead. People are shocked there's a killer free here. They don't know if the idea a crazy is loose worries them more, or if the idea someone's hiding something worth killing over does."

"Bet they think it's my fault somehow," Katie said. She failed to keep her bitterness hidden. Not right up front, but it was detectable.

"Wherever you are trouble seems to find you," Sam replied. "Not fair, and not your fault, I think, but it does seem to be the case. People can't help take notice."

"Why, Sam?" she asked. "Am I like a blind bull in a china shop? I mean, I see now that I haven't been paying enough attention to the other people around me. I'm going to try hard to pay more attention. Only down on the processing line I did my job, just my job. I didn't get any attacks of initiative and try to do more. I kept my mouth shut except to say 'yes, ma'am' and 'yes, sir' and things like that. Even if I was a blind bull in a china shop, I was careful not to move around and knock anything over. I was a very still and quiet bull. Yet somehow despite doing almost nothing someone seems to have got so spooked they decided they had to get rid of me permanently. It's insane."

"Welcome to reality, Katie," Sam said. "It's not fair. It doesn't make sense in truth in any manner that mere mortal minds can grasp. Only most people manage to delude themselves otherwise. They'd go crazy otherwise. Most people stay on a beaten path their parents laid out for them. Usually nothing bad happens to them. If it does, it's inexplicable bad luck. They're happy believing simple incomplete fairly tales about how the world really works."

"Gee, Sam, you know how to cheer a girl up," Katie replied with exasperation. Exasperation tinged with some amusement. That was good. Progress of a sort. "Cynical much?" she finished.

"It's a big world out there. There's a lot happening," Sam said. He wasn't giving in on this. It was unfortunate, but Katie needed to finish growing up and fast. "Too much for any one person to keep track of, let alone fully understand. So everybody prioritizes. And we miss some things and oversimplify others. It's unavoidable, but not anything worth dwelling on. It's just a fact like gravity."

"Gravity's a lot simpler," Katie observed.

"You think so?" Sam asked. "To a poor Earth boy, gravity out here seems pretty complicated. Most Earth people never have to figure the difference between mass and weight. Gravity on a planet always has the same force and comes from the same direction. It isn't always changing on you. It's not different from your head to your feet and doesn't make your head spin."

"So it's great to be a dirt hugging Earth boy, I guess," Katie replied.

"You think so?" Sam asked. "When was the last time you had to worry about a weather forecast?"

"Ah, never?" Katie answered. "Your point?"

"Your friend Calvin in all probability will never need to worry about the weather because he's going to stay on Ceres and ships working out of her," Sam said. "You Katie on the other hand want to go to the Space Force Academy, which for reasons has part of its campus down on Earth's surface. You will gain an intense familiarity with all sorts of weather. Cold weather, dry weather, rainy weather, heavy winds but a lack of breezes when you could use one. You'll doubtless discover a new interest in weather forecasts. That's my prediction."

Katie grinned at Sam. "You think I'm going to make it," she said.

"I'd give you odds despite your own flaws and the Commander's issues too," Sam replied.

Katie nodded at that, then frowned. "About Calvin," she said, "his family's offering me a room to stay in. He messaged me. He says it'd be a lot safer there than in the student dorms. What do you think?"

"I think he's right," Sam said. "Not just him but his whole family. He didn't make that offer without their full support. I also think you're right to be wary of owing him for their help."

"Is that why I don't feel that good about the idea?" Katie asked.

"I think so," Sam said. "Some people are lacking in the basic hard wiring to understand other people or read their emotions. I don't think you're one of those people. You only need some practice using what you have. So you can sense if you take this favor, which is a good idea, you'll owe the Cromwells though I'm sure they'll never be so crass as to say so. Reciprocity. You scratch my back, I'll scratch yours. People assume it without thinking about it explicitly. But boy, they'll get upset if you take and never give back."

"Wow," Katie said. "That clarifies it beautifully and still doesn't leave me any closer to a decision."

"Some choices are plain hard," Sam said. "Worse case you get no good ones and have chose between the bad ones and the horrible ones."

Katie smiled shaking her head. "You really are the cheerful one. It's helping."

"Facing up to things. Having a sense of humor about it. It can do that," Sam replied.

"So I haven't heard from the Commander yet," Katie said. "I expect I will sometime today. If I don't, I'll call him first thing tomorrow. I don't figure he'll refuse to endorse me because he messed up his test and somebody else decided they needed to kill me. He knows that'd be too unfair. Don't think he's going to be too happy either. Figure he'll have something else for me. Any thoughts?"

"We both know you'll take anything he gives you as a challenge and barge ahead full steam," Sam said. "Might be the best thing, but this is getting serious."

"It was always serious to me," Katie interjected in a flat tone.

"There are degrees," Sam replied evenly. "Wreck the rest of my life is a touch different from having no more life. Also this is bigger than just you. Katie, you can be a bit much at times but not to the degree that anybody would actually try to kill you over it. I'm sure Chief Dingle has already asked you but you have to figure out why. Something you've seen or been close to that's that important."

Katie shook her head. "I don't know what it could be," she said. "Lost sleep thinking about it. I have no idea."

"Maybe someone just wanted you off the processing line," Sam said. "We can hope, but I wouldn't bet on it. If you don't take the Cromwell's offer you have to find some other way of protecting yourself from future attacks. Any deal you strike with Commander Tretyak has to take that into account. You hear me?"

"Loud and clear," Katie replied.

"Good. That enough?"

"Yep, guess I've got an appointment to make," Katie said standing to leave.

"Stay safe," Sam said by way of good bye.

"I will."

Sam smiled.

## 8: Katie's New Mission

Katie had to admit the Commander wasn't wasting any time. The Commander must be giving Katie priority over everything else on his plate.

She'd called him as soon as she'd finished talking to Sam. The Commander had answered immediately and in person. Almost like he'd been waiting for her to call. He'd scheduled a face-to-face meeting for only an hour later.

Katie hadn't taken that long to clean up, dress presentably, and make her way to the Admin ring. Katie no longer felt comfortable in the student dorm ring that'd been her home away from home whenever she'd been on Ceres before.

Katie had welcomed the fact it was full of transients who didn't pay much attention to each other before. She liked to be left alone to do as she pleased. Only now it felt like nobody was looking out for her either.

And so she'd reached the Admin ring some tens of minutes early and was killing time in a small parklet not too far from the Commander's office. She was sitting on a square set of faux stone benches that surrounded a small tree with white papery bark. One of only five trees to be found on Ceres. Katie imagined that if she got to the Academy, she'd be seeing a lot more trees. Experiencing a lot more weather too, if what Sam said was true. She imagined it was.

Katie had decided she needed to go to the Academy as a kind of intellectual necessity as required by her plans for her life. She was starting to get emotionally excited about it.

Something moved under a nearby bush. A bush carefully situated in its own planter with the earth around it covered up with an air and moisture permeable fabric. The denizens of a space habitat weren't the sort of people to be comfortable with open containers of dirt.

Planets were apparently full of open expanses of uncovered dirt. With luck, she'd be getting to see some of that.

In the meantime, the parklet which was a static tableau of carefully groomed plant life was showing signs of unexpected movement. Katie peered at the bush, trying to see what it was.

A pair of small green eyes appeared. The eyes had vertical slits for pupils. They were situated in a small furry face with whiskers. Small, sharp tipped ears protruded from a little head. It was a cat. A black kitten.

Katie had seen plenty of pictures of cats, kittens in particular, the network was full of them. They did seem cute. People back on Earth loved to keep them as pets.

Katie had never seen a live cat before.

The creature in question was growing bolder. Its head was now full visible and a tiny furry four legged body was following behind.

Looked like the reports that kittens were much more prone to curiosity than prudence were true. It was insufferably cute. So alive and full of active, fascinated intelligence. The pictures hadn't done kittens justice. Katie felt privileged to be the current object of that curiosity.

Katie held out a hand and made tsking noises.

The kitten perked up and scooted over, jumping into Katie's lap. She managed to suppress a startled jump.

The little thing sat there, warm and furry, looking up at Katie expectantly.

Katie had read cats liked to be scratched behind the ears. Carefully, she tried it.

That worked, the kitten purred. Katie had heard of purring. Even listened to audio recordings of it. She'd never experienced the feeling of something sitting in her lap purring. It was nice.

"Oh, you found Blackie," a young girl's voice exclaimed. Katie looked up to see a young girl. Impossibly dolled up in a frilly dress.

Spacers generally didn't find dresses were practical wear. The young girl also had the stout build of the Earth born.

Most likely the child belonged to a couple doing a temporary two-year tour of service with one of the many Earth agencies with outposts on Ceres.

"More like he found me," Katie said. "He's very cute."

"He's the bestest," the girl agreed. "But he's bad too. He wasn't supposed to get out. We're not supposed to leave home, but I peeked outside and he ran out through my legs." The girl paused for breath after this speech.

Kate gathered Blackie carefully in her hands. He gave a little meow of protest. She handed him to the little girl. "Here you'd better get him home before anyone notices."

"Yes, ma'am," the little girl said taking the kitten and walking off with determined steps muttering placating endearments to it. The little girl had got maybe three meters before turning and yelling back. "I'm Lily. Come visit anytime." With that, she rushed off.

Katie watched with bemusement before remembering she had somewhere to be herself.

\* \* \*

Katie saw that the Commander had the tea service out again. He glanced up and waved her over to it.

"Sorry, I have to finish up here," he said. "I didn't think it'd take so long. There are always more fiddly details to look up and sort out in Space Force paperwork than you expect. Something I imagine you'll find out yourself."

Katie fought to keep from expressing her glee. The Commander was assuming she'd become a member of the Space Force. Was he about to tell her he was giving her the endorsement she'd jumped through so many hoops for?

It was all she wanted. His endorsement and an end to her accumulating reputation as a spoiled, oddball trouble magnet. Katie wanted to move onto becoming a good regular dependable Space Force officer. First stop on that journey being a solid non-problematic, but promising officer candidate.

She sat down and tried to appear composed. Katie refrained from helping herself to some tea. She was patient as the Commander hurried determinedly through some set of screens, his head swinging back and forth looking at various documents and his hands occasionally pecking out or rattling out some entry.

Finally, the Commander sighed and stabbed a key on his keyboard with a determined, gleeful flourish. "Yes, done," he exclaimed.

Making his way over to the little tea table, he shook his head ruefully. "You'll find most of your fights in the Space Force are with red tape," he said as he sat down.

Instead of getting right to it, he insisted on serving both of them tea.

"When settling important matters it's essential to have a calm untroubled mind," he claimed.

Katie fighting impatience knew this was going to be an up hill battle for her. Oh well, the journey of a thousand miles begins with a single step. This was a more positive and pleasant version of the Commander, but a rather disconcerting one too.

"So," the Commander said, "I don't think it's an overstatement to say your latest trial didn't work out as planned."

Katie readied herself to reply. It was hardly her fault.

The Commander stopped her with a flat raised palm. "I know it wasn't your fault," he said. "In fact, I messed up badly. Something I assure you Chief Dingle explained to me at length." He smiled at her. Ingratiatingly. Very disconcerting. "Between you, me, and that bulkhead, at heated length," he said.

"Yes, sir," Katie said. She had no idea how to reply to that. Katie wanted her endorsement and to be gone.

"That said, the way it turned out was a deeply concerning surprise," he said. "Again, in no way your fault. I can see that now. You've been pinned with a reputation as smart and nosy. You don't have to do anything at all for people to react to that."

"I'm starting to figure that out myself, sir," Katie agreed. "I'm beginning to realize that being smart is great, but experience is valuable too. I think I have to work on letting one inform the other."

The Commander smiled. His eyes crinkled up at the corners. Looked genuine to Katie. "That's great. Great, you're learning humility too," he said. "It's unfair to a degree that you have to be figuring all this out as young as you are. If you were a couple of years older, it'd all be much easier. The downside of your excelling academically, I'm afraid."

"Yes, sir," Katie said. She paused. "It's going to be hard throttling back over doing it on the things I'm good at. It's fun being good at things. Didn't realize it made me so annoying and obnoxious. I didn't realize it was unbalancing me either. I can see I'm going to have to work on that."

The Commander nodded. Katie's analysis pleased him. "Well, I think, going by the reports I got back from your supervisors, that you're not doing too badly at that. They were all quite glowing."

"They were?"

"Indeed," the Commander replied. "I dare say you weren't overwhelmed by a feeling of warm acceptance down there. Most of the workers on the line would rather be somewhere else. They tend to dour, grumpy, and skeptical of outsiders."

"They did seem that way, sir," Katie admitted. "But if you did your job like you were told and didn't make a fuss, they were good with that. Not happy or content really, but grudgingly accepting."

"Reminds me of some senior NCOs I've encountered," the Commander said. "They've spent their careers cleaning up after junior officers. They're never over enthusiastic about some new baby officer that's wet behind the ears. If you can somehow manage not to make messes for them to clean up they're quite pleased. Grudging acceptance is the height of their praise."

"Sir," Katie said. "Hope it's not out of place to say it, but that's kind of sad."

This time the Commander's smile seemed sad, wistful really. "I've no wish to crush youthful enthusiasm," he said, "but a life of plugging away to keep things running and not getting much recognition for it isn't uncommon. There are worse fates. It's not nice to say so, but there are plenty of people who don't make any clear net contribution to society at all. World's sufficiently complicated that it's not always easy to tell who's who. That's without getting to the people who are looters and destroyers of what others work hard to build."

"That's kind of depressing, sir," Katie said. "I'd like to think that everybody can make a contribution in their own way if given a chance."

The Commander nodded and took a sip of tea before answering. Composing his thoughts, Katie imagined. "A positive attitude," he finally decided. "That's good thing it gets things done. Not necessarily realistic, but it gets things done. People like to live up to expectations if they can. Most people anyhow, brings us around to the fact that there are bad people."

"Sir?"

"Murder is widely considered a bad thing, Miss Kincaid," the

Commander said, smiling thinly. "Your being on the line flushed out the fact that there's bad people down there doing something they don't want the rest of us to know about."

"That's not a bad thing, is it sir?" Katie asked. "Not fair to shoot the messenger, is it? Not even practical long term if what I've read about history is true."

Another genuine smile. "Not many young people read much history these days," the Commander said. "Miss Ping wasn't a once off for you?"

"No sir, my parents bought me a whole pile of out of copyright old histories to read as recreation. I love them. I'm afraid maybe I've got too much of my idea about what other people are like from them. World has changed, I guess."

The Commander paused to sip yet more tea before replying. Katie followed suit. Seem awkward otherwise.

"Space travel, industrialization, modern communications, and a scientific understanding of how the world works have meant a lot of changes," he said. He spoke in a manner that made it clear he was choosing his words carefully. "Changes to the options people have and the sort of interconnections they can make. Not changes to what people are like themselves. People are still people. So I think allowing for the changes the old histories still have a lot to tell us. I regret more people don't see that."

"Yes, sir," Katie said. "Do they teach a lot of history at the Academy?" she asked, hoping to turn to the topic of his endorsing her application to the place.

Another smile. It truly was throwing her off her stride. Had she been that transparent?

"Not as much as you'd expect," he replied. "Junior officers are apprentice cogs in the bureaucratic machine that the Space Force happens to be. Encouraging them to worry about things above their pay grade is not on the agenda. They're expected to have received a decent historical education in secondary school, which is why I had you take Miss Ping's course. Later on if they appear suitable to higher command, they take in depth specialized courses with a high historical component."

"But not as cadets or junior officers?" Katie asked.

"No, regrettably not," the Commander answered. "I'm enjoying this conversion, but I do have duties, and I can see you're growing impatient." He smiled his disturbing smile again, looking at her with a twinkle in his eye.

Kate realized the dour apparatchik the Commander showed to the rest of the world was a shell for a man who on the inside was a dedicated romantic. How odd. How interesting. How many other interesting things about other people had she been missing by accepting surface appearances?

"One of the many skills you're going to have to develop, my dear young woman," the Commander continued. "Is that of not appearing impatient when a senior officer choses to ramble on at you."

"Yes, sir."

"You want me to endorse your application. Then you want me to let you go your way free from more trials or philosophical meanderings," the Commander said. "Am I right?"

"I would like my application endorsed, sir," Katie replied. "I'm not sure I'd put the rest of it exactly that way." She wasn't going to say she was tired or stressed out and would like nothing more than to hide in her bed reading one of those history books he'd mentioned. Right up until the time came to leave for the Academy.

"Yes, it wouldn't be discreet, would it?" the Commander said. "I wish I could grant your wish. Unfortunately, though it wasn't your fault you didn't finish the qualifying tasks I gave you, I can't. Not without creating bad optics. Right now I'm regretting having asked you to do them and wish I'd just endorsed you in the first place. I didn't and we both have to live with the consequences. It's going to look odd on your record and mine if we don't see this to its logical end."

"Yes, sir," Katie said, trying not to sound glum.

"I'm truly sorry," the Commander said, "and I'd like to make it up to you if I can."

"Yes, sir." This did sound more hopeful.

"Yes, but practically we have a major problem surrounding your safety," the Commander said. "A problem that also looks like my fault. I don't see how I could have seen we have a murderous criminal in our midst and that you'd stumble across them because of me. But seems we do, and you did. And it's my fault. I have the responsibility of fixing it."

"Sir, the Cromwell family have offered to take me in and keep me safe from intruders."

The Commander gave a slight nod. "You have more friend than you think," he said. "However, though I'm not a Belter born, I have learned a little about the culture. You'd owe them a big favor.

More accurately, since you're planning to go off to the Academy your parents would owe them a big favor. Forgive me for saying so, but your parents seem even vaguer about how Belter society works than I am. In the end, the Cromwells would feel slighted and your parents would have even more trouble hiring good outside crew than they already do."

"They've been resisting the whole idea of hiring outside crew," Katie said. She ought to know she'd fought and lost that battle repeatedly.

"I think you know as well as I do that with you gone they'll have no choice," the Commander said. "I wondered for a long time how they kept that ship running by themselves. It occurs to me now that you were doing much of the work that a proper crew would have. I'm sure they love you and are in denial about it, but they've been very unfair to you. It's not merely that they've over worked you and deprived you of a proper childhood. You've understandably developed a great deal of self-confidence, but also a lack of respect for those senior to you. We touched on this earlier. You need to work understanding the value of experience. Also of respecting authority, even when it may be mistaken in some instances. Understood?"

"Yes, sir," Katie said. She tried to tamp down the anger and annoyance she was feeling. Katie had managed fine. "Are those the grounds you're going to deny me your endorsement on?"

"No, they're not," the Commander said. "In fact, I've come around to the idea that you deserve it. You're not perfect and you differ from the typical candidate in ways which will be a continuing source of difficulty in your career. You are ambitious, determined, extremely smart and able. You've shown a precocious ability to be pragmatic and grow personally. Don't let this go to your head. You're going to need all those qualities to succeed. However, believe that if you persist, you have what it takes to become an outstanding Space Force officer."

"Thank you, sir."

"I've hit upon the perfect way to preserve appearances, reward you for your patience, and to keep you safe without you having to incur any problematic social obligations," the Commander replied. He was projecting smug glee.

"Sir?" Katie said, this could be good or it could be bad.

"I've arranged for you to accompany a survey patrol to the Outer Belt," he said. "Little over two weeks. Speaks directly to your ship board skills. You get to see a real Space Force crew in action. Allows you to show you can along with a non-family team. Last, but not least, you can't get safer than being surrounded by loyal Space Force members in deep space. It's perfect."

Katie blinked. It did sound good. "Yes, sir," she said. "Sounds great. Thank you, sir."

"I've forwarded all the necessary paperwork to your tablet," he said. "You'll have to read and sign off on some safety and familiarization documents before reporting first thing tomorrow to the SFS *Sand Piper*. Lieutenant Anderson who's captain will check you know all that sufficiently. Technically he could deny you acceptance if you don't, but I don't think you'll have any problems, even with the short notice."

"Thank you, sir. That sounds great, sir," Katie answered, still stunned by the development.

"Well, that's all. You can go," the Commander said. "You've got some study to do. Goodbyes to say. Your parents need to sign off. That's not going to be a problem?"

"No, sir."

"Good. Best get a good night's sleep too. Off with you."

Katie put down her tea cup and stood. She resisted the urge to jump up and salute the Commander. She was that excited.

Katie left with as much dignity as she could. It was exciting. On the other hand, she didn't have her endorsement yet. Also, if she was trying not to stick out as special this wasn't going to help.

Still, tomorrow she was going to be crew, very junior but still crew, on a real SF ship on a real mission.

It was a dream come true.

\* \* \*

Katie, as was her habit, was running a few minutes early.

She was spending those minutes admiring the SFS *Sand Piper* from the viewing gallery overlooking the spacecraft's berth in the docking hangar. The *Sand Piper*, a Bird class Scout Courier, was small by spacecraft standards. Small enough to fit into an enclosed, fully pressurized hangar.

Katie knew internally she was cramped. The personal space allotted each member of the five-man crew precluded individuals significantly larger than average from serving on her. The sleeping, toilet, and washing tubes provided were simply too small. A feature from one point of view as the ship's crew normally operated under zero Gee conditions with arbitrary unexpected accelerations a possibility. It was important to keep "falls" short.

For all that looking at the ship from the outside and in person, it seemed quite large enough.

A large metallic insectoid like construction that resembled nothing so much as a huge artificial space going dragon fly. The long pair of "exercise pod" booms attached added to that impression. They existed to make sure crew members got their daily dose of exercise under full Gee conditions, but form did not resemble function. They looked for all the world like weirdly formed wings.

A couple of enlisted technicians were methodically scurrying about the ship. Going by their frequent glances at large thin tablet devices, they were going down a set of checklists preparing her for departure.

A red-headed young man with a sub-lieutenant's pair of two narrow rings on the cuffs of his ship suit looked on. Supervising, no doubt. The ship's complement of five only included a single sub-lieutenant, so this had to be Sub-Lieutenant Timothy McLeod.

Katie wondered that Captain Anderson, a senior lieutenant, wasn't supervising the departure preparations himself. It seemed a rather critical thing to be delegating to a relatively inexperienced officer.

"You must be Katherine Kincaid," a voice from behind her came.

Katie turned to see a tall man, Earth stocky, but skinny by their standards, she'd guess, standing behind her. He was trying to project authority, but mainly succeeded only in looking awkward. He was was wearing a Space Force ship suit. Two thick lines on his cuffs and shoulders identified him as a senior lieutenant. A ship's crest identified him as part of the *Sand Piper's* crew. A name tag on his breast read "Anderson".

This had to be Lieutenant Anderson, captain of the *Sand Piper*, Katie's boss, and personal god for the next couple of weeks.

"Yes, sir, Captain," she said. "I thought I'd take a few minutes to look her over before reporting."

For a second a sunray of happiness broke through the man's gloomy demeanor. "She is a beauty isn't she?" he said looking out at his command.

It didn't last long. He blinked and seemed to remember something he'd forgotten. Something that made him anxious. "Do you prefer to go by 'Kathy' maybe?" he asked. Apparently, polite social niceties were on his checklist.

Katie remembered to breath slowly and evenly and to keep her dismay off of her face. Commander Tretyak might have thought it no big deal but Lieutenant Anderson did not appear happy about the disruption her presence meant to his ship's routine. Which naively, she did think was odd. Wasn't carrying the occasional passenger or two part routine for couriers?

"'Katie is fine, Captain," she replied.

"You know how long she is?" he asked.

"Twenty-three meters from the tip of the bridge to the end of her engine nozzles, sir," Katie replied.

"Divided how?"

"Three meter bridge section attached to the front of the sixteen meter main spindle after which comes the four meter long propulsion module, sir," Katie replied. "The main hull is sub-divided into five sections. The three meter long living and utility section, the five meter long cabin equivalents section, the two meter long exercise pod access section, the three meter long cargo section, and, finally, the remaining three meters belong to the engineering space."

Captain Anderson blinked and gave her a confused smile. "Very good. You've swallowed the ship's manual?" he asked.

"I tried to memorize as much as I could," Katie replied.

"Good," he replied. "What about safety? Where are the damage control stations located?"

"There are three damage control stations, sir," Katie answered. "Number one in the forward part of the utility section on the port side between the airlock and the bridge, one meter aft on side seven, the port lower side, to be precise. The number two damage control station is in the after part of the cabins section on the port side. Eleven meters aft on side six, the port middle side, to b precise. The last number three station is in the aft part of the cargo station next to the engineering air lock. Sixteen meters aft on side two, the starboard middle side, sir."

Lieutenant Anderson's mouth quirked. "You did swallow the manual, didn't you?" He paused and stared at his ship for a second. "Book learning is not the same thing as knowing a ship and what to do in an emergency," he said.

"I'm a Rock Rat kid," she answered. "I know how to find the way to an air lock, emergency shut valve, or fire suppression system under variable Gee, and in the dark after being woken from a solid sleep. We all learn that young. Stuff happens; you cope or die."

"Alright then," Captain Anderson said drawling out the phrase, "maybe we'll test you later, but I believe you. It's weird, but I guess kids out here do learn that even if most of them have never seen an open sky or been swimming."

"Is swimming part of the Academy's program?" Katie asked.

"It is, but most of the cadets can already swim before they get there," the Captain replied. He looked at Katie in an assessing manner. "If you're serious about attending the Academy, arriving on Earth early and acclimatizing to it and learning things like swimming and how to hike and run in the outdoors might be a good idea. Even things like a mosquito or two or a bit of mud might be overwhelming if you don't. Believe me you don't need more handicaps at the Academy it's already hard enough. Most of the cadets are Earth born. The Academy sort of assumes that you'll know anything the average Earth born person does, I'm afraid."

Katie was startled. The Captain hadn't seemed that friendly, but he appeared to be offering genuinely good advice. Like he'd like her to succeed if possible. It didn't entirely add up in her mind. "Thank you, sir," she said. "I'll try to see if I can do that."

"It'll help, I'm sure," he replied. He then grimaced thoughtfully. "It looks like you know your stuff, but I do have to make sure." With that, he proceeded to grill her mercilessly on the material she'd spent the night before committing to memory. With no false modesty, she couldn't imagine anyone else managing to satisfy his demands given the time she'd had. It was an anomaly. The material had had a note from the Commander to the effect that although crew were required to memorize everything on the ship down to the square meter and all its various procedures and routines that passengers, which he basically believed she'd be, got off with a quick safety demonstration of what was needed in a dire emergency such as fire or a hull puncture.

And yet here was the Captain expecting her to know what crew members trained for months to learn. Not entirely reasonable, though she wasn't going to say that. Finally he gave it up ending with a half question, half statement about the ship's routine.

"Last, you understand that I don't stand regular watches, but the rest of the crew normally stands them twelve hours on and twelve hours off, one pilot and one sensor officer?"

"Yes sir," Katie replied. It hadn't been clear if she'd stand a watch or not. Technically, she was qualified to stand a watch as either a pilot or sensor officer but she'd have been shocked if the Space Force accepted that in practice. The familiarization material she'd been given had seemed to assume she'd simply be a passenger without any shipboard responsibilities. "I was wondering which watch I'd be doing my mandatory daily exercise with."

Captain Anderson looked at her as if he'd never considered the question. "I tell you what," he said. "We'll keep the pilots Gregorian and Romanov on twelve hour watches, 0800 to 2000, 2000 to 0800, starboard and port. You, Wong, and McLeod get eight hour sensor watches, 2300 to 0700, 0700 to 1500, and 1500 to 2300 respectively. Gregorian, You, and McLeod do your exercise 0700 to 0800. Me, Romanov, and Wong from 1900 to 2000. Okay?"

"Yes, sir," Katie hardly knew what to say. It was like he was making it up on the spot. An impression reinforced by the fact he then took time to enter it all into a tablet. She heard a send ping when he was done. Had he really just altered the ship's entire watch setup on the fly and only told the crew at the last moment?

When he was done the Captain looked up. "Well, I think we'll have lots to keep you busy besides your watches and exercise time, but we'll work out the details later. No sense wasting your time. You want to learn as much as possible, right?"

"Yes, sir," Katie answered. A tremendously useful phrase.

"Good. You got your rations order in on time?"

"Yes, sir."

"Great, but have Sub-Lieutenant McLeod check it got loaded properly, okay?"

"Yes, sir."

With that, the Captain heaved a deep sigh. "Good. Consider yourself as having reported in. Go see McLeod. He'll get you settled in. I'll see you again at departure. Dismissed."

With that, he turned and walked away.

Katie shook her head and made her way down to where Sub-Lieutenant McLeod waited.

\* \* \*

Katie couldn't help liking Sub-Lieutenant McLeod. He was like the puppies she'd seen so many vids of. She knew she wouldn't be able to have a pet at the Academy, but she was hoping to see some real dogs on Earth. Maybe as a junior officer she might be posted somewhere where it was possible. Not likely, but not inconceivable either.

Anyhow, SLT McLeod was energetic and eager to please. He was young, but Katie knew he had to be at least five years older than she was. Most likely at least seven unless he'd entered the Academy early. Still, he gave the feeling of being much younger and closer to her age. He was showing her around the ship. The familiarization and check that she'd done her homework she'd originally expected as her introduction to the *Sand Piper*.

He'd kept up a steady patter since she'd introduced herself. When he wasn't pointing out some feature of the ship, "This is the dining nook. Note it only seats four at a time and has restraints in case of emergency maneuvers. Never leave a drink open or unsecured. Never leave food uncovered or unsecured either," was an example of that, he was elaborating on shipboard life.

"Everybody hates exercise hour. Strapped into a torture device and spun around in open space for an hour. Most dangerous part of the day. RPM is so high that even once you're acclimatized to it, it makes most people feel giddy and a little off. Some of us get sick every damned time. Science is solid that it's necessary for long term health." He'd looked at her briefly then. "Especially for those of us who want to go back to living on Earth. Damned nerve racking and damned unpleasant all the same. Space Force and the Captain don't cut us any slack on it. Twice a day every day and can't maneuver properly with the booms out," being an example of that.

It was extremely informative and Katie was listening with rapt attention. Mostly she'd kept him going with periodic "Yes, sirs.".

Katie had felt his heart felt screed on exercise hour required a bit more feedback. "It's a tough problem, isn't it, sir?" she'd said. "A ship this small and fast was always going to have problems coming up with a good solution. We had a full gravity ring we lived and worked in ninety percent of the time back on my family's ship the *Dawn Threader*, but she's big even by Rock Rat standards and hasn't got great acceleration."

"Is that why you look more like an Earther than a Belter?" McLeod asked. He then promptly blushed. With his fair complexion barely relieved by a generous splattering of freckles, the blush was hard not to notice. No doubt he'd realized that it was kind of personal to ask a young woman about her appearance. Katie also wondered that the crew hadn't been better briefed about her background. They were going to be spending north of two weeks together in close quarters.

"I imagine," Katie replied. "But although I was born out here, my parents are both Earth born. I was conceived there. They're a lot more inclined to tolerating full time full Gee than most Belters. Hopefully it'll make it easier for me to acclimatize to the place."

"Should do," McLeod said, nodding before reverting to full tour guide mode.

The only other break in that came as they worked their way through the cargo module.

"Not much to see here," McLeod was saying, "just a few bins for small amounts of special time sensitive cargo," when Katie spotted something odd. She picked it up and looked it over. Organic, gray, and fibrous; she recognized it as, of all things, a tiny piece of tree bark.

"Damn, the Captain won't be happy to hear about that," McLeod said, looking over her shoulder.

"It's tree bark isn't it?" Katie asked. She didn't bother to keep the surprised wonder out of her voice.

McLeod looked, if anything, more unhappy. "Yeah," he said. He paused to clear his throat. "Captain lets Wong keep wood for his woodworking hobby in some of the unused cargo bins. Strictly speaking, it's not in accordance with regulations. Let me have that." He was blushing again.

Katie gave him the little bit of wood.

McLeod looked at her with concern. "Could you do me a favor?" he asked.

"Of course, sir," Katie answered. She had the feeling trouble had sniffed her out again, but she didn't know what else she could say.

"Could you not mention this to the Captain? Anyone really. Pretend it never happened? There's no reason to embarrass both of them and get Wong into trouble."

"Mum's the word, sir," Katie said trying to pass it off as a small favor.

McLeod gave her such a thankful smile she wanted to pet him on the head.

He didn't seem like a bad guy.

All the same she was going to keep her eyes open and watch her back here.

Something wasn't adding up.

## 9: Katie's Grand Adventure

Twenty-two hundred hours, an hour before Katie's graveyard shift sensor watch, and for the first time in almost a week she wasn't being watched.

Captain Anderson, Lieutenant (jg) Wong, and Lieutenant (sg) Gregorian were all racked out getting some badly needed rest. Lieutenant (sg) Romanov and Sub-Lieutenant McLeod were standing their watches on the bridge. McLeod at least would be genuinely busy surveying the local population of rocks.

If it'd ever been a mystery before, Katie no longer had any doubts why Scout Courier crews were dominated by the young and unattached. Cramped quarters and being adrift in a tiny bubble far from any other life weren't the only things. The routine was brutal and unrelenting.

Even given that Katie had the feeling they'd been working extra hard to keep her too busy to ask many questions or to poke around. Tired themselves out first in the progress. Ha.

Having checked where everyone was, she didn't waste time. It was seconds to scoot back into the cargo area and flip a few bins open. She'd already ascertained that they weren't instrumented. There was no logging of accesses. The Space Force trusted its crews. No place to go with anything, anyway.

Anyhow, what it added up to is if she hurried she could take a peek at what they were carrying, and nobody would be the wiser.

The bit of bark had perplexed her more and more as she thought about it. Wood working was a strange hobby for someone on an asteroid base where importing wood from Earth was bound to be extraordinarily expensive. Also, why pay to ship bark? Why not finished wood that wouldn't have wastage?

What she saw in several of the bins did not answer her question. It was rough wood. Not large pieces of it. It looked like a mixture of very large sticks and small tree trunks, a variety of types, though she knew next to nothing about types of trees. A lot of bark, and it'd be hard to make a single, good sized plank out of it.

What was Wong making? Walking sticks? Small figurines? Didn't make sense, but she couldn't take time to ponder it any more than she could ask Wong outright.

She scooted right back to cabin section. The sleeping tubes came in pairs, but there was no other passenger. She had a whole "cabin equivalent" to herself. The sound proofing between the "cabin equivalents" was excellent, so nobody noticed she wasn't bunked out for the few minutes her little recce took.

She was back up after a short nap to grab what the crew still called "midnight scran" despite it being an hour earlier. Then eight hours of a sensor watch surveying the local rocks. Exercise hour, breakfast, and some proper sleep.

As she lay her head down to rest, she wondered what was going on.

One thing for sure, she wasn't asking any questions.

* * *

The sensor watches had proved to be surprisingly interesting. The *Sand Piper* worked through its survey sectors at a significantly faster pace than the *Dawn Threader* did. Neither did the Space Force crew take periodic breaks from their surveying. They kept at it twenty-four seven. They did after all have the crew to allow that. They also had military grade gear. Much better than anything that had to be commercially viable.

Also, Katie had to admit the Space Force officers were much better trained on that gear than her parents were or she had been. She'd thought she was pretty good, but McLeod in particular had shown her a few tricks useful in interpreting the spectrum reflected by odd pieces of rock. Even Romanov who was the pilot during her watches had proven to have useful advice. He wasn't drawing a sensor watch now, but he'd done his time.

In particular since the Space Force valued speed in resolving the nature of sensor contacts, he'd shown her quick rules of thumb that helped nail down what something was composed of much faster than what she'd been used to. Theoretically, quickly distinguishing between a rock and something artificial and metallic could be the difference between life and death for a Space Force crew.

Lieutenant (jg) Samuel Romanov had also proved to be good company, full of stories about his hi-jinks on Earth and at the Academy. Katie was finding them entertaining as well as informational. Katie wasn't sure if the informational part was intended. She was learning a lot about Earth and the Academy, and even better about how the people there thought.

So it was a surprise when she finished their survey of the current sector early, and Romanov didn't look happy.

"Well, isn't that impressive?" he said, his words not fully agreeing with his body language or tone. "I didn't think there was any chance you'd get that far along in just one watch."

"You guys have been really helpful," Katie said. "I've learned a lot here."

He smiled wanly. "Glad to have been of help." He stared at his console, digesting the information about what she'd done. When he looked up, his smile didn't make it to his eyes which looked a bit glassy. He wasn't blinking enough. How odd. It occurred to her Samuel Romanov wasn't used to being anything but honest. "I think it wouldn't hurt to go over these bodies here again," he said. "Use the tactical fire control radar and ping them hard. It'll be a useful learning exercise. Take the rest of the watch. Save me the trouble of moving on to the next sector. Captain didn't have that sector scheduled until Gregorian and Wong were on anyways."

Katie looked at him, uncertain how to respond. As much as she'd like getting to play with the tactical radar what he'd said didn't make a lot of sense unless the point was to keep her from being on watch during the survey of the next sector. No way she was going to say that.

"Yes, sir," she said. "This is going to be fun."

*  *  *

There were two layers of sound insulation between Katie in her sleeping tube and the rest of the *Sand Piper*. The tube itself was well insulated and the cabin equivalent space had an additional layer of sound proofing. There was no need for the crew to hear the sounds of each other dressing, showering, and crapping. The quarters were claustrophobic enough as it was.

So when the ship started to maneuver to dock with something, Katie didn't hear anything in the normal range of the human auditory system. That was blocked out. What wasn't blocked out was the lower and higher frequencies and the tiny tremors transmitted through the frame of the ship itself. Things most people would never notice. That majority of the population that hadn't lived their entire lives on board a space ship.

Katie was space born. She'd learned to touch a part of her ship's frame and feel what was running at much the same time she'd learned to walk. As she'd grown older, she'd learned the feel and patterns of different sorts of operations. Learned to feel them even in her sleep.

So when the *Sand Piper* began to maneuver for a rock rendezvous, Katie didn't need to hear anything or be watching a data display to know something was up. She didn't even need to be awake. The change in the ship's normal feel was enough to wake her.

It was Gregorian and Wong's watch. She'd gotten to know both of them to a degree during watch change overs. Wong had been distant and reserved if polite on the rare occasions he spoke. But Iris Gregorian, the pilot, had been friendly and helpful. She'd been full of advice and stories about what it was like to be a woman in the Space Force. Things like, "Doesn't matter about your personal plumbing the Space Force expects you to put it first. All outside interests, including family, are second to its needs. It's harder on us girls than the guys."

So in the normal course of events, Katie would have been surprised Iris hadn't let her know about a maneuver Katie might be interested in observing.

Given the crew's odd behavior ever since she'd joined, surprise wasn't the emotion she felt. Rather an alert wariness was. If they hadn't told her what was going on, they didn't want her to know. She didn't bother to pop out her tube and go to the bridge to check it out.

Rather, she logged on to the *Sand Piper*'s internal network from the terminal in her sleeping tube. Usually used for messages and bedtime entertainment, it was in fact capable of much more.

Whatever the nature of the skullduggery the *Sand Piper*'s crew were involved in, they were complete amateurs at it. The Captain could have locked her out of everything except messages and the entertainment library when she'd first come on board. She'd have never known that wasn't normal. Nobody let children and random passengers remotely control engineering from any arbitrary terminal after all.

As it was Katie wasn't sure the Captain had even thought of it. By default, the crew gave every evidence of being highly trusting and indifferent to security. As a concerned citizen and prospective future Space Force officer, Katie was rather alarmed. She couldn't help thinking the Space Force was vulnerable to attack. It'd be a soft target for criminals or terrorists.

Right now it was very convenient for her. She brought up the navigation screens and outside cameras without any problems. She'd checked a couple of days ago and there didn't even seem to be any logging. If you couldn't be bothered to review logs, and why would you, it was a nuisance.

The cameras showed the *Sand Piper* laying itself alongside a large rock the size of the ship itself. Once the *Sand Piper* had settled in at a fixed distance from it Katie felt the very slight shudder thump of the external air lock cycling. A short while afterwards a pair of figures and a train of large cargo bins appeared and drifted towards the anonymous space rock. Reaching it, they messed about for a while before returning with a different set of bins in tow.

At that point Katie was spooked enough to log out, turn down the lights, and pretend to herself she was sleeping.

There was little doubt now. The *Sand Piper*'s crew were smugglers. She shivered. Depending on what it was they were smuggling and to who it could be worth as much as her life if they learned she knew that.

She had most of another week in close contact with them, during which she had to pretend she didn't.

After that, she didn't know.

Did she report it to someone? To who?

Maybe, in fact, almost certainly thinking cynically, it'd be better to pretend it'd never happened. That she knew nothing.

Maybe some day she'd learn to be that cynical.

But not yet.

\* \* \*

Sometimes Katie hated herself. Her expectations were too ofte harsh and uncompromising. She tried to soften them for other people. It wasn't reasonable to expect everyone else to go to great efforts, even take risks, to act the way she thought they should. She didn't always succeed.

With herself, she was less forgiving.

Which is how she found herself, risking possibly her life and without doubt her future plans and happiness, making another near midnight trip back to the cargo section. Despite there supposedly being no night or day in space, the *Sand Piper*'s crew seemed to regard the hours between 2100 and 0600 as nighttime. A time when anyone not required on duty should be in their bunks sleeping or at least relaxing.

Convenient for her, though she'd have welcomed the excuse not to be making the quick minutes long trip that she was.

She found strangely odd looking cargo containers in the ship's cargo bins. Opening one she saw it was full of thick rectangular almost square slabs roughly twenty centimeters a side. They had puffy, rounded edges. She recognized them as alien, Star Rat, hand held data access devices. Packaged with them were multiple packages that looked a lot like plastic pegboards with transparent coverings. In each peg hole there was a small hexagonal crystalline rod, each with a pair of little labels, one with alien symbols, the other in the Latin alphabet. Space Rat data shards.

Technology the Space Rats had claimed they couldn't legally give humans. She didn't doubt the hardware was also full of data they also said they were prohibited from passing on to humanity.

Geez Louise, this was severely above her non-existent pay grade.

She scuttled back to her sleeping tube as quickly and quietly as she could.

So she wasn't sure why the Space Rats wanted fresh sticks from Earth although she had read they were beaver analogs, so maybe that had something to do with it. It was very clear that the *Sand Piper* was part of a ring smuggling things to and from them. She wondered who was in on it.

She knew where the incriminating evidence was. Who could she tell about it? Safely. She couldn't be sure who it was safe to talk to. Who was in on it and who wasn't?

Yet another risk that she wished she wasn't going to take.

But she had to, to be able to live with herself.

This could be big.

Correct that. This was big.

\* \* \*

Guy Boucher ate his lunchtime meal of red curry and rice with a methodical slowness.

He watched Commander Yuri Tretyak across the table while doing so.

The Commander was going on at length about the brilliance of what he'd done with the Kincaid girl. It took only the odd grunt and word of encouragement to keep him going.

Guy had long wondered if the Commander could be for real. He'd been leaning to the theory that he was. That as amazing as it seemed that the Commander really was as clueless and out of touch with reality as he appeared to be.

Under long sustained observation, the man had been consistent. Oblivious to what was going on under his nose. Convinced as a newly hatched school graduate from a sheltered home that the world worked the way those in authority said it did. That those people only had everybody's best interest in mind. That all the rules and regulations they promulgated and the people they used to enforce them existed solely for the benefit of the greater good. He stopped just short of believing in Santa Claus and the Easter Bunny. Guy wasn't sure about the Tooth Fairy.

Guy thought it was incredible that anyone of at least average intelligence who'd been out and about in the world for more than a few years could be so naïve. Nevertheless, the Commander had never once slipped out of character. Guy didn't believe that anyone could have such an inhuman degree of acting ability either. In the end, he'd come down on the side of the idea that the Commander was a natural innocent. Did lying to himself serve some psychological purpose? Looked like it.

Recently, he wasn't so sure of that analysis.

Recently, the Commander had made a series of decisions regarding the Kincaid girl that had proven very inconvenient for Guy.

Opinion on Ceres had long been ambivalent regards her. It hadn't been able to decide between two possibilities. Was she was some sort of child prodigy that had trouble coloring within the lines? Or was she plain out a troublemaker with delusions of grandeur who couldn't be bothered to try? Guy had started working quietly in the background on swaying opinion to the downside regards her. Preparation for a more open move when the time was ripe.

The Commander, apparently unbeknownst to himself or the girl herself, had put a spike in that wheel. The whole Miss Ping episode had crystallized opinion around the idea that the girl was some sort of genius. Not an ill intentioned one either, even if she did have a habit of being awkward.

Everybody with kids, or even the kids themselves if they had any ambition, knew who Miss Ping was. She was the primary obstacle to getting a secondary education that'd be recognized outside of the Belt. But as harsh as she was, and as difficult as her course was, nobody had ever thought she wasn't fair in how she imposed her Draconian standards.

Kincaid had managed the unprecedented feat of testing out of the course. She'd also somehow managed to keep Ping sweet in the process. It was the talk of the rock.

A fact the Commander was somehow, ostensibly, unaware of.

"Another great point about sending her out on patrol with the *Sand Piper* is that's there no conceivable way she can somehow manage to cut the exercise short," the Commander was saying. "Not like what happened with Miss Ping or on the line."

Guy grunted in reply. Was this guy serious?

The grunt was the only permission the Commander needed to continue his spiel. He sounded for all the world like a salesman for Belt tours by prospective Academy candidates.

He was going on about how sending the girl off on the little ship guaranteed her safety.

If the Commander wasn't on the up and up Guy had to think he was being deliberately provoked.

Billy was an ongoing loose end to which the Kincaid girl was attached. If he had it to do over again Guy might have promoted her candidacy to Yuri in the interests of getting her off of Ceres and somewhere far away as soon as possible. As it was he'd elected for a more final solution.

Unfortunately, he'd missed her on the line. The processing line had had at least the advantage of not being anywhere near the core of Guy's operations. The same couldn't be said of the *Sand Piper*.

Guy felt like he was being herded, and he didn't like it. If he hadn't known Yuri Tretyak so well as a person it would have been a conviction not a feeling. The Ping thing could have been happenstance. That's what he'd figured. Stuff happened. You coped and overcame.

Kincaid had been dangled in front of him on the processing line like so much bait. It rankled that he'd fallen into the trap and not got the bait both. Still, it could have been coincidence.

That the next place the Commander sent the poor girl was the *Sand Piper* was starting to look like enemy action.

Guy had a hard time thinking the Commander was so clever and such a great actor. He had an even harder time thinking that he'd be willing to use the Kincaid girl in such a ruthless and cynical manner. Only the evidence for it was piling up.

In any event, clueless clown or ruthless schemer Guy had a counter for the Commander.

Guy had no hope that the girl would fail to notice the smuggling the *Sand Piper*'s crew were engaged in. Even less hope that she'd keep it under her hat like any more sensible and less principled person would. You could place money on that bet if you could find anyone dumb enough to take it.

What he could do, what he was going to do, was make sure that the inevitable accusation when it came backfired.

That done and the Commander would have to either reveal himself as not on the level or he'd have to sacrifice Kincaid.

If the Commander chose to blow his cover, then Guy would arrange for his removal. An accident would be too suspicious, but his long overdue promotion back to a post on the far side of Luna maybe not so much. Guy would enjoy congratulating him on it. It'd be tempting to hint it was because of strings Guy had pulled with friends back in-system. He'd resist that temptation.

On the other hand, if the Commander acted in character with what he'd shown so far Kincaid wouldn't be dead, but she'd be so disgraced she might as well be.

In either case, nobody would be making wild accusations about the *Sand Piper* and her crew again any time soon.

And Guy's plans would proceed apace.

He'd be not only rich, but powerful locally, and influential system-wide.

Guy smiled at the Commander.

"Does sound good, Yuri," he said.

\* \* \*

Katie had always enjoyed good health. Something she now realized she'd never appreciated as much as she should have. Her ongoing belly ache told her that. It wasn't any bug. It was worry and stress straight out.

Well, at least it was almost over.

She was with the rest of the crew on the bridge for the docking approach to Ceres. Normally she'd have happy to have been there. She'd done this dozens of times, up into the hundreds for her whole life, on the *Dawn Threader*, but only rarely on other ships and never before on a Space Force one.

It was an adventure and a chance to learn all rolled into one.

But all she could think about was the message queued up to go once the *Sand Piper* had docked.

The one addressed to Commander Tretyak with the greatest urgency.

She'd debated sending the message to Chief Dingle as well, or maybe just to him. She didn't know how far up the rot in the Space Force went.

She also didn't know much about the Police Chief.

Commander Tretyak for all his flaws she'd seen quite a bit of. He gave every indication of being on the level despite being somewhat hide bound in his thinking. Also, it made no sense for him to have sent her out on the *Sand Piper* if he'd known the crew was involved in smuggling. He was her best bet.

Her message had asked he come down to the docks right away. That he institute immediate and full surveillance of the docks before doing so.

She didn't think there was anything she could say to the man that'd convince him one of his crews was involved in smuggling.

He'd need to see hard evidence for himself.

She'd need to lead him to those cargo bins and show him the alien tech before the smugglers managed to move it.

That should do the job.

The fecal matter would surely and truly meet the air impeller at that point.

All she could do was not too much of it would get splattered on her.

She had to think people were right.

She was a trouble magnet.

\* \* \*

It was a grim parade that Katie was leading.

The Commander, Captain Anderson, and a couple of MPs.

The Commander had brought a whole five man squad of MPs with him to greet the *Sand Piper* on her arrival home. He'd left the sergeant in charge of it with the other two MPs back on the docks outside of the *Sand Piper*'s airlock, along with the remainder of the Scout Courier's crew.

Katie had had to march past them on their way into the ship. They'd been lined up at parade rest. Katie wondered that such blank faces could look so unhappy. They'd pointedly avoided looking right at her. She'd become a non-person.

She'd never felt so bad about doing the right thing. Wasn't sure she'd ever felt so bad. Didn't add up. Some regrets she could see. But she was doing the right thing. They were smugglers. The Space Force had been infiltrated and subverted. It could not stand. She wished fervently it could have been someone else doing the fixing. All she felt was awful. No satisfaction. No sense of victory. No pride in a job done well.

At least as grim and somber as they were, the Commander, and the MPs didn't have invisible waves of disappointed condemnation rolling off them and all over Katie's raw nerves.

She'd be ever so happy when this was over with.

The short trip through the *Sand Piper*'s air lock and aft to the cargo section felt like forever.

Nobody spoke.

Once they were all assembled in the now small feeling space, Katie pointed. "That bin there, those there, and there," she said. "They're the only ones I looked in. They had alien tech in alien cargo containers. Data pads and data shards. Probably some of the other bins, too."

The Commander motioned an MP to open the first bin Katie had indicated.

It was empty.

The others all glanced at each other.

The Commander had the MP open all the other bins.

They were all empty too.

"We're done here," the Commander said flatly.

An MP took Katie by the arm.

## 10: Katie on the Carpet

They were alone. In the Commander's office. They'd left a pair of MPs on guard outside.

Katie was standing at some civilian semblance of attention in front of the Commander's desk. He'd not offered her a seat, and she knew enough not to take one.

The Commander had managed to maintain his dignity and the appearance of calm until the door had closed behind the MPs. He'd then sat himself down in his chair, anger apparent in every line of his body. Currently, he had his elbows on his desk and his forehead resting on his clasped hands. Even if Katie hadn't been able to see his complexion was flushed dark red, she'd have known he was furious.

That he was trying to compose himself before speaking.

Katie couldn't help thinking that if less than an hour ago she'd deleted the message she'd instead, in the end, sent him, she'd be seeing a very different version of the Commander now. A happy, congratulatory one. She'd heard the universe wasn't fair. She was beginning to believe it.

As it was she'd done the right thing, but she now had no idea how she could prove she wasn't in fact a brazen self-aggrandizing liar. If she was anyone else looking in from the outside, that's what she'd believe herself.

As things stood, she wouldn't give herself another chance to win an endorsement to the Academy. Yet she had to convince the Commander that's what he should do.

So she had a goal. Only no idea of how to achieve it.

In the time she'd spent pondering how hopeless her situation was, the Commander settled down. His complexion returned to only a little more florid than normal. His breathing settled into a more regular, slower pattern.

The man had been mad. He looked up from his hunched up over posture and grimacing, took a deep breath. He sat up straight and inspected her coldly. He did not seem pleased with what he saw.

"Sir?"

"You will be quiet and listen to me," the Commander said, his tone implacable and harsh.

"Yes, sir."

One of the Commander's eyes twitched. "I don't know what to think of you, Miss Kincaid," he said, "up to this point you always seemed to be in trouble, but it never appeared to be your fault."

The Commander paused. Katie resisted the urge to fill the silence with affirmations of her innocence. The Commander didn't give the impression of someone who wanted to hear it. He'd said as much, hadn't he?

"A couple of hours ago I had every hope I'd be giving you endorsement to the Academy," he said. "The preliminary reports from Captain Anderson were very positive. It would have given me great pleasure to have been able to have done that. And you blew it with your ridiculous accusations against the *Sand Piper*'s crew. Against people who'd shown you nothing but the greatest consideration, as far as I can tell. You've gone too far this time."

"Sir," Katie replied in haste, trying to get her protest in before he could shut her down. "That's it, isn't it? Whatever else you think of me you don't think I'm stupid, right?"

"No," the Commander answered with a quick shake of his head, "make this quick. You've wasted enough of my time."

"So why would I do something so stupid and self destructive? I'm not a liar, sir," Katie said. She couldn't keep a degree of heat out of her voice. She prided herself on facing reality head on and not lying about it. "The lie would have been conveniently ignoring what I saw. All I had to do was keep my mouth shut and I would have gotten everything I wanted. Blowing the whistle on the others, I didn't want to do that. They're not bad people, whatever they're wrapped up in. Something this ugly makes everyone look bad. There was no upside for me." The Commander started to fidget. Katie wanted to bludgeon him with words until he saw things her way. She knew she had to give it up. "Why would I tell such a stupid lie that was bound to hurt me as well as everyone else?"

The Commander sighed slightly. He was regaining control of himself. He leaned back in his chair. Thinking. Katie could tell he could see the logic of her words. "I don't know," he said. "There's rather a lot I don't know. I'm no psychologist. I have learned over the years that people follow their hearts and their brains follow making up rationalizations. It could be these messes you get into are cries for attention. Attention your parents have neglected to pay you. They are somewhat self-involved, you have to admit. Perhaps because of that you haven't felt as loved as you could have. It might be that you don't feel you deserve the success your abilities allow you. Perhaps you sabotage yourself because of that."

"I think I'd know if that was true, sir," Katie said. "I'm not so silly."

The Commander smiled thinly and without humor. "And there you show how young you are. I say again; our brains follow our hearts. We're the first people we lie to."

"Seems a rather romantic notion, sir," Katie said. She kept most of an acidic edge out of her voice. It seemed a grandiose and unlikely statement, and she failed to see how he could believe it. How he could have come to the conclusion in the first place. Worse, this odd notion was threatening her future.

"It's called experience, Miss Kincaid," the Commander replied. "To be specific and concrete since you seem to like that, I'm not quite as stupid as many of you appear to think I am."

"I'm not one of those people, sir," Katie hastened to say.

"Thank you, Miss Kincaid," the Commander replied dryly, "I appreciate the endorsement."

Katie winced at the word endorsement, though she doubted the Commander had used it with malicious intent.

"In any event a fondness for keeping things simple and routine doesn't make me stupid or unobservant," the Commander went on, "I'm fairly intelligent and when I attended the Academy I had the pleasure of meeting some of the smartest people alive."

"Yes, sir," Katie said. She was eager to hear this.

The Commander gave another grimace in lieu of a smile. No, he wasn't unobservant. "Invariably no matter how perceptive an individual normally was or how skilled at logic, they made their decisions based on what they wanted emotionally. The real thinking came later in the rationalization and implementation stages. Some of the most successful cadets simply skipped the supposed analysis and jumped right to those stages. It was frankly rather disturbing how well that worked."

"You're naturally cautious, sir," Katie observed.

The Commander's expression showed a little genuine humor this time. "If you were more so, you'd have kept that thought to yourself," he said. "Someone more egotistical may have been offended and you're already in my bad books."

"Sir."

"Anyhow, people believe and think what they want to. The really smart ones come up with better rationalizations. So it's not far fetched to think you've may have done something stupid and self sabotaging for emotional reasons without being aware of it yourself. I think so and so will many other people with a few more years under their belts."

"I see, sir," Katie replied. Though if she was honest it was not that clear to her. She could follow the logic given his premises, which he claimed to base on personal experience. If she wanted to convince him of anything, she did need to understand his point of view.

"So, do you have anything else to say for yourself?"

"Sir, accusing the *Sand Piper*'s crew of smuggling was really going to hurt them," she said.

"Go on," the Commander grunted.

"I mean at the very best even the possibility they're smugglers hurts their careers and if proven they'd be fined at least. At worst, they could be drummed out of the Space Force and spend years in prison."

"And yet you did accuse them."

Katie gulped. She hadn't liked this from the beginning, and she still didn't. "I did, sir," she said, "knowing how bad it could hurt them despite rather liking them all from our short acquaintance. Sir, say what you will but I don't have record of wanting to hurt people, do I?"

"Billy Boucher?"

"Sir, I can't prove it, but Billy Boucher and his gang were

bullies, but they've graduated to really hurting people," Katie said. "They're criminals. They like to hurt people and they enjoy profiting from it. If Billy wasn't Guy Boucher's son you'd all see that."

"I think the key point there," the Commander said, "is that you can't prove that. Those are yet another set of very serious accusations."

"Yet they're true and a lot of people on this rock know it too."

"You're not helping yourself with this line of attack."

"Objectively, sir, I have no history of doing things that'll hurt other people. I think Miss Ping's report and the ones you got from my supervisors on the line all back that up, right?"

The Commander nodded noncommittally.

"Anyhow, leaving my character aside, there's something wrong going on here that's not my fault," she said, "and the proof is someone trying to kill me on the line." There he couldn't deny that fact or that logic.

"Miss Kincaid, it could be argued you have shown a profound and consistent indifference to the effect of your actions on other people, even if up to this point you've failed to be actively malicious," the Commander said.

Katie colored. She thought it was unfair, but it was hard to argue with a perception.

"Regards the incident on the line, whatever happened it failed to kill you and did kill Johnny Applebaum," the Commander continued grimly, "It could be hypothesized that you staged that attack yourself to attract attention and confuse matters. That indeed you're guilty of Johnny Applebaum's murder, deliberately or otherwise."

It took Katie a second to absorb what the Commander had said. "You can't believe that!" she burst out.

"Don't tell me what I can or can't believe, Miss Kincaid," the Commander replied. "I could, but as it happens I'm not inclined to. I don't think you're that good of an actress or that self deluded from what I've seen of you. The fact remains that the argument could be made. Your logical position is not as good as you'd like to think it is."

"So what do you think, sir?" she asked.

"I'm uncertain of what to think," the Commander said. "I do believe I've tried to give you a fair chance to prove yourself a worthy Space Force Academy candidate. What has resulted is a series of messes. It's been said you tell the tree by the fruit it bears. Seems like a good rule of thumb."

"I see, sir," Katie replied. She did too, and it didn't look good.

"Right now," the Commander went on, "I couldn't do much for you if I wanted to. Publicly accusing a crew of smuggling and then failing to substantiate the charges is that serious. I can't endorse you now. I can't even afford to indulge you further."

"That bad?"

"That bad," the Commander replied. "You're lucky it's not worse. If you weren't still a minor you'd be looking at charges and likely a few years in a prison somewhere. It's that bad. So you don't get my endorsement. I don't want to have you darkening my doorstep again. Clear?"

"Clear, sir." Katie was shocked by what he'd said. She couldn't see how she could dig her way out of this.

"Furthermore, I don't have the power to confine you to your quarters, but I suggest you stay in them as much as possible until your parents return with your ship. I suggest you board her and then stay off of Ceres in the future. You're not welcome here."

"Sir," Katie responded. This seemed excessive.

The Commander stood and taking one of her elbows in hand guided her to the door. Opening the door, he spoke to the MPs there. "Miss Kincaid is free to go now."

The MPs looked at her blankly.

They seemed disappointed they weren't getting to haul her off to jail.

\* \* \*

Commander Yuri Tretyak liked to do his job and let the chips fall where they might.

He'd found that worked in the long term. Up to now. Now he wasn't so sure.

The Commander was sitting in his office alone. He'd dismissed Kincaid and canceled all the rest of his appointments for the day. Yuri Tretyak was in no mood to deal with anyone. Yuri needed time to fume and get the anger out of his system. The rules he'd so trusted had failed him. They'd proved inadequate.

The rules on endorsing Academy candidates were quite explicit. There were no rules. There wasn't even any guidance. The matter was one in which district commanding officers were expected to use their own personal judgment.

The results of that had left the Commander heartsick and angry.

It'd wasn't that he had any doubts about what his gut told him about the Kincaid girl. It wasn't that his judgment disagreed with his gut. No, they agreed. The girl was a superior candidate if too young yet to be ideal. Kincaid was also a disastrously poor fit for the Space Force, at least as it currently was.

It was a circle that had refused to be squared.

Yuri had hoped by setting the girl a series of tests designed to highlight her weaknesses that she'd come to see the problem herself and withdraw her candidacy voluntarily. If not her failing them would have justified his refusing her his endorsement.

If she'd succeeded at them proving him wrong, well, he could have lived with that too. He'd have admitted he'd misjudged her and given her the endorsement she wanted.

Only somehow, Katie Kincaid, bless her soul, had managed to find a third way every time.

Katie Kincaid had created a situation where he had no rules and no routines to guide him. She was calling his very understanding of the way the world was into question. Yuri didn't appreciate it.

In fact, to be honest with himself he was not reacting well at all. Yuri was angry. He'd been angrier. Yuri had acted in haste out of that anger.

And now he'd boxed himself in and left himself with no good choices.

It would have offended the crew of the *Sand Piper* even further, and he'd not seen the need for it, but after they'd failed to find contraband where Kincaid had said she'd seen it he should have shut the *Sand Piper* down, sealed off access to her, and searched the little ship from top to bottom. Draconian, but it would have been the only way of being absolutely sure there was no substance to the Kincaid girl's accusations.

Furthermore, he should have taken the ship's logs all into custody, especially the message ones, and gone over them with a fine-toothed comb.

Yuri hadn't and now it was too late.

Yuri hadn't lied to the girl. He'd tried to play it straight all along. He really did think the most plausible explanation for the repeated messes she found herself in was that she created them out of some deep unconscious psychological need. A need created by the de facto child neglect of her irresponsible self absorbed parents.

It was speculation. Yuri couldn't know that. He wasn't a mind reader or a psychologist. Like he'd told Kincaid herself, people tended to believe what they wanted to. It wasn't an explanation he liked, but it was the least uncomfortable one he could think of. Not an argument in its favor.

One thing he had learned about Kincaid from direct observation was that she was an uncompromising idealist. It took one to recognize one. He couldn't believe that she was a con-artist who'd deliberately created the embarrassing outcomes to the tasks he'd given her. Logically that ought to be on the table, but in reality he couldn't see it being so.

Yuri had long ago decided people were in the main good and well intentioned, barring a few bad apples. Not perfect, mind you. Everyone has flaws and limitations, and there was such a thing as plain bad luck. But in the main good, and in the main, they managed to muddle through okay. The same with the system, or rather systems. People were better off working together. Doing so in more than small groups wasn't natural, but it paid off and so over time people had worked out systems for it. The systems weren't perfect, and sometimes not fair, but overall everyone was better off for them.

And so Yuri Tretyak worked hard at working within the system despite its imperfections and his own deep desire not to compromise and always do the best.

Katie Kincaid on the other hand barely seemed aware that there were systems. The idea that she needed to respect them was apparently not one that had yet occurred to her. If she hadn't managed to pull Yuri's world down around his ears, he might have even found her Mr. Magoo levels of obliviousness amusing.

Katie Kindcaid had proved that she was bright and disciplined with Miss Ping. The attempt on her life on the processing line was a red flag. As was her accusation of smuggling by the *Sand Piper*'s crew. They could be explained away. Yuri had outlined how to her himself. People will believe what they want to and accept elaborate rationalizations to allow it when necessary.

On reflection, he didn't believe it. The girl was smart and capable, but only fifteen years old with only limited experience outside of her family's ship for all that. He didn't think she had it in her to fake the accident. On reflection too, it didn't seem credible she'd have made the smuggling accusations for any other reason than she believed them to be true. The Kincaid girl wasn't stupid enough not to realize how much damage they'd do to her. Yuri simply did not believe she was psychologically damaged enough to make them up despite that.

Yuri didn't want to believe there were murderers abroad on Ceres or that corruption had become so entrenched in the Space Force, right in his own command at that, that a whole crew could be complicit in it either.

But it was one or the other.

Only he'd already decided and come down on one side.

While acting in anger and based on less than full evidence.

And now there was nothing he could do about it.

It might be he'd made the right call. Only now he couldn't tell.

If by some magical means he did learn the truth it didn't matter.

Any evidence would have been disposed of by now. Yuri had put his imprint on the idea the Kincaid girl was a trouble maker. One who falsely accused innocent people of serious crimes in order to garner attention.

Yuri regretted it now, but his only course of action was to persevere in what he'd already decided. To do anything else would just muddy the waters.

Maybe it was unfair to the Kincaid girl. Yuri didn't know. It didn't matter.

There was nothing Yuri could do anymore.

However little he liked it.

\* \* \*

It was unfair, and Katie was outraged.

Katie had marched herself back to her room like she'd been told to. She'd thrown herself onto her bed, a luxury after more than two weeks of a sleeping tube, and allowed herself to melt down in a full blown emotional fit.

Katie hadn't done that since she was a toddler. It wasn't something you could afford on a short crewed spaceship. It felt good. She felt guilty that it felt so good. She'd worked so hard to contain her emotions and do what was expected of her and what had it got her? Nothing. Less than nothing.

Katie was so far down in the hole that on Earth she'd have been in China. Seemed like a geographically biased and Earth centric expression of the sentiment, but who cared? It didn't matter.

Nothing mattered anymore.

Nothing she did mattered anymore. Katie was finished.

Why not indulge her feelings?

Because it didn't matter anymore.

Nothing mattered.

Katie's life was over before it'd even got started.

She might as well be dead.

Dead people couldn't possibly hurt so much. Katie's Dad was vaguely religious, but he hadn't passed his faith on to her. Katie would have liked to have believed in an afterlife where people could still feel something. Only she didn't really. Katie had loved science, the dinosaurs, the infinite cosmos, the intricate but ultimately useful explanations for how things worked, since she was a child. She recognized science wasn't religion now, wasn't a replacement for it either, only she couldn't believe in her father's faith and science both.

It was one reason she'd set her sights on being some sort of hero, the great leader sort to be precise. If she herself couldn't live on, then maybe the memory of her life and the results of what she'd accomplished could.

And now she was stymied before she'd got even a good start.

For no fault of her own. She'd helped those who seemed to need it. She'd stood up to injustice. She'd done her best at every task she'd been given. When she'd learned of criminal activity, she'd reported it. Her reward?

Disgrace, and an end of her hopes for the future.

It looked the Katie Kincaid she'd worked so hard to become was dead on arrival. Dead with a stake through her heart, with garlic and salt sprinkled all over her.

Dead. Dead. Dead.

She cried.

Katie couldn't do that. Fearless leaders do not cry. Neither do people who expect to become Space Force officers. The Space Force might be a corrupt collection of glorified traffic cops, like the Commander suggested. Well, maybe not the corrupt part. She really hoped he didn't believe they were corrupt. That would be too disappointing. Katie had really wanted to believe he was a straight shooter, however misguided in choosing his targets.

Good cops, bad cops, bureaucrats, or fearless leaders Space Force officers were not people who allowed themselves to break down when faced with emotionally trying challenges. No, they rose to the challenge and if they felt overwhelmed, they kept that to themselves.

That was the standard she'd set out to emulate, and she couldn't bring herself to abandon it.

No more than she could bring herself to abandon life, despite its being so painful and seeming so hopeless right now.

She felt empty.

She didn't feel like giving up.

Didn't feel like much of anything, but that included giving up.

So she'd let her life go on a little longer. She still had her freedom and her health.

Maybe her mind was still intact. She didn't think she was crazy. She could still think despite all her plans so far failing.

She'd rest. Get some sleep. Tomorrow perhaps she'd feel better. She wasn't sure what to do.

She couldn't quite bring herself to believe how badly things had gone.

Tomorrow morning, bright and early, after a good night's sleep she hoped, she would set out to figure out where she was. That done, she could maybe plot a new course into the future. Or maybe she'd give up on planning and live each day as it came, as so many much happier people seemed to.

Anyhow, life went on.

Only she didn't know what sort of life it'd be anymore.

\* \* \*

Sam, like everyone else on Ceres, had heard of the fiasco down on the docks with the *Sand Piper*.

It'd only been hours, but news that juicy traveled fast.

Sam had learned not to have expectations. Expectations led to disappointment and unhappiness. Neither useful emotions.

Couldn't say he was pleased, though. Hope is a useful emotion. He had hoped he'd be seeing Katie about now, all happy after a successful and interesting patrol with the Space Force. Sam himself had a strictly limited love for being trapped in a small tin can in close quarters with other people of dubious personal habits and having his butt worked off. Katie, however, he could easily see her thinking it was all a great adventure.

It did not seem to have worked out that way.

Sam didn't know how the trip had gone, but it hadn't ended well.

Sam liked to have contingency plans for all possibilities. Katie accusing the entire crew of the *Sand Piper* of being smugglers had not been one of the ones he'd considered.

Some sub-lieutenant with two left feet and a math degree had once told Sam that surprise equated to information.

Well, Sam was feeling awfully well informed.

Unlike most of Ceres' population, Sam didn't think Katie had gone off of her tiny little rocker.

Sam paused in his work. Work was good for worries. Keep your hands busy and your mind will follow. It'll spend less time chewing bitter cud over things that can't be changed.

On the other hand, if your mind insists on haring off after mental rabbits, and down the rabbit hole there's not much you can do about it. You can refrain from working inattentively. Inattention leads to mistakes, waste, and destruction. At least it did when working on the power armor Sam had broken his teeth on as a budding mechanic. Now it'd only diminish the good reputation he'd built up with Ceres' mining community. Still not a desirable outcome and a man has his pride after all.

Katie was Katie. Katie had no off switch. For all her brains, she was anything but subtle. Katie was also as rigorously honest as the day was long. If Katie said she'd seen something, she had.

Which meant there was something deeply wrong going on on Ceres. Far more than he'd been aware of.

Sam still didn't know what.

At first he'd thought it was as simple as someone having it in for Katie. For some unexceptional minds that the exceptional exists is enough to be an unbearable insult. Katie was quite exceptional. The rumors circulating around the time the news had come out about her outstanding performance on the standard tests had seemed too much alike, as having too little natural variation, to be the organic product of envy. He'd suspected a co-ordinated campaign by someone. He'd hoped, not expected, it'd all blow over given time.

The incident on the line could have been unconnected. It did suggest Katie had stirred up a real crazy. Only Sam wasn't taking that suggestion anymore. The *Sand Piper* mess suggested more than a lone crazy that had it out for Katie.

Somebody might not like Katie, but this was more than that. Only he couldn't think what. The only connection between the incidents was Katie herself.

Sam looked at his hands. They weren't talking.

What he wanted to do was visit both Chief Dingle and Commander Tretyak and insist they launch full investigations of Katie's allegations. Get to the bottom of matters and clear the girl's name.

Only Sam had a feeling the rot went so deep and was so pervasive it wouldn't work out that way. If who ever was determined to keep their secrets had been willing to resort to murder at the mere chance Katie had stumbled onto something it was a certainty, they'd fight back harder and more viciously when the walls started to close in. As "who" appeared not to be an individual but an entire criminal organization, that was a problem.

Intervention at this point could result in him and Katie being terminated.

Only thing he could see to do was to wait and hope an opportunity appeared.

Hope wasn't a great plan.

It was the only one he had.

## 11: Katie in the Dumps

Calvin had read books where the characters talked about how receiving bad news like a kick in the stomach. He'd thought it was some kind of literary exaggeration.

Live and learn. Calvin had had Billy and his boys punch him in the stomach at times when Katie wasn't around. He knew what that was like. The news Katie had accused the *Sand Piper*'s crew of smuggling and then been marched to the Commander's office with a pair of MPs in trail had hit him worse. It hurt. Physically hurt. He'd had to sit down on the floor.

One of his sisters had come by and seen it. His sister hadn't teased him. She'd just looked and marched off blank faced. So, it was bad.

Katie was in deep.

Calvin had thought her leaving Ceres and Calvin behind was bad enough. This was worse.

The Belters had a saying. "You can't do good business with bad people," they said. They refused to do so. Reputation was precious in the Belt, without a good reputation you couldn't do business. If you couldn't do business, you couldn't live. It wasn't life or death exactly. Passage back to Mars or Earth to start over at the bottom of the multitudes there was always possible. Most Belters would have preferred death.

Right now Katie's reputation was looking very bad.

It was unthinkable to Calvin that Katie would lie and make up accusations about innocent people.

It was also unthinkable that the entire crew of the *Sand Piper* was complicit in smuggling.

Calvin's world made no sense anymore.

The only thing he could parse out was his hopes, and Katie's had just been trashed. Katie's future looked bleak. That bothered him more than his own hurt feelings.

He wished he could see some way he could help her.

Calvin would offer what support he could.

It wouldn't be much.

Calvin's family didn't believe in Katie the way Calvin did.

Calvin's family would be worried about the stink of her bad rep rubbing off on them.

He couldn't see that it'd be enough.

*  *  *

Katie was sitting on the edge of her bed feeling sorry for herself. She told herself this at least was progress from huddling in her bed, whimpering in pain. Katie had never quite believed in mental pain before. She'd equated it with malingering. Katie was going to be more open minded in the future, she promised herself.

Katie sighed. Time does heal, she guessed. It was annoying all those nostrums and sayings older people had been plaguing her with for her whole life actually contained some truth. She was sure it was only some. So, how was a girl supposed to tell the difference between the wisdom of experience and nonsensical old fairy tales? Katie couldn't see any way.

Katie guessed it wasn't unreasonable to cut herself some slack given the situation she was in. It'd only been a few hours. The *Sand Piper* had timed its return to Ceres for early morning local time. She'd had the morning to destroy her reputation, get called on the carpet by the Commander, and then hide in bed feeling all weepy and sorry for herself.

Katie had made herself go to lunch. That'd been a mistake. Most of the people there just looked right through her. She wished Billy Boucher and his hangers on had done that.

"You'll be lucky if anyone lets you clean their toilets after that stunt," he'd said among other things. It'd had the extra sting of hard to swallow truth. The world was surely going to hell in a hand basket if Billy was making sense.

Katie had shoveled her food into her mouth, chewed, and swallowed despite having no appetite, and ignored him. It hadn't seemed to discourage him. He knew he'd made his point. Having done so, he'd rubbed salt into her wounds by talking about their new jobs with his followers. Seemed his Dad had hired Billy and his whole crew to work in his warehouses. How nice for Billy.

Billy was a success and Katie was disgraced. Sure didn't seem fair to Katie. Wasn't much she could do about it. Mechanically, she returned her dirty dishes to the scullery and went on her way. Back to her empty little room where she could mope in undisturbed peace.

And here she was, sitting on her bed, not lying in it, and that was progress. Hey, progress!

She had to get the brain cells moving. Assess, plan, and act. Do something.

There'd been messages waiting for when she'd returned. Most were the ugly things she could have expected. Some simply told her in dignified language people like her weren't needed and weren't wanted on Ceres or in the Belt generally. Some expressed the same sentiment in much more obscene and insulting language.

The worst one was from Miss Ping. It hadn't been insulting. It hadn't suggested she slink off. No, it'd been dryly reasonable. Miss Ping had said she hoped what she'd heard wasn't true.

Katie believed Miss Ping tried hard to be fair, however harsh she was, if Miss Ping doubted her she didn't have much chance with more emotional, less fair people.

It really didn't look good.

Katie was tempted to open a link to her parents. Only she knew they were stretched thin doing one in two watches. They didn't need the extra burden. Also, they'd be less than useful anyways. Katie's parents had never worried about their reputations and wouldn't understand the problem. They'd believe Katie's side of the story, but would have no useful advice. Her parents would say just ignore it, we know the truth. They'd not understand that wasn't enough.

So she guessed that left Sam and Calvin.

Katie had no idea what to make of it or what to do.

Maybe they would.

Couldn't hurt.

Get her out of her room, too.

Wasn't like there was anything more the Commander could do

to her.

* * *

Calvin was buying Katie a burger again.

Fries too, and he'd gone so far as to splurge on a chocolate milk shake from real re-constituted milk. The expenditure was not getting great returns. Neither of them were happy. It was fascinating in a macabre way.

Calvin had never seen Katie either discouraged or listless before. He was seeing both now. All things Katie interested Calvin. Calvin never tired of Katie or trying to figure out what made Katie tick. Seeing her so down in the dumps held a certain interest. The sort of interest a vivisection or one of those train wrecks in old videos held. It was like opening the cold storage and finding a new colorful sort of mold had developed on what you'd been planning to eat for dinner.

As novel as Katie's actual mood was what was causing it wasn't.

Part of it was she was realizing how much having a bad reputation hurt. She'd never worried about that before.

Calvin had no doubt she'd noticed everyone else in the dinner looking right through her. That they spoke to her only when necessary and with short clipped words when they had to. That they looked at Calvin with pity.

Katie could be pretty oblivious to the people around her and their moods, but she wasn't that oblivious. She had to be feeling it, even though Calvin was sure she'd deny it if asked. Not that she was dishonest, only that she had a strong tendency to believe what she wanted to. What she wanted to believe tended to be what she thought would get the job done. Whatever the current job at hand might be.

His girl had her flaws.

Besides that of not really being his girl.

Katie finished her methodical chewing of the latest bite she'd taken of her burgers. She swallowed. She gave Calvin a rictus of a smile. It was hideous. Calvin decided to bite the bullet.

"Katie," he said, "I know you're not used to being depressed. I know you're unhappy and you're not used to that either. I'm sorry, but most of the rest of us get used to not winning all the time. It happens. You pick up the pieces and figure out how to go on."

"Commander Tretyak isn't going to give me his endorsement," Katie answered. She spoke in a flat tone and spaced out her words as if she thought Calvin wasn't understanding. As if he was stupid or hard of hearing. "Without it, particularly after what happened with the *Sand Piper* there's no way I'm getting into the Academy. Isn't that clear?"

Calvin crushed a flash of annoyance. She was under a lot of strain. "It is," he said, "also he doesn't want to see you again, let alone given you more chances to change his mind. Rumor is he told you he would have had confined you to your room if he had the power. Suggested you stay there anyways."

"I don't know how rumor figures these things out, we were the only ones in the room," Katie said. "He must have blabbed to someone. That's right, though. Not just '*no*' but '*no*' with ice cream and a cherry on top like Sam would say."

"I think that refers to ice cream sundaes, which are supposed to be really special. They have them here if you'd like me to buy you one. It'd be bound to make you feel better."

Katie gave a very slight, but real smile. She shook her head. "Thanks, Calvin, for putting up with me. You're a real friend. You're already doing too much. I'd feel bad taking advantage of you even more. Still, you have to admit it's bad."

Calvin nodded. "It is," he said, "and I'm not sure you're adequately taking the damage to your reputation into account either. It's not just accusing the *Sand Piper* crew of smuggling either. Somebody has been working hard to blacken your reputation since at least that fight with Billy. It's working too. You're going to have to start to fight it, but, yeah, it's going to be hard, and it's going to take time. If you don't, you're going to find out you can't do business here and you'll have to leave Ceres and the Belt, eventually."

Katie grimaced. "Guess I should think about that," she said. "Seems far in the future and I've got enough disasters for one day already. I feel tired and unfocused when I try to tackle the problem. It's like a hard surface my mind skitters off of. Like I can't get any purchase on it. It's not like any other problem I've ever had."

Calvin reached across the table and laid a hand on one of Katie's. Looked at her directly. "It's going to be hard. I won't tell you different," he said, "but you're only fifteen. You've got time. Lot's of it. As well as a ton of talent and plenty of brains. You've hit a single dead end. What you've got to do is stop pounding your head against the wall at the end of it. Even your head isn't harder than the proverbial brick wall." He grinned at her. He willed her to lighten up and see a little humor in the situation. Humor was a great curative his Dad had always said. His parents had always preferred gentle teasing and mild sarcasm to direct harsh reprimands.

Katie did indeed produce a smile, but it was a thin one, and her eyes were dead and implacable. "You want me to give up."

"No," Calvin said, he was afraid not in entire truth. "I want you to give yourself a rest. I want you to take a step back and reassess your goals both immediate and longer term. You might need to choose a new direction, but that doesn't mean your life is over. It's bad, but you can fix it given time if you're willing to try."

"Yeah, so you think going to the Academy is a lost cause," she said. "You figure everyone thinks I'm a demented loose cannon of con-artist now too. I really don't have a lot to lose right now, do I?"

Calvin didn't know what to say. Nothing he said was helping. "You have your whole life in front of you," he finally ventured.

Katie smiled wider and thinner and nodded. Who knew a nod could be so grim, or so determined. What was she thinking?

"What?" he asked.

"Only got a couple of months at most before it's Fall back in Earth's northern hemisphere," she said.

Calvin interrupted. "Again. I'm sorry, but someone has to say it. You have to be reasonable. There's no reasonable way you can straighten things out in time to get into the Academy this year. You have to pick some more reasonable goal, at least for the short term. There'll be other years."

"Not likely I'll get another invitation in those other years," she said. "Not after this mess."

"Don't do anything desperate that you'll regret," he said.

"You say you think this gets back to Billy," she asked.

"It could be just coincidence," Calvin said, "but it was about then it started to seem like someone was grinding an ax, not just passing juicy gossip along."

"Not like Billy to be clever or patient for that matter," Katie mused.

"Mr. Boucher dotes on Billy," Calvin said. "Guess that's why Billy's such a spoiled jerk. I've heard rumors Mr. Boucher can be a little dirty if he doesn't get his way. Sneaky, but things tend to go wrong for you if you cross him. Nothing anyone can prove. Hard to believe, but I guess he could be behind it. Not that it matters. We can't prove it and our word against his means we lose."

"Yeah, but it makes sense," Katie said. "That's been the worst thing for me about all this. I can deal with things that make sense, but none of this does. Not to me."

"Doesn't make sense to me either," Calvin replied. "I mean, think about what happened on the line. Why would any one try to kill you for getting in a fight with their kid? I mean, he could have simply reported you to the police. You did give Billy a good thumping and even if they stuck to the truth, Billy and his buddies, and some expensive lawyer hired by his Dad, could have made you look real bad. Me too. Still owe you for not letting them beat the crap out of me. Always will."

"It was the right thing to do," Katie said, as if that explained it all. "Even if you hadn't been a good friend."

Calvin wasn't sure whether to be happy Katie still saw things in such black and white terms or not. "Thanks anyways," he said.

Katie stared through the diner and people around them. What she saw in the distance Calvin didn't know. "And you know I don't know how smuggling by the *Sand Piper* could be connected to Billy and Guy Boucher?"

"I'd guess they're not," Calvin suggested.

"See, Calvin, I don't think I'm that big of a trouble magnet," Katie said. "I think it's an unlikely coincidence that I should land in two such big pieces of trouble in such a short period of time. I believe it makes sense to assume that the simplest explanation is that they're parts of the same mess. Only we haven't figured out the connection yet."

"Katie, I'm not sure how you could do it, but please don't do something desperate that's going to land you in any worse trouble."

Katie patted his hand. Gobbling the last remnants of her meal she jumped up.

"Thanks, Calvin," she said. "I mean, turns out I'm even deeper shit than I thought, but I think I'm starting to figure it out. Gotta go."

Katie all but ran out of the diner.

Calvin was left with the bill and a nasty feeling.

\* \* \*

Sam was chipping coral off of a water valve when Katie arrived in his shop shortly after lunch.

It was an interesting job. You don't encounter much in the way of sea life in space normally. Or seafood, which was one reason the Braga's high end seafood restaurant, *"The Port"*, had such cachet.

Only Mary Braga, the woman who'd spend her life raising large white fleshed ground fish on an asteroid, had been getting old for some time. She'd been forgetting things for most of that time. Finally, the younger Bragas had noticed. Rather too late in Sam's mind. She'd been forgetting regular maintenance for some time from what he could see, she'd also forgotten to pass on her vital knowledge, acquired by years of patient hands on trial and error, of how to grow cod and other prized fish in smallish tanks in space. Right now the Bragas were panicking with the realization that the secret sauce of their successful business might have slipped through their fingers.

Sometimes you don't realize what you have until it's gone.

Sort of like the invincible self confidence and can-do attitude Katie had always displayed before.

The girl entering his machine shop right now was not the old Katie. This new and not improved Katie was slightly hunched over, not at all bouncy, and had a generally defensive and grimly unhappy air about her. Some of the old determination remained, but Sam worried about what it'd end up being directed at. Or who.

At least she wasn't huddled in her room feeling sorry for herself. Sam wouldn't have blamed her one bit. She was, after all, a young girl who'd been left to deal with crushing developments all on her own. Well, with limited help from himself and the Cromwell boy, but there was only so much they could properly do.

Sam could give advice. If she was here, it was for advice and she'd at least listen to it.

"What's that?" she asked. "I don't think I've ever seen encrustation like that."

"Hello to you too, Katie," he answered. "I'm doing fine, thank you. How are you?"

Katie fought it, but she smiled. "I've been better, but I'm coping," she said. "So are you going to tell me what you're doing?"

Sam lifted the valve and displayed it, and the stony life coating it to her. "This is coral. Probably the only coral any closer than Earth herself. Came from one of Mary Braga's fish tanks."

"Wow, she sort of let it go, didn't she?"

"She's old," Sam answered. "Your energy seeps away. Then your memory starts to go. You get creaky. Sometimes you can stop caring. Your future is all behind you and there's not much to look forward to."

"I was already depressed."

"You're still young," Sam said. "You have no idea what a blessing that is. Some people will say that youth is wasted on the young. That's going too far, but it's true youngsters like yourself don't appreciate what you've got."

"Gee, I feel so lucky."

"You should," Sam said. "You have good health and abundant energy. You have years of it in front of you. Almost infinite possibilities are open to you. You haven't made most of your choices or most of your mistakes yet."

"Somehow I feel like I've made a good start on the mistakes front," Katie said. "I'm not so sure about all those possibilities either."

"Look, you aren't perfect," Sam said. "You've had some setbacks. Right now your reputation is in the gutter because people think you falsely accused innocent people of a serious crime."

"I didn't do that," Katie said. "I don't blame people for being mad at me for what they think I did, but, Sam, you have to believe me, I know the *Sand Piper* was smuggling. I don't know how they hid the evidence. I don't even know how they knew they had to. But they did. And they were smuggling. It's the simple truth."

"I believe you," Sam said, "but I know you better than anyone else I suspect. I suspect even your parents look at you and just see their little girl and not the very upright young woman you are. Given what they know, you can't blame people for thinking what they do."

"I don't really," Katie said, "but you know that doesn't help. It only makes me feel worse."

"Do you really believe in your own mind that you did anything wrong or even made any serious mistakes," Sam asked.

Katie hesitated like she didn't want to say what she was about to. "No," she said, "no, I don't. Only the way it's worked out and from what everyone else thinks I must have, mustn't I have? Only, I don't see it. Which really doesn't help. How can you fix a problem you don't see?"

"And you're not used to self doubt," Sam observed.

Katie blushed. Would miracles never cease? "I guess it's something new for me," she said.

Sam grinned. "Take my word for it. It is," he said.

"I'm here for advice and any information you might have," she replied with an attempt at being serious, "but I was also hoping you'd try and cheer me up a little."

"Oh, you can't handle the information that you're less than perfect?" Sam answered. "Oh, poor Katie!"

Katie tried to look angry, but it was clear she enjoyed the teasing. "Do you have any useful observations?" she asked.

"It's going to take time, lots of time, and hard work to get your reputation back here on Ceres," Sam said. "On the other hand, you know in your heart of hearts you're not actually guilty. Bad luck happens. It's not so much you made some serious mistakes. That can happen too, but not in this case, I think. No, you somehow managed to stumble on to something that's landed you in the sights of someone nasty and powerful. You've gone stepped on someone's toes. Now they have it out for you."

Katie frowned. "Emotionally," she said, stretching out the words, thinking in the pauses between syllables, "that's reassuring. Only practically if I'd made mistakes than I could have fixed those mistakes. Bruised ego, but solved problem. If I've offended someone. Someone, but I don't know who or why. Then what am I supposed to do?"

"Well, first you have to accept the enemy has a vote, and be realistic," Sam said. "The ball's not in your court. You have to be careful and patient. Means you're not going to the Academy this year. There's not enough time to turn things around and make it to Earth for the northern hemisphere Fall. Accept that and move on. Behave like a responsible, honest person and people will see that and adjust their view of you over time. You're going to be a minor for another two years. Nobody is going to hold you fully responsible until you hit your majority. With luck, whoever attacked you has what they wanted and will leave you alone from now on. Don't assume that, be careful and alert. If they attack again, that'll tell you something you can use to fight back."

"That feels like letting the bad guys win," Katie said.

"The enemy not only gets a vote sometimes, sometimes they get more of one than you do," Sam said. "Only the young and inexperienced think they can fight, and if their cause is good, always win in the end. It simply isn't so. Consider this acquiring experience."

"Next you'll be saying 'growing up'," Katie muttered. "No Academy this year likely means no Academy period. If someone is working against me for some reason why would they stop now?

What happened to *'when on desperate ground, fight'*?"

Sam sighed. "There's wisdom in Sun Tzu, just like there is in many old writings that have survived the test of time," he said, "but they're not complete blueprints that can always be followed without interpretation. First, consider whether your situation is truly desperate. Are you truly certain you can't choose different, more attainable goals? Are you certain patiently waiting and rebuilding isn't your best option? One unfortunate accident in a dangerous industrial setting is not a sustained to the death enemy attack."

Katie's face twisted. She didn't want to argue, but it was evident she wasn't buying it.

"Sun Tzu also advocated making many calculations in the temple before embarking on a campaign," Sam said. "He held it was foolish to fight when the odds were heavily stacked against you."

"I'm not sure I have the choices you think I do," Katie said. "If I want to go to the Academy, and I do, I can't let the chance to go this year pass. As for going to war, it seems to me like the bad guys already have. Only I haven't been fighting back. Maybe it's time I did."

Sam didn't sigh. It'd have been too much like acquiescence. "I think you understand what I think," he said.

"Yeah," Katie said, "and I appreciate you're not trying to make my decisions for me. I'm going to think over what you said, promise. Right now, I think I better go and tell my parents what's happened."

"You've waited?"

"Yeah, I was really hoping it wouldn't look as bad if I waited a bit."

Sam nodded. Katie wasn't much for empty words.

"I'll talk to them," she said. "Then I'll think about it all really hard. Okay?"

"All I can ask," he said.

"Great. Later," she replied. With that, she turned and marched out. A little straighter and more certain in her movements, but a lot more determined and even more grim.

Sam wondered what he'd achieved.

## 12: Katie's Desperate

Katie's mother answered Katie's call with her professional negotiation smile. That smile was quite a nice smile, pleasant and warm, and although not precisely fake, didn't truly reflect her mother's rather cold analytical and very pragmatic nature. Very pragmatic about everything except her father. It was not a smile her mother used with Katie. Not anytime before.

Katie knew beyond any doubt she was now in deep trouble. She should have got her head out of her butt and called earlier to preempt the news of events from reaching her parents before she could put her own spin on them. However difficult that would have been and however little she'd felt like doing it, that's what she should have done.

"Hi, Mom, how's it going?" she chirped.

"Katie, kindly cut the BS," her mother replied.

"Yes, Mother, I have some bad news," Katie said.

"Indeed," her mother said, glancing off to the side at something, "wait a second while I get your father on the line."

"Won't that mean waking him up?"

"Yes."

Yeah, she was in deep, deep trouble.

It didn't long for her father's bleary face to appear in a box on her screen. "Hi, love," he said.

"Hi, Dad."

"Good," her mother said. "Now, Katie, explain."

"Well you know how Commander Tretyak wasn't willing to endorse my application to the Academy without my doing something to prove myself, right? We've not got the best reputation with him, you know?"

"Yes, dear, I'm aware our frictions with the good Commander adversely affected your plans for your future. Sorry about that. I'm also aware he had assigned you some extra work, including a stint on an industrial processing line where you almost got killed. A piece of news you neglected to inform us about. We had to hear about it from the Cromwells."

"Sorry, Mom, I didn't want to worry you. I wasn't harmed and nobody could have expected it. It was the first serious accident reported in years."

"Yes, we're well aware of the processing line's deficiencies regards the reporting of safety incidents. We also understand a man was crushed standing in the place where you were supposed to be. That's not what you're calling about though, is it?"

"You know how Commander Tretyak wrangled me a place on a Space Force patrol, right?"

"It required our permission, dear," her mother replied. "A heads up since you seem determined on venturing out into the wider world. Most of it is much more formal than the Belt. No matter how pro forma asking for something non-routine ought to be, people appreciate actually being asked. In high society back on Earth, which you'd have to have dealt with if you'd gone to the Academy, they have little rituals for how to do it. Rituals you're supposed to have absorbed as a child if you're the right sort of people. Also have them for giving thanks once the favor is done."

Great, a lesson on etiquette from her mother. Only maybe she really needed it. She didn't like how her mother assumed going to the Academy was now off the table. She took a breath and thought before she spoke. "Yes, mother," she answered, "I was inconsiderate and took you and Dad for granted. I'm sorry."

"Good. Apology accepted," her mother replied. Her father just nodded in his little inset screen. "It sounded like something you'd enjoy a great deal. We also thought it'd help keep you out of trouble." She paused to sigh. "In fact, we thought it was a kind of peace offering from the Commander. What happened?"

"Right off the Captain ambushed me with a grilling on safety rules, ship layout, and operations. You know me, comes to memorizing technical stuff, I'm a child prodigy."

"Yes, dear, I used to find it cute as well as useful," her mother said. Her expression softened. She'd been proud of Katie's ability.

"So, now I think he thought he could make it look like I'd be a safety hazard if they took me on the patrol," Katie said.

"They didn't have long to react, did they?" her mother asked.

"Commander dreamed it up and put the orders together in less than a day, I think," Katie said. "It was a great idea."

"For you and him, a lot to ask of the crew even if they didn't have anything to hide."

"Right off I noticed some bits of bark about."

"Bark?"

"Yeah, bark like off the outside of trees. Sub-Lieutenant said another crew member did wood working, but not to talk about it. Seemed odd," Katie answered.

"There was wood?"

"Little tree trunks, maybe a meter long with all the bark still on them, filling several containers back in the cargo hold," Katie said. "I snuck a look."

"I've warned you about being nosy," her mother said. "Some things we're all better off not knowing." Her father grimaced. Katie took after her father in believing in the truth, and nothing but the truth was an unadulterated good. Her mother was more of a *"The truth? You can't handle the truth."* sort.

"Yes, Mom," Katie replied. "Anyhow, I saw them swap it for some other cargo containers over the ship's system when they thought I was asleep. Later snuck back again and found new containers that were full of Star Rat tech."

Her mother frowned. "This wasn't just a suspicion based on a misunderstanding then?"

"No, ma'am."

"When did you decide to alert the Commander?"

"Well, I decided right away, but I waited until we docked to send the message."

"It never occurred to you he might be in on it?"

"I don't think he would have sent me on the patrol or Captain Anderson would have tried to spike it if that was the case."

"And it didn't occur to you that if the whole crew was in on it, it must be part of a large well organized operation?"

"Didn't think it through that far."

"So you haven't realized that it was naïve of you to think they wouldn't realize you'd figure out what was happening and anticipate your trying to rat them out?"

Katie blushed. She was certainly gaining experience in being embarrassed. "No, ma'am."

"Can I also assume it didn't occur to you that if you successfully revealed evidence of smuggling, there'd be a big stink? That that stink would stick to everyone concerned. Stick to you. Stick to the Commander. And last, but not least, stick to your family?"

"I didn't think it was relevant, ma'am."

"Not relevant? We have to live here, young lady," her mother said, biting off the words precisely. Katie had never seen her so angry. "I don't believe we ever had to tell you that Santa Claus, the Easter Bunny, and the Tooth Fairy were all pretty fictions. You figured that much out on your own. You couldn't also manage to figure out that people don't always want the truth brought to the surface? Especially if that truth puts them in a bad light. Maybe lands them in jail? It never occurred to you that there might be a lot of people who'd want to discredit you and bury your very inconvenient and dangerous truth? I thought you were supposed to be smart, Katie?"

"It was the right thing to do," Katie asserted with as much determination as she could muster.

"Regardless of the consequences?" her mother asked. "Your being able to see yourself as a knight in shining spotless armor was more important to you than going to the Academy? More important than your reputation? More important than the Commander's? More important than the careers of the crew who did nothing that actually hurt anyone? And lastly, more important than your family's ability to make a living here?"

"I didn't do it to look good," Katie replied quietly. She was hurt. "We can't know what the consequences will be."

"Katie," her mother said with exasperation. "I'm sorry. Maybe we expected too much of you. We certainly thought you'd have longer to grow up, but you need to do it now. Okay, let's say I believe you there's a big smuggling ring operating. Who's in on it? How high does it go?"

Katie blinked. Her mother had jumped from one point to another without finishing. She never did that. She'd said she'd been doomed to go into finance before running off with father, but Katie had always thought she'd been destined to be a lawyer. She'd always been that relentless, that rigorous. "Whatever is up, Commander Tretyak is not in on it," she replied, repeating a point she'd made already herself. "Don't think Chief Dingle is. He was too interested in getting to the bottom of what happened on the line. Don't know about anyone else. Kind of suspect Mr. Boucher of being involved, but no real proof."

Her mother frowned. Katie had no doubt she wanted to know where Katie's suspicions of Guy Boucher originated, but also wanted to stay on track. Katie now regretted all the rabbit holes she'd led her Mom down as a mischievous, overly clever youngster. After a long pause her mother spoke, "You're going to suggest that this smuggling ring isn't that entrenched and we just need to wait for it and all will be sunshine and roses again, aren't you?"

Guilty as charged. Hey diddle diddle, straight up the middle. "They've got to be running scared if they're picking on little girls," Katie replied. "Sooner or later whatever is happening is going to be unearthed. Who's the stink going to stick to then? Better to be on the side of the angels in the long run."

Her mother stared at her. Katie knew she was supposed to be discomforted. She knew she was supposed to show she understood she'd stepped in it. She wasn't backing down. "Katie," her mother said in the end. "You know, dear, that I was being groomed to be an investment banker back on Earth?" She shivered.

Katie supposed she wasn't the only one who felt emotional about the plans her family had had for her. Odd to think of her mother as a young woman. "Yes, ma'am," she answered, "not that you ever talked about it much."

"It would have been a living hell for me," her mother said. "You see, I do have some sympathy for your feelings. That's not the point though. The point is that it means risk assessment and management. You understand?"

"Yes, ma'am," Katie replied. "You're saying you learned how to pick your battles. You learned to understand when to take a chance and when to pass." It occurred to Katie her mother was a more interesting person than she'd realized.

"Exactly dear," her mother said. "Along with exciting little details like the time value of money. Believe me when I tell you serious investors spend a lot of time worrying about things like long-term fundamentals versus short term market irrationality."

"Yes, Mother," Katie replied. "I believe you." She wondered where this was going. Some sort of rambling metaphor to make a point?

"We had a saying; *'the market can be irrational longer than you can stay liquid'*. Also *'that in the long run we're all dead'*. Don't tell me about the *long run,* if we don't make it through the *short run,* the *long run* doesn't matter."

Wow, she'd never realized her mother was this hard headed and cynical. Logically, Katie guessed she had a point. Only it didn't help Katie's cause. "Long run, Mom," she answered, trying to sound reasonable to offset the bluntness of her words, "I don't think I want to stay in the Belt for the rest of my life. I'm going to be eighteen in only a little over two years and I'll be able to do what I want."

"Fine, dear," her mother retorted, "but it works both ways." Her father's face in its little insert was looking distressed. "We'd rather leave the *Dawn Threader* to you in good time, but if we have to mortgage it to hire outside crew, so be it."

Katie hadn't realized that was the choice involved. She'd thought they could afford crew out of operating revenue, especially with the increased efficiency they would allow. Not the time for that debate. "Yes, ma'am," she said.

"What you have to understand is that if that it doesn't work out for you in the wider world you may not have a place to come back to," her mother said. "Same if you go to the Academy and don't make it through. Be careful what you want."

Katie took a deep breath. "I understand, Mom," she replied. "I may not know as much about risk as you do, but I'm not completely clueless. I have to start making my own choices sooner or later."

Her mother shook her head in resignation. "You understand we would have preferred later," she asked almost plaintively. Her father nodded in agreement.

"Yeah. Yes. I'm sorry," Katie replied. Her eyes stung. Katie really was sorry. Why did it have to be so hard?

"Very well, dear, we'll ignore the Social Service demands we should keep a tighter leash on you. You can have more rope," her mother said. "Please, pretty please, do not use it to hang yourself. Okay?" Her father made a praying gesture by way of silently making the same plead.

"I'll do my very best, Mother. I promise."

"We love you, but we're very tired, and there's nothing more useful to say," her mother said. "I think this talk is at an end."

"Yes, ma'am."

"See you on the other side, love," her father said.

With that, the connection was broken from the other side.

Katie had got what she wanted.

It felt hollow.

* * *

Calvin was meeting Katie after his family supper. Calvin had been let out of clean up duties for it. His family was happy he wasn't spending yet more of his limited allowance in Bob Burger's. His family were also happy he was meeting the girl somewhere closer to home where they could keep an eye on the pair.

That closer place being the large kid's play park in the residential gravity ring his family occupied a good part of. He was sitting on a bench with a good view of a brightly covered play structure waiting for Katie. Earlier in the day the bench would have been in use by young mothers watching their broods running about and screeching. Now the area was quiet except for the odd older body relaxing after dinner.

Calvin was hoping to convince Katie that her proclivity for tackling problems head on wasn't the appropriate approach for her current difficulties. That trying harder wasn't the right approac right now.

Katie needed to understand that doubling down wasn't the answer to every losing bet. That that was a strategy that only worked if you had infinitely deep pockets. And that nobody had infinitely deep pockets.

Katie needed to understand that accepting your losses once you were too far down, and walking away wasn't shameful, that it was merely prudent. Everyone had limits, and you needed to accept them.

Here she came. Not as bursting with extra energy as usual, which was sad. Determined though. Katie spotted him noticing her and gave him a big grin. It was good to see.

"Hi there. Sit," he said, patting a place beside him on the bench.

"Hi," she said, sitting down. "This is a lot nicer than the dorms."

"Dorms are temporary. Families live here," he answered. "Some for generations now. You still have a room here if you want it, you know?" His parents wouldn't be overjoyed about honoring that commitment now, but they would.

"And your sisters and the rest they'd watch me like a hawk the whole time I was here, wouldn't they?"

"You'd be safer," Calvin replied. "And maybe you'd find you liked the company of some girls roughly your own age."

Katie looked around at the park's play structures and grass like she found them fascinating. "Maybe, but I'm not sure I'd be comfortable hanging out with people who think maybe I'm a liar."

"I don't think you're a liar," Calvin said. "And my family, even thinking I've a crush on you, they trust my judgment. They're giving you at least the benefit of the doubt. Not everybody is against you. Also, I think the truth will come out in time. You only have to be patient and wait."

"Maybe it will. I'm not sure. Only I don't have much time if I'm to get into the Academy."

"Katie, I'm crazy for you. You know that. I want the best for you. Not sure what that is, though. Maybe it's not going to the Academy. You should give it some thought."

"I'm sorry. I don't feel the same way," Katie replied. She wrung her hands and contemplated them. Looking for Calvin didn't know what.

"I know that. It's okay," Calvin said.

"Is it? I don't know," Katie replied. "Anyhow, I'm not perfect. Boy, do I know that. Only this whole mess, it's not my fault. Someone is out to get me. It's not just something I've stumbled into, I think. It feels personal. Someone hates me. What have I done to make someone hate me? Who could it be? Why?"

"You think that sounds crazy, don't you?"

"Yeah, but Calvin, I know you won't think so," Kate said. "Thanks."

"You're welcome," he replied. "Billy is the only person I know that has a real hate on for you. Everyone else is only reacting to bad things they've heard second hand. By the way, did you hear the news about Billy and his buddies?"

"Not sure. What is it?" Katie answered. "Also, why do I think it can't be anything good?"

"I don't know. They all got jobs. Honest work down in the warehouse district. Courtesy of his dad, of course."

"Guess with Chief Dingle and the Commander distracted, Mr. Boucher figured nobody take much notice," Katie said with disgust. "Billy was bragging about it at lunch. Took great pleasure in grinding it in. Important to have the right parents."

"Yeah."

"You know, it makes sense in a way, but it's also odd," Katie mused. "Not just Billy, but all his shiftless buddies, too?"

"He said it was more for added security, but also has them doing odd stevedore jobs too."

"It smells. Might bear some looking into. Thanks."

Katie's sudden enthusiasm rang alarm bells in Calvin's gut. "Katie, you don't need to go provoking Billy more."

"I promise I'll try to avoid Billy."

"You don't need to stir up more trouble."

Katie jumped up. She hugged him. "Don't worry," she said, and ran off.

Damn. It was nice she was happy. Nice, she was happy with him.

Only backing off and keeping a low profile didn't seem to be on her agenda.

Calvin hoped she'd be careful.

\* \* \*

Sam was working on a docking grapple, waiting for Katie to appear.

Katie had called during breakfast this morning full of a large fraction of her normal vibrancy. Looked like she'd gone from scary, semi-suicidal funk yesterday morning to having blood in her eye. Sam knew she'd talked to her parents, and that that had not gone that well. Details uncertain, but even Dave, and especially Allie, Kincaid had their limits. Katie was close to finding that out.

Apparently, she'd been talking to Calvin Cromwell, too. Sam wondered how the boy's parents felt about that. Somehow that'd got her even more fired up. Odd because though he didn't doubt the boy's courage he was a cautious soul. Calvin had a comfortable place in life. Lots to lose and not much worth taking risks for.

Sam doubted Katie appreciated that. He doubted Calvin realized how much Katie had to keep moving forward on the other hand. They were good kids. It was sad to see them at such loggerheads. Calvin would never understand how Katie had to leave. To take a progression of risks to achieve her goals. Katie didn't see how Calvin could potentially provide the base for the leaps of faith she'd be making. How he could be the port in the storms she'd be bound to be facing.

They were both too young. Too young and destined to part ways as far as he could see. To get truly maudlin, he could see them both looking back twenty years from now and feeling regrets over what could have been.

Enough of that.

He had a docking grapple that needed some focus before Katie appeared and distracted him.

It'd been abused. A pilot got to acting like a hot shot, came in too quick, messed up, but managed to correct. Mostly. Engaged with too much force along not quite the right vectors and all of a sudden the docking mechanism needs some looking at.

Thank the gods of commerce for operators who thought it was cool to abuse their gear. It went a long way to keeping Sam in business and profitable.

Of course, he wasn't just using his Mark I eyeball. The damage wasn't likely to be so gross as to be visible to even his expert eye. Sam had the thing mounted on his measuring and scanning table.

The specialized lidar it had would check the dimensions of the grapple down to the nanometer. That'd pick up any subtle distortions.

Sam stepped back and triggered the descent of a seriously heavy shielding bell over the piece of docking machinery. The hard radiation it took to analyze the state of the metallic objects' insides was nothing you wanted to be exposed to, even if you weren't planning on having children.

Kate came just as he was in the process of checking the shielding. He waved her to silence, and back to the farthest corner of the shop. The inverse square law is your friend.

When he was done and the scan finished, he turned to Katie who'd been waiting quietly and nodded. "Sorry about that, I thought I'd be done before you arrived."

"It's okay," Katie replied. "I think I was a little early."

"Something you're eager to discuss?"

"Yeah, you know I was really depressed because I thought the world was out to get me. I couldn't figure out why. None of it made sense. Usually I'm good at making sense of things. I guess it scared me I couldn't."

"It happens to all of us," Sam replied. His goal her was to keep her from either panicking and running off and doing something self destructive. Or getting cocky and running off and doing something self destructive. Get her to stay in the nice safe moderate middle. "Thing is not to panic. Not to freeze either, act if it's necessary, but don't go off and make things worse. You see?"

Katie scrunched up her face. "I understood all your words and some of how they went together," she said, grinning.

Sam sighed. "Look at this grapple. Why do you think it's in my shop?"

"Some would be hotshot jammed it in too fast at the wrong angle?"

"Bingo!" Sam said. "Don't be that hotshot."

"You know, Sam," Katie said. "Some of your metaphors are a bit thin."

"Not so," Sam said. "You simply haven't matured enough to appreciate them."

Katie grinned again. It was good to see her back in some semblance of her normal spirits. "Calvin pointed out something interesting last night," she said.

"Oh?"

"Yeah, this whole thing has felt strangely personal from the beginning," Katie replied. "And weirdly close, too. I mean if I only accidentally got too near something sensitive and someone overreacted because of my reputation for, ah, curiosity then wouldn't the cold blooded sensible thing to do be backing off and letting me go off to where I wouldn't be a problem?"

"Say again, girl?"

"Too many coincidences. Too much over reaction. I figure even if I don't know it, I've got to be close to something big to merit such a strong reaction."

"The smuggling accusation wasn't a little misunderstanding," Sam said.

"Yeah, but I think somebody set me, and the crew of the *Sand Piper* for that matter, up to look bad," Katie said.

"That makes sense to me," Sam said, "because I believe you when you say that you saw smuggling. Anyone else might think you're spinning paranoid fantasies."

"Take the smuggling as a given," Katie said.

That she didn't react to the idea a lot of people were beginning to think she was a paranoid nut told Sam she was intensely focused on a particular train of thought. It could be penetrating that focus of hers. It also left her open to being sideswiped. It worried Sam. "Okay," he said.

"The crew of the *Sand Piper* were amateurs," she said. "They're not running this scam. So someone else is. That someone els tipped them off that I was going to report them."

"Plausible, maybe true so far," Sam allowed.

"So, that someone didn't have to mousetrap me," Katie

asserted. "They knew ahead of time I was slotted to go on the patrol or Captain Anderson wouldn't have tried to disqualify me at the risk of annoying Commander Tretyak. Sensible thing would have been to cancel the transfer this time. Failing that, they could have warned the crew to be far more careful. Finally, failing that, they could have squished the message to the Commander so there was no way he could do an inspection in enough time. They didn't. They made sure to cause me the maximum embarrassment."

"Sounds paranoid to me," Sam said. He smiled as he said it.

"For some reason getting me disgraced and out of the picture was worth extra attention and complication," Katie said. "Why was the extra risk worth it? Because I was already a significant threat without being aware of it is the only explanation. Questions are how? And to who?"

"Let me guess poor old Calvin gave you a clue."

"Yep, Billy Boucher."

"I've never heard much good about Billy," Sam replied. "I've never heard he's too smart, good at planning, or even very cunning. I don't think Billy Boucher is running a smuggling operation."

Katie put her hands on her hips and gave Sam a stern look. She knew he was being deliberately obtuse. "Not Billy," she said. "His dad, Guy. The head of logistics. I mean to some not naturally on the up and up it's the perfect position for a little skimming and a nice side operation providing things not legal to people not entitled to them."

"Could have just said stealing and smuggling," Sam observed.

"I got into a bad scrap with Billy," Katie said. "He's not the sort to let that go, but Guy had to think any formal light thrown onto Billy had to risk spilling over on to him and whatever he's been up to, right?"

"Allow all your other suggestions and it adds up after a fashion," Sam admitted. It was circumstantial and even if Guy was guilty as charged, he was a leading light on Ceres and wouldn't go down without a fight. Sam didn't like this train of thought.

"He's given Billy, and all his friends too, jobs down in the warehouses," Katie said. "He doesn't seem to like loose ends."

Sam didn't like that thought at all. "If you think you're one of those loose ends, it behooves you to be careful young lady," he said. "Get a room with the Cromwells or get back on the *Dawn Threader* and stay there. Don't remain vulnerable. Don't stick your neck out anymore. If there's anything to this tale of yours he's waiting for you to give him a chance."

Katie snorted. "I'm not soft or stupid."

"Perhaps over confident at times," Sam suggested. "Seriously, if you've provoked Guy, or someone of similar power, you're outmatched. You need to watch yourself and not give them any openings. Understood?"

"I understand the reasoning," Katie said. "You don't think mine is outright crazy, do you?"

"I'm afraid not," Sam said. "Though like I said, that's because I'm willing to accept your version of the facts. Look if this is all true like you say it's not going to stay hidden indefinitely. You just need to lie low and let it blow over. If Guy is a crook, I guarantee you he has a plan for leaving the table with his winnings."

"Right," Katie replied. "Aren't you the one who likes to say *'In desperate ground, fight!'*"

Sam had no idea what she was planning. Not specifically. Could be she hadn't figured it out herself yet. He could guess the nature of it. "Don't throw away your future, the problem will solve itself," he said.

"Maybe, maybe not," Katie said in a distracted tone, staring at the docking grapple without seeing it. "Only I'm a problem someone wants to solve. I can't leave them the initiative. I have to solve them first."

"You don't have to fight this fight now at what must be bad odds. You don't know your enemy, and I'm not sure how well you know yourself, you're riding for a fall, Katie. Defense is stronger than attack. Give it time. In the long term this'll sort itself out."

"You have to get through the short term for the long term to matter," Katie observed. "Anyhow thanks for listening me out."

"I hope you listened to everything I said."

"Of course, Sam," Katie said, waving good bye as she left.

\* \* \*

Katie felt new. Her whole world did. Nastier and more complicated than it had been before, but clearer and sharper in its outlines. It made some sense again. Katie might not like the sense it made, but the pieces made a coherent picture once more.

Katie hadn't had any clear idea of where she was going when she'd left Sam's shop. As she strode down the corridors of the ship chandling gravity ring where the many support businesses required by the Belt's fleet of mining rigs and transports mainly resided she realized she'd better think about what he'd said.

She felt of a twinge of fear. Sam was no worrywart.

If he believed she was under threat and needed to watch her back, then she needed to do just that.

Katie needed to find a place nobody would expect her to be, where she'd not be noted, but it'd be hard for attackers to isolate her, and act if they did find her.

Without thinking she'd been walking towards the docks. The docks were a familiar and favorite haunt of hers. She switched directions. She'd try the admin rings. Katie had rarely been there before with the major exception of her visits to the Commander. It had several areas open to the general public including the records office. She'd spend the day in the records office.

There might be information she could use there. At the very least, it was a place nobody would expect to see her, and she could make plans in peace.

Katie would take a not obvious route there and see if she could lose anyone who might be tracking her at the same time. She found a noisy crew of miners who having finished their official business were looking to start a little recreational drinking prior to lunch. After months of being guarded and consistently responsible a little limited irresponsibility could be an addictive drug.

Katie didn't understand the feeling herself. She'd had ample opportunity to observe the fact of its existence though. A fact that might have caused her parents some concern if they'd been aware of it. They'd not ever spent much time on Ceres. They'd not paid that much attention to the people around them during their limited time on the rock either.

In any event, the miners didn't pay much attention when Katie inserted herself on the edge of their group and followed them down the lifts into the tunnels.

Katie flitted down a side tunnel when nobody was looking and out of the view of what few security cameras there were.

She'd move patiently through side and mainly maintenance tunnels stopping frequently to listen for the presence of any other people.

Katie had had time to think. So she now had some idea of what was going on. It was scary, but it gave her something to work with.

Katie had decided on a course for her life that was bound to put her into scary situations over and over again. She wasn't going to let that stop her now when she was facing her first major obstacle.

She'd almost doubted her own sanity when the idea occurred to her that the reason for the attack on her on the processing line was because of her fight with Billy. That it had been connected to the rumors Calvin had told her had been spreading before her success Miss Ping had seemed just as far fetched.

That it explained just how disastrously her reporting of smuggling on the *Sand Piper* had gone appeared like the workings of a mind eager to displace responsibility even to her.

Only, if she trusted in herself it all fit together.

Guy Boucher was head of logistics on Ceres. People did some ordering and moving about of products on their own, but for most of the movements of things on and off of Ceres, people were happy to let Guy and his people handle the nitty-gritty details.

It was a position of some trust and opportunity. Opportunity to abuse that trust and skim a bit more off the top of transactions than formally agreed to. Also to a really ambitious crook the smuggling of illegal goods promised much higher profits. Evidently Guy had failed to resist those temptations or never tried.

But even crooks have their soft spots. To Katie it looked like Billy was Guy's soft spot. If he'd had a properly pragmatic understanding of his son, the boy would have never been allowed to become the arrogant bully that he was.

Guy was lucky Billy hadn't brought him unfavorable attention earlier. Katie guessed he had some awareness of that fact, and had overreacted to the fact that a formal investigation of Billy's bad behavior might ooze over on to his own activities. Billy might not be overly observant, but no doubt he knew things Guy didn't need spread around. Things that Billy wouldn't have the good sense to keep to himself if questioned closely.

Katie suspected the loyalty between father and son went one way. In his heart of hearts, she suspected Guy knew that too.

A hard hearted crook would have come down hard on Billy by way of solving the problem. If Guy couldn't do that taking it out on Katie made the next most sense.

Which was all great in that it made sense.

Only what could she do about it?

Not much through formal channels. A direct public accusation wouldn't get far either. Her reputation was in tatters. It would have been a stretch for a fifteen year girl to successfully accuse one of Ceres' main leaders anyways.

Could be Sam was right and she should accept the reputation hit and the loss of the immediate chance to attend the Academy.

Have faith time would tell and all would come out. Come out for the better in the end.

Sam hadn't pointed it out, but if Katie truly believed the Space Force was going to be more needed and bigger in the future they were going need more officers than were currently being graduated from the Academy.

That meant that a second invitation mightn't be as unlikely as Katie feared. It also meant routes into the officer corps through other channels might open up. Maybe she could go enlisted or join a planetary service and transfer into the Space Force officer corps indirectly.

It was a strategy of waiting and hoping.

Hope was not a plan.

Katie intended to be somebody who made things happen. Not somebody who waited for them.

So far she'd been constrained by her hopes of getting into the Academy to trying to appear respectable and trying to stay out of trouble. Well, those hopes had been dashed. She wasn't so constrained anymore was she?

Katie needed proof to show people that Guy was a smuggler and at least an attempted murderer. If he'd managed suborn the *Sand Piper*'s entire crew, she had to think he was an extortionist, too. From what Calvin told her he was a spreader of vile malicious slanders too.

But she needed proof. Proof more convincing than her word and a wild conspiracy theory.

Where to find it?

That wood the *Sand Piper* had dropped off, it must have come from Earth. Odds were the Star Rat tech was going back that way. Hard to distribute that sort of thing invisibly on a community as small as Ceres. Besides, Earth was where all the big money was.

Not too likely the schedules of the patrols of Space Force ships and those of transports back to Earth lined up precisely. There'd be transshipment somehow anyways. That meant there had to be some place where the illegal product was kept at least for a while between ships. Someplace controlled by Guy where he could prevent nosy outsiders from seeing what he was doing.

The warehouse district was the obvious answer. The warehouse district Billy and boys had just been hired to work in. Likely for the exact purpose of keeping nosy unofficial investigators out. With the additional benefit of keeping Billy busy and out of trouble of course.

The warehouse district's security was rather lax, but it wasn't open to the public either. Katie was going to have to finagle access somehow and find out where they were storing their contraband. Then she was going to have to make sure Chief Dingle, and the Commander got to see it before it could be moved this time.

It wasn't going to be safe.

Katie was going to have to do things that weren't technically legal to achieve it. Even if it all succeeded the manner of her success probably wouldn't impress either the Commander or the Academy's admissions board. She'd be risking everything.

Katie had arrived now within sight of the lifts to the main admin ring. She eyed the ring of brighter light around them from the shadows.

She had to be cautious here.

But she also had to move forward.

## 13: Katie All In

Katie was in the Warehouse Workers' Labor Exchange Office. The working day was about done and she'd been a busy girl.

Spent the better part of the morning, and all of what should have been lunch, ransacking the records office for information. There'd been only limited information publicly available regards the warehouse district.

Katie had got her big break when a clerk she'd run ragged forgot her ID pass beside Katie when going to eat. It was definitely neither fair nor legal for Katie to have used that pass.

Despite what others thought, Katie believed herself to be honest and not given to random impulses. You couldn't have told it by what she'd done. Katie had taken the pass and used it to get the warehouse district layouts she'd been looking for. That done, she'd noticed she had write permissions to all of Ceres' routine records. She couldn't alter existing records without raising alarms, and she had no doubt anything she did would eventually be detected.

All the same, she could create any routine record she wanted and it would pass for a time.

Right on the spot, she formulated her plan to infiltrate the warehouses. Katie quickly created a new, fictitious person similar to herself, but with a blond bob, an earlier birth date, and newly arrived from Earth. Katie had gotten away with that. At least so far, and now she was committed.

Katie either managed to at least partly justify what she'd done or she was in even deeper trouble.

"Bob, close the doors," a bored clerk called out. To the supplicants crowding the office, he made an announcement. "No more applicants. We'll process everyone already here. It'll take about forty minutes. Please be patient."

So within forty minutes Katie would find out if her final most dangerous and most important gamble of the day was going to pan out.

Katie's second earlier gamble hadn't been risky, but might have the worse consequences in the end. Katie had full access permissions for conducting ship's business on the behalf of *Dawn Threader* incorporated. Katie had full access to the ship's account. Her parents trusted her not to abuse that trust. Katie had done just that, renting a small storage room in the warehouse district in the ship's name.

That done, she'd gone to a nearby beauty salon and talked herself into being taken immediately without an appointment. Claimed a big date. She'd had all her long red braids cut off and was now sporting a blond bob. A bit of make up covered up the few stubborn freckles that remained from when she'd been younger.

Katie had often been told she resembled the iconic Anne of Green Gables. Not any more.

"Karen Jackson," a clerk called. That was what Katie was calling herself. Katie got up and carefully slouched towards the counter. She didn't want to show any hint of the ebullient energy she was famous for.

"That's me," she said, arriving there.

"ID," the clerk asked.

Katie handed over the papers she'd printed off in the records office.

The clerk frowned. "These are temporary and there's been no confirmation of your identity from your home town of Chicago on Earth," he said.

Katie gave a heavy sigh. "Admin clerks back in Chicago aren't as efficient as they are here. All political appointments," she said. "One reason I left."

The clerk smiled slightly. "Welcome to the final frontier," he said. "You want a temporary permit to register for on call work down in the warehouse district, right?"

"Yep," Katie said. "I understand from a guy I was talking to in the transients quarters that you can grant them at the cost of a slightly bigger fee." She'd actually gained the information from court documents in the records office. It was a bribe and a scam, but apparently one tolerated between periodic crack downs.

The clerk hesitated briefly and then relented. "That's right. Cash, since you've no local payment means."

Katie handed over the requested fee, which amounted to a fair portion of her limited savings.

The clerk gave her a twisted smile. "You realize your information will be checked within the week? That if it is false you're subject to heavy fines?"

"Figures," Katie said.

"And if you can't pay them confinement and then deportation will result?"

"Here's hoping those twits back on mother mudball don't lose my records," Katie grumbled. "In the meantime, I need to pay for food and shelter. You guys even charge for the air."

"Better be here early then," the clerk said. "First come, first served, and the work is irregular if you're not the boss's son."

"Okie-Dokie," Katie said.

"Okay, stand on that spot, and I'll take your ID picture."

A couple of minutes and Katie had papers and a new, albeit temporary, pass to the entire warehouse district.

It'd been necessary. The pass she had for *Dawn Threader*'s storage didn't give access to the full area.

Katie walked away and let herself out of the office. The concourse outside was crowded with staff returning home.

Katie had taken the first steps in her plan.

All she needed to do now was actually get into the warehouse district and find the smuggled goods she was sure were there.

It shouldn't be too risky, but she'd leave information drops with what she had so far on deadman switches. If something did happen to her, it'd give her accusations much increased credibility. Not that it'd do her much good at that point. Still, Katie believed in fail safes and she wasn't doing this just for herself.

Also there was the tiny issue of being on not just one clock but two. Neither of them of an exactly determined duration. There was no saying how long the goods the *Sand Piper* had been smuggling would remain in place before being moved again.

Also her various transgressions with both the *Dawn Threader's* funds and the fake Karen Jackson identity were bound to be discovered within a few weeks, maybe even days. She needed to find the contraband and justify them before then.

No pressure.

\* \* \*

Katie had almost not gone back to her room out of concern who might be waiting for her on the way. In the event, the slap dash way she'd put her plans together meant she needed to.

Katie had done so carefully. Taken a round about route and peered around corners before turning them. She'd felt like an utter idiot. Conspiracy theory or no, she was spooked. Katie had gone so far as to wait outside her door and listen for possible lurkers inside.

If Billy or his dad had nefarious plans for her, they weren't apparently acting on them tonight.

Katie had carefully packaged up all the information she had and her speculations as to what Guy Boucher was up to. Some packages she set up for timed release unless she intervened with a pass phrase to prevent it.

As an extra layer of paranoia in case they decided it was worth hacking the school computers and trashing the local storage in her room, she decided to leave packages with Sam and Calvin.

Katie would use fear of hacking as her excuse. If either of them thought she was risking her life in the slightest they'd been on her door step within the hour. All the things she'd risked doing would be for nothing.

"Calvin," she said to start the first call when he answered. "Would you mind doing me a favor?"

Katie could see he wanted to ask what before agreeing. Finally, he broke down. "Sure," he said. "Why are you wearing a black wool cap?"

"Worried Billy still has it in for me," she said. "Red hair stands out, you know. I just want you to keep a package of information for me. Encrypted back up in case someone tries to hack me. School system is not secure, you know."

Calvin looked skeptical, but uncertain as what to object to first. "Okay," he said.

"Great," Katie exclaimed, before stabbing the send button for the queued archive.

"Thanks, later," she said, logging off as soon she saw the indicator that the package had been transmitted successfully, and before Calvin could mount a response.

Now Sam. Sam might not be so easy to buffalo.

Perhaps it'd be better to pre-record her message to him. Wrap the messages several deep. Something innocuous this evening, a fuller explanation for tomorrow morning and, of course, the timed message for a couple of days after that. By then, this should have all worked out or ended in some sort of disaster.

"Spent most of the day in the records office," Katie said. "At first, I was just hiding like you suggested. Then I figured I'd look around. I think the Bouchers being smugglers theory is a good one, and it kind of spooks me. Just in case I'm overreacting and I think better of it in the morning I'm putting a time lock on this data which documents what I found and what I think it means."

Katie reviewed the recorded message. It might fool him. Katie wouldn't bet on it. It occurred to her she needed to move her schedule up. Meant some late night shopping in the last few hours before the shops closed. Then she needed to hole up somewhere else. She could use ship's funds to rent a transient sleeping tube down by the warehouses and docks. Put her on site to get started early tomorrow.

A good plan. Katie packed light, but carefully, and got on with it.

Sneaking out of her room was almost as nerve racking as sneaking into it had been. At this rate, she'd drive herself genuinely crazy without the Bouchers having to lift a finger.

Some more ship's funds later, and some fast shopping in a disreputable shop, and she had a whole duffle bag full of little hard to see surveillance cameras.

Katie ended up having to rent a storage locker down by the docks as well as a sleeping tube for the night.

It was physically similar to the one she'd had on the *Sand Piper*. Didn't smell anywhere as nice.

Katie was on the clock, though. Tomorrow was going to be busy again and more fraught even.

She cleared her mind and fell asleep.

She didn't dream.

She didn't even have nightmares.

\*\*\*

Katie had had absolutely no problem getting into the warehouse district. As the agent of a ship renting storage there, she was waved past the guards and through the checkpoints restricting access to it.

Katie's second pass as Kate Jackson, temporary warehouse worker, got her out of the area she was technically confined to and into that where she knew Guy Boucher had rented several large storage spaces in his own name. Seemed careless, but doubtless he had some excuse in the unlikely event anyone asked about it. The records office had been a font of information that few had any access to.

Katie had seen her share of crime vids set on Earth in past centuries. Warehouses were a popular venue for action scenes. The warehouses on Earth were large open sheds in effect. There were some larger spaces in the warehouse district of Ceres, but for the most part it was a warren of large corridors lined with accesses to a variety of rooms hollowed out from the asteroid's interior. Unlike the transit tunnels, the warehouse district was finished in a rough way. The storage rooms were essentially airtight steel boxes. Along with heavy duty doors that locked, this kept thieves out. Also smaller vermin, and allowed simple climate control, and preserved air pressure in case of a decompression event. Given the proximity of the warehouses to the docks, this last was a small, but distinct, possibility.

In any event, Katie had spent the balance of the morning slinking around those warrens distributing small cameras as she went. The cameras self organized into a distributed network as they were deployed. It neatly overcame the lack of regular communications in the warrens. Generally, a mixture of rock and steel walls isn't great for RF propagation.

But as long as Katie was careful to place the cameras at regular intervals, either very close or with a line of sight to each other, she could access all of them.

Katie had just hit pay dirt.

The line of cameras she'd placed first thing that morning in the corridor leading to the spaces the Bouchers rented showed Billy and his buddies opening one of those rooms. They conveniently left the door behind them open. The cameras didn't have sound, but she could see them laughing at something as they did so.

Through the open door she could see containers. Star Rat containers with their signature fat corners. Like the ones she'd seen on the *Sand Piper*. Might be the exact same containers for that matter.

Katie couldn't believe her luck when Billy opened one of them, clearly showing the alien tech within. Looked like he was playing with the merchandise.

She made sure that was recorded and started on the long trek back out of the district. Wait until the Chief and Commander saw this. They'd have to believe her then.

Katie had made it half way back, moving slowly and cautiously when she turned a corner to find Billy, Marvin, and another couple of Billy's buddies waiting for her.

"So what do we have here?" Billy asked.

"Looks like a trespasser to me," Marvin said. Did they have a script for this show?

"So we're allowed to like do a citizen's arrest and detain her, right?," Billy said.

"That's right, it's our civic duty," Marvin said with a snicker.

Katie had seen enough she turned to run and found herself facing another three of Billy's buddies.

They were all carrying packing blankets like large thick dirty quilts in their outstretched hands. She was blocked off from escape and she could hear Billy approaching from behind. Billy was clumsy and Marvin useless in a fight, they'd hamper the other two young men she was more likely to break through that way. She turned back and found herself facing Billy, who was holding a blocky black pistol like thing in one outstretched hand.

"You didn't really think you could sneak in here unexpected, did you?" he asked. "We were ready for you." He didn't waste anymore time monologuing before zapping her with the taser.

As she lay twitching on the deck, they grabbed her and rolled her up into one of the smelly packing blankets. Marvin hovering at a safe distance whined. "Careful. Careful. Remember what Mr. Boucher said, we can't bruise her."

It took three of them and the packing blanket, but by the time she'd stopped twitching she was securely swaddled and unable to move on her own. They moved her a short distance and being strangely careful manhandled her through a door. When they unceremoniously unrolled her, she found she was in a small room. Billy stood, the taser pointed at her as his buddies backed out around him. "Don't move or you get it again," he said.

"You won't get away with this," she answered. "You can't hide the evidence this time. I'm telling the Chief, the Commander, the entire rock for that matter, as soon as I get out."

"Who says you're getting out?" Billy asked as he backed out of the room.

"I disappear and they'll be all over your case."

"I don't think so. It's going to look just like an accident," Billy said, slamming the door behind him.

At which point, Katie realized the little room was airtight.

Katie looked around for the escape switch or an emergency alarm. All of these spaces were supposed to have at least one of them. There was a heavy piece of machinery, a three-D metal printer of some sort, in front of of where they should be. She squeezed in beside it and looked in behind. The switches were smashed. "Accidentally" not working, no doubt.

Katie spent a hectic, breathless half hour trying to get at them and activate one anyways. It didn't work.

They'd seen this coming. They'd planned well.

The room had less than a day's air, but Katie knew she'd start succumbing to carbon dioxide poisoning from her own breathing well before the lack of air became a problem. Probably best to do as little breathing as possible. On ship they'd have had emergency re-breathers, but there was nothing of that sort here.

Katie was trapped.

She only had a few hours to escape.

\* \* \*

Katie was in shock. Aghast. Was this it then? The end of all her dreams?

Had the bad guys in fact won?

Wasn't the way it was supposed to go. Guess life wasn't an uplifting story after all.

Katie couldn't believe it. Only it's kind of hard to argue with immediate physical facts. Katie was locked in an airtight steel box and her time was rapidly running out. Along with her air.

She wanted to cry. Or shout. Or scream. Or pound the walls in frustration. Or failing all that curl up into a tiny ball and go to sleep. To hope when she woke up, the nightmare would have ended.

Being short on time and breathable air both she couldn't afford to do any of that.

Katie had to think. Might not do any good. Wouldn't hurt to take a few minutes for it.

She sat on the floor and took a deep breath. She calmed herself.

Did a mental reset.

As far as she could tell there were three ways this could end well for her. Getting the emergency buttons to work was one. Somehow getting the locked door open was a second. Third and last, someone could come by and let her out.

Katie had already wasted a half hour on the first and most obvious approach. That'd been an error. Sure it'd been worth checking out. Crooks are human. They make mistakes, but this had obviously well planned in advance. Likely by Guy, who would have been careful to brief Marvin properly so that Billy wouldn't mess it up. The taser, the blankets, their care not to visibly bruise her, and the machinery in front of the switches to make it look like an accident they weren't working. It'd been carefully planned. It was exceedingly likely they had made sure those emergency switches were useless.

Katie should have realized that sooner.

What about someone rescuing her in time? Was there anything she could do to help with that? If there'd been any signal inside what was in effect a large Faraday cage, maybe she could have used the phone on her handheld computer. If the entire warehouse district hadn't been such a signal desert already. It just wasn't a place people frequented. It was for storage.

She should consider leaving a message on her handheld. Would in the end maybe, but she had little doubt it'd be the Bouchers or someone working for them that would "find" her body and that they'd handle that. So not a top priority.

Katie's deadman switched info dumps would serve the purpose as well if they worked. No point wasting time on that. Wasn't going to do her any good.

Maybe constantly yelling would alert any passer-by. Only there wasn't likely going to be any passer-byes and it'd use up her limited air that much faster.

Scratch that idea.

Alternatively she could try to be calm and do as little as possible to stretch out her remaining time, hoping that'd give people more time to realize she was missing and come find her.

Only no one knew she was missing or where she'd gone. She'd done too good a job of giving all her friends the slip, and her family was not only far away but unaware of the trouble she was in.

Not much hope there.

So what did that leave? The second option of somehow getting through a locked solid steel airtight door. That was her best option. Ouch.

Katie had the toolkit she always carried. Was there some way of getting at the lock's mechanism? Of doing the modern equivalent of lock picking?

Bet Sam would know.

Katie got up and went over and looked at the door. She tried to move the door handle. It didn't budge. She looked at the place where she knew the locking mechanism lay.

It hadn't been that long ago, had it? That she'd been in Sam's shop watching him work on one of them. Sam had told her quite a bit about them.

Katie remembered him showing her the heavy metal plate protecting the locking mechanism. She wasn't going to be hacking her way through something like that.

She also remembered him saying that wasn't a lock's greatest vulnerability. That the power to the fail safe mechanism was.

That was it.

That was the lock's point of greatest vulnerability.

Katie looked around. There it was. A simple "armored" electrical cable coming through a tightly packed port and then running into the door frame. The cabling armor was simple thin metal, not even continuous. Some flexibility was needed.

It practically wrecked a perfectly good screwdriver and took some hard work, but eventually she managed to hack through that cable.

This time when she tried the door handle, it did move.

As did the door.

The outside air seemed so much sweeter.

## 14: Katie Outnumbered

Having managed to escape the airtight little storage room and having taken a few blessedly sweet lungfuls of non-stale air, Katie realized she had no idea where she was.

In a corridor of the warehouse district, to be sure. Only where, exactly? Katie had been wrapped in a packing blanket and unable to see anything when they'd put her in that little room. Katie didn't think they'd carried her far. She must be close by where she'd been ambushed by Billy and his thugs. Close to the space where the contraband was stored.

Her goal at this point was to escape the warehouses and make it to the Chief or Commander with the news of what she'd found. First, she needed to figure out exactly where she was. Use that to plot a path out of the place. One that avoided encountering Billy and his crew ideally. One run in a day with that lot was more than enough.

Katie looked around and listened. There. There was one of her little cameras. Not easy to see the sneaky little things. She could hear faint voices off in the mid-distance. Billy and buddies, she'd guess.

The camera would give her access to its entire network and let her figure out where they were. Show her a good route around them too, she hoped.

Katie bounced over and jumped up to grab the camera from the ceiling wall corner she'd placed it into. She landed slow and light. She didn't weigh more than a few kilograms here in the warehouse district, which only had Ceres' minimal natural gravity.

Katie attached the camera to its controller and began to scroll through the images the network had collected in the last couple of hours. With glee, she noticed she had full records of Billy and his boys not only accessing the storage room with the alien contraband, but of actually handling it. This would prove they were smugglers beyond any doubt. As a bonus, the camera had also captured them ambushing her and locking her in the little room. Add attempted murder to the charges.

That was great, but where was Billy right now? It was taking a little effort to place the images. One piece of warehouse corridor tended to look much like the next. One image showed Billy and the others working in the contraband storage room. Moving the evidence? Katie didn't know. Also wasn't clear where that was from here. She tried to remember the exact layout of the cameras she'd dropped and which numbers corresponded to what locations.

Distracted by that problem, it was a surprise when a shout came. "She's out, boys!"

One, just one, of Billy's young accomplices had appeared at the end of the corridor. He was visibly hesitating. Torn between running back to warn Billy and the rest and trying to take Katie on by himself.

The first was what was wise. A young buck's pride argued for the second. Fleeing from a one-on-one fight with a young girl smaller than you doesn't look very brave. Looks kind of cowardly, in fact.

Katie didn't hesitate.

Sometimes it's a problem that it's so easy to build up a lot of momentum in low gravity. This wasn't one of those times. Katie made full use of the distance between her and Billy's accomplice. Harry, if she remembered correctly. Note to self in the future don't fail to learn your enemy out of disdain. In the event, Harry stood his ground. A mistake. Crouched low, more pushing forward than stepping or hopping, Katie built up velocity and momentum with each thrust of her legs.

Katie hit Harry right about his knees in an overpowered tackle. Higher up would have been better. She took more of his weight than she would have liked. Harry himself was flipped sidewards and down, doing an involuntary sliding face plant.

Katie granted her would be murderer no mercy. She twisted and awkwardly grabbing his head in one palm, smashed it several times into the floor they were sliding along.

There was blood. Harry's shouting ceased. She didn't pause to assess the situation more thoroughly.

There was more shouting coming from the other thugs. Who were blocking the only route she was sure of out of this place.

Katie couldn't give them the time to get their acts together.

Another of the thugs appeared from the direction of the shouting. Tom, she thought. She hadn't seen Marvin come to think of it on the camera. Billy's boys weren't reacting in a co-ordinated way, thank heavens. Could be Billy really did need Marvin to do his thinking. In any case, she still didn't have time to waste. She wasn't looking a gift horse in the mouth.

Grappling the comatose Harry and pushing him in front of her, she started to regain the momentum she'd lost when she hit him. Tom reacted even more perfectly than Harry. Perfectly for Katie's purposes.

Tom kept moving towards Katie. He hesitated only to the extent of slowing down a little in the last moments before she hit him. Apparently Ceres born as they were Billy's boys weren't that used to very low gravity. If they'd done any serious fighting at all it hadn't been in low Gees.

Katie smacked her opponent right where she wanted to this time. Tom and Harry took all the damage. Tom was flipped backwards. Flipped hard. She had a real talent for smashing heads against floors. They slide slowly along the floor with Katie on the top of a human sandwich with Harry in the middle and Tom on the bottom. Neither of the thugs was making a peep.

Grabbing Harry, Katie continued forward. Careful not to build up too much momentum again. She had a corner to turn. Katie figured she'd reach it before Billy and the rest of his thugs.

Probably Billy wasn't moving at all. He'd let his buddies go forward without backup. Probably waiting to use that taser again. From a safe distance. Well, she had the counter to that in her hands.

Going to be tricky mind you to keep Harry between her and Billy, but if she managed it Harry would take the shocks intended for her. Sure sucked to be Harry.

Katie tried to slow as the corner approached. Not with complete success.

A problem as it meant she was being dragged by Harry's body when they cleared the corner and fully exposed to being tasered by Billy. He'd hung back near the entrance to the contraband warehouse space like she suspected. That much was good. Close in and outnumbered, his size would have been an issue.

Katie desperately tried to twist Harry around between them.

Billy had another of his buddies with him. Rich, most likely it occurred to Katie, as she struggled for life. Rich got proactive and started off towards Katie, only to be pushed hard to one side by Billy. "Get out of my way," Billy was yelling.

Rich twisting towards Billy was caught off guard by his leader pushing him into the corridor wall. He hit it at a bad angle. For him. Suited Katie fine. Katie was feeling very appreciative of Billy's buddies habit of hitting hard surfaces with their heads. It all seemed surreally slow.

Must be the effect of the adrenaline the fight was driving through her system.

Billy fired his taser at her just as she managed to bring Harry into place between. He hit Harry, not Katie. Harry twitched with the shocks and Katie could feel them too. Hurt, but she powered through it, using Harry as a battering ram for a third time.

She was getting good at this. Her hit on Billy smashed him backwards hard.

Katie didn't have time to observe her handiwork. Rich was getting back up. Using the pile up of Billy and Harry as a pivot, she drove Rich right back into the wall with a foot to his face. He slid down it like a character from a children's cartoon.

Katie was just about done in with exertion, but the fight wasn't over. Billy didn't seem to be moving, but she made sure of him by kicking him as hard as she could in the nuts, which got only a subdued grunt. She pulled Harry off of Billy and kicked Billy in the head for good measure. She couldn't risk his getting back up.

Billy's taser fell from his limp hand. She picked it up and turned to face the remaining pair of Billy's boys who'd been working inside the warehouse space. They were standing there with their mouths gapping open. Apparently not quick thinkers. Good thing.

"All right hands in the air and kneel down," she shouted, waving the taser at them. They seemed slow. "Now!" she yelled, pointing the taser at one of them. That galvanized them into hastily doing as she'd directed.

Katie noticed some heavy duty packing tape to one side. She tried to remember the names of these two. Only one name came to her. "Gerry, you get the packing tape and tape your buddy up," she said. She wanted nothing more than to taze the two of them and then to kick both their heads in while they lay twitching on the ground. The murdering bastards deserved it.

Katie managed to fight the urge, but her anger must have shown on her face because a white faced Gerry hastened to do her bidding.

Once he'd finished taping up his partner, she tazed him anyways. Didn't kick him while he was down, though. Only taped him up without bothering to be delicate.

Katie looked around in shock.

All her enemies were down. Not moving. She wasn't entirely sure they were all still alive.

All she wanted to was to lie down herself and get some badly needed rest. She was wiped. Hollow.

She couldn't. She needed to go for help.

So she did.

\* \* \*

Katie was feeling numb and grimly satisfied. And tired. Very tired.

Katie would have liked to gone somewhere not so busy and to have gotten some sleep. She couldn't. After she'd met both Chief Dingle and the Commander along with their dozens of subordinate officers and led them back to the warehouse full of alien contraband, the Chief had been clear.

"You stand right here," he'd said, "and don't say anything to anyone." The Commander standing beside them had nodded affirmation.

The police and Space Force personnel didn't seem to fully trust each other. They were working in pairs. There were now dozens of witnesses to the fact that someone had been smuggling alien contraband.

That someone quite clearly including Billy and his buddies who had been collected up by medical teams and carted off. One medical technician had also peeled off and looked Katie over. Another one of them had reported on the status of the young men to the Chief before leaving.

The Chief had come over to Katie to pass on the information. "Listen, don't say anything," he'd said. The Commander like some sort of uniformed bobble-head doll nodded affirmation. He did some review of the full dump of camera footage Katie had given both him and the Commander copies of. "You're lucky," he'd said. "You're not a murderer." He paused and looked straight at her. "I'm sure a claim of self defense would have held up, but you won't have to be making it. They're all still alive and stable now."

Katie nodded. He'd said not to say anything.

"You have a pass to be here?" he'd asked next.

She handed it to him.

He inspected the fake ID. "This looks like an error in records. I'll see it's rectified without any further fuss."

The Commander nodded approvingly off to one side.

"Stay here and wait. We'll try not to be too much longer," the Chief had said before going off to supervise his uniformed minions. The Commander trailed behind quietly. He spared Katie a quick wink as he did so.

Looked like a hint she'd not be in too much trouble. Ought to be a relief, but she was too numb to feel it. Satisfaction, she could manage that much.

Finally all the containers in the storeroom were opened and their contents cataloged. The Commander and the Chief held an animated conversation off to one side that Katie couldn't quite make out. For all their animation, the men kept their conversation low.

Having reached some sort of conclusion, they came over to Katie.

The Chief looked at her with sympathy. "You don't look good," he said.

"Thanks."

The man's mouth twitched a quick smile. "You also need work on your deference to authority," the Chief said. His tone warm if matter of fact. He seemed amused, if anything. "As am sure the Commander can attest, it's something expected of junior officers in the Space Force."

The Commander nodded. "The Chief is correct," he said. "After this, you're going to get your chance at going to the Academy. Going to mean a lot of work." He smiled. "You've convinced me you're up to it, but it's not going to be easy."

"That's it?" Katie asked. "That's all?"

"No," the Chief answered, "it's not. For one, we're going to have to take you into protective custody for a while until we've secured Guy and all of his accomplices."

"Including the crew of the *Sand Piper*," the Commander said. "That's one of my tasks." Not one he looked happy about.

"I'm sorry about that, sir," Katie said.

"Yes, but the less said about it the better," the Commander replied.

"In fact, you shouldn't volunteer any information even to me or the Commander," the Chief said. "You shouldn't discuss any of it with anybody else at all. Not with Chief Williamson, not with Calvin Cromwell, not with your parents, not with anyone. This is going to be an ongoing investigation for some time. I strongly suspect for security reasons most of the details will end up classified. To that end, we believe our superiors will be happy to overlook any technical legal infractions on your part in exchange for your discretion. Understood?"

Katie in an ideal world would have liked to have believed a lawyer and an open legal investigation would have been better. She wasn't at all sure that was true in reality. She'd settle for trusting the two men had both her best interests and that of the public in mind. "Yes, sir," she responded.

"Good. Let's find you a decent place to get cleaned up and rested."

Sounded good to Katie.

\* \* \*

Guy had a temper.

It'd flared when he realized what was happening.

Guy had felt great satisfaction when Marvin had come calling with the news they'd captured the Kincaid girl and she was being dealt with. He didn't believe in counting his chickens before they were fully hatched just the same. He'd sent Marvin, along with his escort, back to Billy with a message that they were to remain on site and not to do anything before Guy got there. From what Marvin had said Guy suspected the girl had been collecting data electronically and Guy would have also bet his bottom credit her disappearance would be swiftly followed up. He had to make sure that follow up didn't find anything.

Guy followed behind Marvin and the other kid after barely five minutes. He'd sensed something was wrong even before he saw them detained. There'd been too many officers of the Space Force and police around and all heading in the same direction.

The gig was up.

And so Guy was angry. Not normally so. It wasn't the cracking under a load of frustration and exasperation hot sort of anger that expressed itself in violence against things, and at times people, he felt.

No, it was the intense anger of being in immediate danger. The cold controlled intensely focused and utterly ruthless anger that scared even him in his calmer, more rational moods.

The ruthless anger that told him Billy was a lost cause. The anger that told him he wasn't too old to have other children. The one that informed him he needed to be someone else, somewhere else, and that he needed to move on that need now.

Guy had escape plans, of course.

His implacably cold pragmatic anger told him he needed to use the riskier one of them. The slower, more uncomfortable and costly one.

Ceres was too small, and he was too well known there. He had to leave. He had a plan in place to replace a regular crewman on one of the transports that plied a route in system. It was one that would have stood up to regular scrutiny. It would have been a rather boring, but not uncomfortable trip back to the vicinity of Earth and the substantial back up resources he'd stashed there.

Guy didn't allow himself the luxury of thinking that plan would work.

No, he was going to have to take a position on a small cramped mining rig owned and manned by some truly disgusting reprobates. Ones hopefully rational enough to realize they'd get paid more in the end if they didn't try to back stab him.

Then it'd be many months in space in cramped quarters and a complicated, uncertain path back to the inner system. Who could be sure what assets would survive his being out of contact for all that time? It certainly wouldn't increase his political capital with his associates back on Earth.

Still, it was the best choice.

Chief Dingle and the Commander would both be looking for him. They'd soon have the whole rock locked down hard.

And so, Guy was on his way to the seediest part of Ceres, where he knew he'd find the men he needed.

It should work out, and with time and effort he'd rebuild.

Guy would be more careful this time.

Among other things, he'd keep an eye out for Katie Kincaid.

He had a feeling the little girl was going to make a big splash.

* * *

Commander Tretyak was nibbling at a spicy faux chicken wrap. It was a very late lunch he was enjoying in his office. Reacting to the mess Katie Kincaid had found in the warehouse district had consumed most of his day so far, including his regular lunch hour.

The Commander had very mixed feelings about the whole thing now that he had had a little time to think about it. That his friend Guy Boucher had turned out to be a crook, not just a smuggler, but one who'd at least attempted murder hurt. He hadn't enjoyed having to put the crew of the *Sand Piper* under house arrest either. As for his career, well, it was just as well he enjoyed his position here on Ceres.

That their dragnet had yet to dredge up Guy was cause for concern. He assumed the man couldn't have gone far. They had after all sealed off the entire base as soon as they'd realized the magnitude of what the Kincaid girl had found. So, he expected they'd find Guy sooner or later, but he'd have felt better if the man wasn't still at large.

Oddly, he felt more sad than angry about the whole thing. Embarrassed, too. He'd had a certain view of the SDF and the people here on Ceres, and it'd now turned out it'd been wrong. Turned out that he'd been naïve. It made him sad that the world wasn't as a nice of a place as he'd thought. He could cope though, and he didn't blame anyone for it. He didn't blame himself that much either. Given a choice between naïve and cynical, he'd still chose naïve.

The Commander did regret not catching the situation earlier. In particular, he regretted the hard time he'd given the Kincaid girl.

He still thought she'd be a source of disruption in the Space Force. Only now he was inclined to think that might not be a bad thing.

He was annoyed at the Space Force right now and at SFHQ in particular. As soon as he'd realized there was proof of Kincaid's allegations this time he'd informed SFHQ with a highest priority message.

Their immediate reaction had been to ask him to keep the whole matter as confidential as possible. There was an old adage that sunlight is the best disinfectant. He wasn't convinced, but the bureaucracy's inclination to bury the news of anything and everything it might find embarrassing didn't impress him.

It did mean that the Kincaid girl was likely not going to be held here on Ceres and subjected to a whole series of awkward questions. The leadership of the Space Force doubtless understood it wouldn't like the answers that'd be made public as a result of that.

It should leave him free to give her a solid endorsement to her Academy application.

In the meantime, her initiative meant he had a lot of paperwork to fill out. He'd be here well into the evening.

\*\*\*

Calvin's family were giving him a lot of room.

It'd taken most of the day, but by the time supper time had rolled around the rumors had solidified. Katie Kincaid had found something down in the warehouse district. The police and Space Force MPs were both all over it. Guy Boucher, the crew of the *Sand Piper*, and Kincaid herself were nowhere to be found. The consensus of the rumor mongers was that Kincaid had found proof of her earlier accusations. It was the talk of the rock.

One of Calvin's sisters had breathlessly relayed the entire story to the family over dinner.

Calvin's first reaction had been one of joy and relief for Katie. His happiness was only somewhat moderated by concern for Katie's safety and the risks he didn't doubt she'd taken. His sister had insisted that only Billy and some of his buddies were in the hospital though, so that was good.

Then the implications of the whole thing began to sink in and his mood had rapidly soured.

Calvin's mother had quietly told him he was excused his clean up duties and suggested he might want some personal time. She'd waved the rest of the family away with sharp gestures.

Calvin had thought Katie's hopes unrealistic. He'd figured that once she realized that she'd look at both the idea of remaining in the Belt and him differently. He'd been wrong on the first count. He shivered. He wondered if he'd been wrong on the second too. Would she have left the Belt and him anyways, even if she hadn't got into the Academy?

It bothered him that he hadn't trusted her judgment. That he'd been hoping for her to fail. He didn't feel good about that.

Calvin had never doubted her honesty. Meant the smugglers were real. Meant she'd most likely emerge a hero from this. A hero the Commander had been unfair to. The Commander would be falling all over himself to make amends. Odds were her Academy endorsement was in the bag. Assuming she'd got through whatever had happened in one piece.

There was no clear publicly available information about what had happened down in the warehouse district. Technically, he didn't know where Katie was. She could have been hurt or even killed.

He didn't think so.

Katie was a survivor. Somehow he was convinced that however battered she might be, she had survived.

When the dust settled, he couldn't help thinking she'd be on her way to the Academy and out of his life.

Calvin was happy for her.

He was sad for himself.

He felt bad about that, but it was what it was.

He remembered some silly book they'd all been made to read about a seagull. It'd said something saccharine about letting what you loved go free.

It'd made no sense to him at the time. Now he understood.

Who'd have thought insight could be so painful?

Where to go from here? Well, if he was hurting he had to think Katie was feeling pretty battered emotionally too. It may have worked out in the end for her. He hoped and thought so, but she'd been through a lot.

So as much as it hurt at times he'd be a good friend.

Calvin would let her know he was happy for her.

Support her any way he could.

Like any good friend would.

## 15: Katie Endorsed

Katie resolved never to get sent to prison. She didn't take confinement and not having anything to do at all well.

The quarters the Commander had arranged for her were not luxurious, but they were comfortable, and more than adequate. Designed for transient Space Force officers they were in fact much nicer than her school dorm room.

Unfortunately, besides a limited standard set of entertainment programs and some games, there wasn't much to do in them except rest. She wasn't allowed to communicate with anyone. She couldn't even let her parents know she was okay. The Commander had assured her he'd pass on the news but that it was critical the details of what had happened not get out.

He'd said it was because they needed to try to catch as much as Guy Boucher's criminal network by surprise as possible.

When she'd first got here, she hadn't minded much.

She'd been too tired.

She'd fallen on the bed as soon as she'd been left alone. Not undressed or crawled under the covers or cleaned up or eaten, just fallen on the bed and slept for most of eight hours straight. She'd then woken up long enough to shower and change into some brand new pajamas that had been left for her.

There'd been snacks too. She wondered she'd been so dead to

the world that she'd not noticed their being delivered.

Not for long, she'd scoffed some of them down and gone right back to bed for a few more hours. She'd never realized it was possible to have an appetite for sleep before.

Now it was the early hours of the day after her adventure down in the warehouse district. She didn't feel like sleeping anymore.

She was alone with herself.

Chief of Police Dingle and Commander Tretyak were the only people she was allowed to talk to. They were doubtless getting some well deserved sleep.

There was no one to talk to but herself. Her unconscious mind had begun the process. The first eight hours or so of her sleep had been the deep sleep of physical exhaustion. More akin to a coma than normal sleep. Later, she'd recovered to the point of having fitful dreams about her experiences of the last few weeks.

Her dreams had featured graveyards. She'd stumbled about in them. Lost. It hadn't been nightmarish. The pervading emotion hadn't been fear. Not even apprehension. Her feelings had included frustration. The dominant theme, however, had been puzzlement.

There'd been a particular gravestone she needed to find. Weirdly not that of a person. No, she'd been looking for where her application to the Academy was buried. Somehow, if she could find it and read the inscription on it, she knew she could resurrect it.

Dreams were strange, she couldn't help thinking.

But as odd as they were, those dreams didn't come from nowhere. Somewhere in the back of her head she was trying to make sense of all that had happened.

When she thought about it, she felt silly. It was obvious. Graveyards were her mnemonic device for remembering safety manuals.

Was there a safety manual for life? One for Academy applications? Not likely, but that's what she'd been looking for. She was a spacer. A conscientious, hard-working crew member on a spaceship. Had been for her whole young life. She lived by her safety manuals.

Her parents were nominally her superiors and her mentors. In reality compared to her they were amateurs. Born and brought up on Earth, they'd learned how to be spacers, rock rats, as adults. It was why so many of the other rock rats and Belters couldn't take them seriously.

To people brought up in space, they gave the impression of playing at being spacers.

It occurred to Katie that this was tremendously unfair. That her mother and father had learned a difficult and dangerous profession despite being ill prepared and done a creditable job of it. One for which they failed to get credit for. Not even from her. It embarrassed her to realize that. She resolved to be more appreciative in the future.

Be that as it may, it was beside the point. This wasn't about them. It was about her.

Another realization. She'd never taken her time on Ceres seriously. The mandatory stints on Ceres had been vacations from her real duties for her. Ouch. Blind and stupid of her, considering her future depended on how she performed while on Ceres.

While on board the *Dawn Threader*, she had responsibilities. She had her safety manuals to tell her what those were. On Ceres, her responsibilities had been limited. The explicit safety manuals for them much more so.

Yet another realization. She'd made up implicit manuals of rules to follow in lieu of explicit ones provided by others. Having decided on an explicit set of rules to follow, she hadn't been very flexible. Not flexible in her own behavior. Not flexible in her understanding of and sympathy for other people's behavior.

Was there a manual for apologizing to all and sundry for being a clueless brat? She could use one right about now. She wished she was still tired. She'd have liked the excuse for crawling back into bed. Crawling back into bed and hiding there for the rest of eternity.

Another learning experience, she now had a much better idea of the difference between physical and moral courage. In fact, she could now break moral courage down into intellectual and emotional courage. Katie was convinced she had plenty of physical courage and intellectual courage too. Yesterday she would have said she had plenty of emotional courage.

Today, not so much. Today it occurred to her she'd been armored in ignorance and a moral certitude dependent upon on it. Now that ignorance was showing cracks and the moral certitude was melting away.

Now she was having to face up to the fact she'd behaved badly. She'd been rigid and arrogant with everybody she'd ever known, with her parents, with her teachers, with her fellow students, and with her friends. She wondered that they, Calvin and Sam in particular, had been willing to put up with her.

Guess she must have some compensating qualities. That was nice. The thought she owed them all extensive apologies, and she had no idea where to begin, was not.

The realization that she was afraid of having to face them and make those apologies was also not pleasant.

Sam would joke about it.

"Suck it up, buttercup," he'd say. He'd have no patience with all this angst. She was going to miss him. Her parents hadn't done as poorly by her as she'd been inclined to think, but she hated to think what her life would have been like without Sam. If he hadn't set up shop on Ceres or been willing to humor a girl left there on her own, she'd have no clues at all.

She didn't know how she could ever repay him. Suspected she couldn't.

Guess all she could do was try to pay it forward.

Try to do better in the future.

There that was a plan.

The start of one, anyway.

\* \* \*

Commander Tretyak hadn't had much sleep. He felt good, ready to face the day, despite that. A few hours' rest, a hot shower, and a clean uniform can do wonders.

On one level, the day hadn't started well. A quick video chat check in with Chief of Police Dingle revealed that Guy Boucher remained at large. It was beginning to look like he'd had a contingency plan for being discovered. If so, they'd likely lost him. Along with a good fraction of his more important collaborators. Most of the names they had were those of the smaller fish who didn't know much.

Chief Dingle had some hopes of getting some circumstantial evidence out of Marvin Minakowski and Billy Boucher as they'd been around enough to pick up things. On the other hand, Guy had obviously had the sense not to tell them more than he had to.

The Commander had been disappointed to hear all that, but not terribly surprised. It didn't diminish his pleasure in the fact that he'd finally be able to put the Kincaid conundrum to bed in a fashion he could feel happy about.

With Guy and the other big fish having slipped their net, there was no longer any excuse for maintaining the news embargo they'd imposed. From what Chief Dingle had said, the rumor mill had already rendered it moot. The Chief would be putting out an official news release anytime now.

The Commander would be releasing a short statement of his own. It wouldn't say much more than that *Sand Piper*'s crew was under arrest given new information regards the accusations they'd been involved in smuggling.

It also formally apologized to Katie Kincaid for earlier doubts about her allegations, the Space Force's failure to more throughly investigate them, and his own personal failure to take them more seriously.

His superiors wouldn't be happy. He thought it likely he was doing them a favor in the long run, but he didn't expect them to see that.

Kincaid herself should be arriving in his office soon. He cared a lot more about what she thought at this point.

A knock came. Speak of the devil. He smiled to himself. The girl was trouble. He couldn't bring himself to hold it against her anymore.

"Come in," he said loudly enough to be heard through the door.

Kincaid entered. Determined as always, but looking unusually tired and worn.

He waved her over to the tea table. "Don't imagine you want to spend any longer here than necessary," he said, "but I'd like to make this session a pleasant one. I have several good pieces of news. So sit down and help yourself to some tea while we go over them."

She sat and poured herself tea as directed.

As he sat down across from her she focused on putting precisely the right amount of milk into it.

He nodded and poured himself some too.

She looked at him expectantly.

"First thing, in case you're still worried," he said, "you're free to go once we're done here. You can keep using the room in the officer's quarters for the rest of the week if you wish. Might be safer. More comfortable, perhaps. You've been through a lot. I'd like to make it as easy on you from here on in as possible."

"Great," Katie said. More relieved than enthusiastic.

"Okay," he said. "Second thing, I'd like to apologize in person for doubting your word and all the hassles I've put you through."

Katie blinked and looked pensive. It was an odd look on her. "So would I," she said. "Thinking about this morning after I woke up, I realize I've been an arrogant brat. I regret that. I apologize."

"Well done," the Commander said. "I appreciate it. However, not fully justified. The bottom line remains: you were innocent of any bad behavior and you were right about the Bouchers and the smuggling both. You were almost killed twice. After that, I allowed your reputation to be smeared. You could have been smoother and more understanding at some points, but that would have been a lot to ask even of someone much older. I'm sorry about what happened."

Katie nodded. "Thank you, sir," she said. "All the same, I think I'll try harder to be more considerate of other people's points of view in the future."

The Commander nodded in turn. "It can't hurt," he said. "Sadly, what I've said earlier about the Space Force is true. It's political. You will have trouble fitting in. It'll be work."

Katie lit up. She grinned at him. Her posture straightened. The whole melancholy mood she'd been displaying since she'd arrived evaporated. She knew what his words implied. She knew she was getting his endorsement. She'd be going to the Academy.

"Yes, I'm endorsing your application," he said. "I will add the facts that I believe that, in addition to your outstanding technical and academic skills, you possess exceptional strength of character, an unusual willingness to learn, and an extraordinary degree of persistence even in the face of seemingly insurmountable odds."

She looked at him in apparent disbelief. Opening her mouth to speak, she failed to produce any words at first. Finally she said, "That's very fulsome praise, sir. I'm not sure I deserve it."

"It's not the sort of thing you'd usually say to someone's face," he said. "It is the unvarnished truth. I'd be remiss not to include those facts in my report on you."

"Thank you, sir."

"Don't thank me yet," he said, smiling. "It's all true, but they won't appreciate those virtues as much as they'd like to think they will. It's not going to be easy for you at first. Cadets and inexperienced junior officers might be right about the occasional thing, but they're still expected to know their place. They don't have a lot of power. They're not always taken seriously. You will have to learn to choose your battles."

"Yes, sir," Katie said.

He took a sip of his tea. "This is the statement I intend to release," he said, pushing a piece of hardcopy over to her. "Do you see any problems?"

She read it quickly. "No, sir. I appreciate the public apology. I hope this clears my name."

"It should help," he said. "Unfortunately, when things go wrong, some of the mess sticks to everyone."

"Noticed that, sir," she replied.

"Do try not to get more experience with it," he said, smiling thinly at her.

"I'll try."

"Finally, you're free to talk about what happened. Our authority to challenge your right to do so is limited," he said. "However, both myself and the Chief would appreciate if you said as little as possible. It's still a dog's breakfast. The Academy and SFHQ aren't officially involved, but you want as little controversy attached to your name as possible. It's not usually a good thing for the little fish to catch the big fishes' attention."

Katie grimaced. "Yes, sir," she said.

The Commander allowed himself a small sigh. "It is, sadly, the way of the world," he said. "I suspect you want to change the world, but maybe not everything all at once, young lady."

"I see, sir."

"Anything else you'd like to discuss?" he asked.

"No, sir."

He stood, holding out his hand for a shake. "You're free to go then," he said.

She stood and shook his hand. "Thank you, sir," she said. "I think you've been fair. More than fair at points. Thank you."

And she left.

\* \* \*

It wasn't until after lunch that Katie appeared in Sam's shop.

He'd been waiting for her. Working on something new, rather than fixing up something old as usual.

Mining rigs were tough. Built to last, but even the toughest, best-build parts eventually need replacing. The thruster block Sam was replacing wasn't much more than a solid piece of metal with parts of it strategically drilled out in the right pattern.

Years of constant use, a certain amount of perhaps unavoidable abuse, had eroded away portions of its predecessor. To the point now that it needed to be replaced.

Even the best things come to an end.

Sam was happy for Katie. The rumor mill made it clear her reputation had been rehabilitated. She was the hero of the day. Sam had no doubt that meant the Commander would endorse her Academy application, and that she'd soon be off to terrorize a different segment of humanity.

He chuckled to himself.

The girl did have a way of making her presence felt.

"What's funny?" she asked from the perch she'd taken on one of his high stools.

"Rumor has it," he said, "that you've managed to go from outcast to hero. Figure means you're getting to go the Academy this year after all. That right?"

"Guess so," she said, like she'd like to disagree but couldn't. "People on this rock sure like to gossip. I don't see how come I got to be the bad guy, and I don't see that I'm such a hero either. Only people seem to like to exaggerate."

"Not just Ceres. The Academy?"

"Commander Tretyak says he's going to give me an endorsement." She fidgeted. "A good one. So that chick's not hatched yet, but the odds look good. Excellent, I guess, only it's been such a roller coaster ride I'm afraid of getting ahead of myself."

Sam paused to line up his milling tool before replying. "Smart not to get too far ahead of yourself. You're learning. You can never be entirely sure of anything, but I'm guessing you've got this in the bag. Congratulations."

"Thanks." She didn't seem quite as thrilled as Sam would have expected.

"Leave early, and you can try riding on a real roller coaster."

Katie grinned. "That'd be neat. There's so much we read about life on Earth, and see on the vids, but haven't seen for real. Open sky, oceans, lakes, forests, the big cities, and roller coasters, it's going to be quite the adventure."

Sam smiled. "Literally a whole new world."

"Yeah, it boggles the imagination."

"You're going to feel overwhelmed at times," Sam said. "For all that a spaceship is a complicated thing it's a lot smaller than a whole planet. Also makes more sense."

Katie frowned. "You're not sure I can handle it?"

"I think you'll manage," Sam answered, "but there will be times when you doubt that yourself. When that happens look around you and see all the other people that manage to deal with what's got you stumped and feeling inadequate."

"Never been accused of feeling inadequate," Katie said, smirking.

"No, but you're a growing girl," Sam said. "One about to venture out into the wider world. You're going to find things are different from what you're used to there sometimes. Sometimes it's going to be hard to cope with it."

"You're sure?" Katie chewed on her lower lip. "Any advice?"

"Nothing specific." Sam abandoned the effort to talk and work both. He pulled up a stool of his own and sat facing her. "The parts of Earth and the people I knew you aren't going to be seeing much of. Thank your lucky stars for that. After that I was an enlisted marine. You're going to be a Space Force officer. Different sort of creature."

"You've taught me a lot about life."

"I've tried. I hope it'll be useful. It won't be enough, I'm sure, you're going to have to learn a lot more on your own. Like I told you when it feels hopeless, the thing is to look at the people around you. You won't find many superhumans. What you'll find is regular humans who take for granted things you mightn't know the least thing about. People who know and understand some useful things you don't, but nothing magical. Have the humility to learn from them, but don't let them intimidate you."

"Don't intimidate worth a damn, you know that."

"Yes, that's what I was chuckling about." Sam gave Katie a wry grin. "Believe me, you will be overwhelmed at times. Only there are going to be plenty of times when you're the one overwhelming other people. Might be an idea to be careful about that."

"You think so?"

"I do. It's a big world out there. You're going to look back at your time here on Ceres and the *Dawn Threader* and it's going to look cozy. Bet you a beer."

"You know I don't drink. I'm only fifteen."

"And when you come back from the Academy, you'll be a young woman past the age of majority who's been out for a few drinks with friends and colleagues many times."

"Wow, I suppose I could be," Katie replied, eyes wide.

"Rule in the military is that if you're old enough to risk your life for the cause, you're old enough to vote and drink."

"Guess that makes sense."

"Yep, and don't know about the officers for sure, but in the ranks a lot of things get worked out over a few cold ones in the mess. I suspect same is true in a more elevated way for officers. Don't forget the social aspects of what you're doing, girl."

Katie looked at her hands clasped in her lap. "Going to miss your advice, Sam. Going to miss you."

"Going to miss you too, Katie."

"That it?"

"You're going to be busy. Keep in touch best you can."

"Will do. Promise."

Katie hopped up and left.

## 16: Bon Voyage Katie

It wasn't ideal.

Katie wasn't going to get to hug her parents goodbye.

Almost everyone seemed to agree that it was best she get to Earth as soon as possible, that she'd need the longest period of acclimation there possible. Everyone including the Academy's Admissions Board who'd expedited the processing of her application since it'd been sent less than two days ago.

Her application to the Academy had been accepted. The regular transport in-system was leaving later today. Katie would be on it.

Katie looked around the dorm room she'd lived in whenever on Ceres. It'd never been her favorite place, but she knew she was going to miss it. It'd be years before she got back to Ceres, and it'd belong to some other student by then. She didn't know what her new life would be like, but she was already losing parts of her old one.

Her tiny cabin on the *Dawn Threader* she wasn't going to get to see again at all any time soon.

The *Dawn Threader* with her parents on board wasn't going to make it back to Ceres before she left.

Which was why it was only "almost everyone" that agreed she needed to leave for Earth as soon as possible. The brief text messages she'd exchanged with them made that clear. They wouldn't stand in her way. They were going to let her do what she felt she needed to. Didn't mean they agreed with it, let alone felt happy about it.

Now that she was about to leave home herself, Katie realized what a wrenching experience it must have been for her parents. They'd not only left everything they'd ever known behind, they'd also cut all ties. They'd started over from scratch in a very different world. They'd had the capital to buy the *Dawn Threader* and to start a business with her. They'd known almost nothing about being spacers or what that business required. There been nobody they'd known on Ceres or in the Belt.

Why had they'd taken such a risk? One that was bound to be so hard. Hard even if it worked out. She'd never thought to ask.

In a few minutes she'd have a last chance to do so, if not in person, at least without a long time lag. At least for a long time.

Only it was a chance to say goodbye and paper over any hard feelings.

Not an appropriate time to be opening old wounds.

Katie had read how partings, an inevitable feature of departing on a trip, could be wistful. This was her first personal experience of it. Once again words did the reality no justice.

Enough of that. She waited. Her terminal beeped. She hit the appropriate key.

"Hi, Mom! Hi, Dad!" she chirped. She felt like such a fake.

Her mother smiled at her. Her real smile. It was good to see. Her father, one arm wrapped around his wife's shoulders, waved to Katie with the other. Whenever together they liked to be touching.

"Katie, it's good to see you well," her mother said. Behind her, Katie's father nodded.

Katie had never thought a simple standard greeting could be such a minefield of possible implications.

Her mother smiled. "It's just a greeting, dear." Katie's dad grinned behind her in confirmation. "If we'd known all the trouble you were going to get into, I'm sure we would have been worried sick. I'd beg you to be more careful in the future, but I don't like to waste my breath. Water under the bridge. We're going to miss you. We want you to remember us fondly and do your best to stay in touch."

"I'll try, I promise, Mom," Katie replied.

"Good," her mother said. "I know you will be very busy, but if you could make a point of dropping us regular, quick updates, we'd appreciate it. I know at your age I didn't want to hear how I'd always be my mom's baby, but it's true. It'll make me feel a lot better to hear you're okay from time to time."

"I'll make a point of it," Katie said. "I never meant to hurt anyone's feelings."

"We know, love," her father answered. It was her mother's turn to nod in agreement. "It'll just make us feel better to hear from you occasionally. Heavens know you do seem to find trouble when we're not watching you."

Katie thought that was odd. She'd always thought she was the one keeping them out of trouble. "I'll keep a better eye out in the future," she said. "Never realized how sheltered I was before."

Her mother nodded. Her father tried to keep the concern he was feeling off his face. Katie knew them too well.

"It's a big world out there," her mother said. "I'm not sure it's ready for you, but you were going to have to leave the nest sooner or later."

"I would have preferred later, too," Katie answered. "If I'd known how well I was going to do on the standard tests or how the Admissions Board would react, I think I would have found an excuse not to do them."

Again her mother nodded. It was a pensive nod. "You couldn't have been expected to have known," she said. She paused. "But let it be a lesson. Sometimes some things we do are more critical than we realize. Try to spot things like that ahead of time and figure out how to handle them."

That was her mother, she liked to strategize. Her father was more into doing things on principle. He followed his heart where it led him.

"Follow your heart, but keep your eyes open," he said.

Katie nodded. "I will."

Her mother grimaced. "Which I guess brings us to the least pleasant part of this little talk," she said. "You were out of line in your use of our ship's funds. I suspect you broke a few other rules, maybe laws, but neither Chief Dingle nor Commander Tretyak are talking. You're forgiven, dear."

Katie felt herself color. "Sorry, Mom, Dad," she replied. "Thank you."

"I wish you hadn't felt it necessary," her mom sighed and looked past Katie briefly. "Maybe we should have trusted you more and supported you better too. Water under the bridge again."

"But?" Katie knew there was going to be a "but".

"But people won't necessarily be so understanding in the future," her mother said. "Usually when you break trust, hard and fast rules, or laws like that there are consequences. Severe consequences. Understood?"

"Yes, ma'am. Understood," Katie answered.

"I'd have rather not mentioned it, but I'd have been failing you not to," her mother said. Her father nodded in glum agreement.

"Thanks, Mom."

"You're welcome, dear," her mother said. Her father smiled wryly. "Your ship leaves this afternoon?" her mother continued.

"Fourteen-thirty hours," Katie confirmed. "I'm all packed to go. Going to have lunch with Calvin and then I'm off."

"Well, we won't keep you," her mother said. "Love, dear."

"Love, Katie," her father echoed.

"Love, Mom. Love, Dad," Katie replied.

And they broke the connection.

\* \* \*

Lunchtime. It'd be Calvin's last lunch with Katie for years, he suspected.

She was going to be buying the burgers, fries, and milkshake to share this time. The *"just like in an Earth diner"* milkshake. Calvin liked them, even though Katie thought it was some sort of snotty scam.

It occurred to Calvin that Katie would soon have the chance to see what a real Earth milkshake made from real, fresh cow's milk was like. He'd have to remember to ask her to write and tell him what they were like.

Calvin would've also liked to have asked her how things were going with her parents. He didn't quite dare. He wasn't clear on the details of the chicanery she'd gotten up to in her efforts to expose Guy Boucher's smuggling. But he had a feeling she'd abused her power over the *Dawn Threader*'s accounts. If so, her parents had forgiven her. Forgiven her to the extent of allowing her the funds to pay for the meal they were about to have. And to the extent of paying for her trip to Earth and her stay there prior to reporting to the Academy.

Calvin's parents had never said as much, but he knew they thought Katie's parents' hands off approach to raising Katie had verged on neglect. All the same, it was obvious they loved her and were willing to do all they could for her.

That was good.

He would miss her. Here Katie was going off to her future as an independent person, and he'd never given the issue of what he planned to do as an adult serious thought. He guessed he'd been thinking he'd hitch his wagon to Katie's, and follow her where ever she went. Hadn't thought that through. That wasn't happening. Oddly, he felt a sense of relief.

It seemed harsh to think it explicitly, but he figured now that friends, family, and loved ones would always take second place in Katie's life. Second place to whatever mission she thought she was on.

It wasn't that she was a bad person. It was that she had priorities.

He wouldn't bring it with up her, but she was leaving her parents somewhat in the lurch. The two of them couldn't keep running the *Dawn Threader* on their own. He'd have to talk to his folks about it. Maybe he could talk the Kincaids into giving him an internship as a crew member or something. Him and one or two of his sisters, perhaps. That way it wouldn't be like they were hiring strangers as crew.

It was a whole new world, and he had a lot of thinking to do.

He was still grappling with the enormity of it all when Katie appeared.

"Hi!" She gave him a big grin as she sat down. "The works?"

Calvin grinned back. It didn't take that much effort. "Sure. Bacon cheeseburger, large fries, and a large chocolate milkshake to share."

"Sounds great." She waved the waitress over. In contrast to the last time they'd been here, the waitress appeared without significant delay and wearing a warm smile.

Once they'd ordered Katie looked at Calvin. "Wow. It's really happening."

"Don't imagine you'll be getting back often," Calvin said.

Katie made an effort to look sad. She was too excited to make it convincing. "Nope, Space Force will reimburse us all the costs of my travel to the Academy. Heck, all the costs of my outfitting even. There's a chance they'll even pay for my acclimatization period. But not trips home, even if there was time." She paused.

Calvin took the opportunity to get a word in edge-wise. With Katie wound up, he wasn't going to get many of them. "That's very generous all the same."

Katie shook her head slowly, like she was baffled or annoyed or both. "It is. Isn't such a big expense for most candidates, and to be frank, most of them are well enough off to afford it anyways. Only I guess from what the Commander has said the Academy wants it to look like it's open to every one equally even if they're not well off or live out in the boonies." She frowned. "Politics," she said with disgust.

Calvin had never been much interested in politics himself. His parents made a point of discussing them, both the general civic kind and the office politics kind, at the dinner table. They said being a responsible adult meant paying attention to politics. Paying attention and considering them even if you didn't actively engage in them. Guess it was getting to be the time both he and Katie needed to start paying attention. "They're part of life," he said.

"Yeah, and if I want to make a difference, I know I'll have to get involved," Katie said. "At least as a cadet and junior officer I'm supposed to look apolitical. From what the Commander says, I' have to start paying attention right away because I have a lot of catching up to do. Guess politics is like cleaning the sanitary facilities, it needs to be done, but it's not clean or pleasant."

"A fine topic for the dinner table," Calvin said deadpan.

Katie giggled. Calvin thought he could maybe count the number of times he'd seen Katie giggle on one hand. "Like sports, I guess. Everyone has a team, and there's lots of complex detail to argue about. Oh, Calvin, I don't know anything about Earth sports and I'm told everybody has to participate in them at the Academy. I was so focused on getting in I never thought about what it would involve."

"Not much zero-Gee racquetball on Earth, I guess."

Katie looked blank as she considered the issue. "Nope, swimming, football, basketball, and track and field mostly, I think."

"I'd give that some thought," Calvin said.

Their food came at that point and the conversation languished as they both ate and considered the enormity of what Katie faced.

After they were down to the milkshake they were sharing, Calvin was the first to speak. "You're going to be incredibly busy, if not completely overwhelmed," he said.

"Looks that way," Katie agreed. "I'll make a point of staying in touch. Short messages periodically, at least. You do the same."

"I will."

"Good."

"I'll keep an eye on your parents, too. Don't imagine they'll be willing to tell you if it gets rough for them."

Katie grew solemn. "Nope, Pollyanna's their role model. Worries me. Appreciate it."

"Maybe me and some of my sister's will beg them for an apprenticeship. Sell it like they're doing us a favor. Truthfully, they would be even though they need the help too."

"I hope that works out." Katie sighed. "I don't want them running my life. I don't want to run their lives. I do worry."

Calvin knew altogether too well that Katie would make hard choices in order to pursue what she thought was important. He refrained from pointing that out. "You have plans to do something with your life that requires going away," he said. "We all understand that. We all wish you the best."

Katie smiled sadly. "Thanks, Calvin, you're a great friend."

"I try."

The milkshake was gone. The waitress came, and Katie paid the bill. She didn't have that long before she needed to board her transport, *The Solar Star*. She didn't want to be late. "Guess that's it," she said, standing.

Calvin stood too and took a step towards her. She gave him a hard, sharp hug.

"Miss you," she said.

"You, too," he answered.

And with that she turned and left.

\* \* \*

They were finally on their way.

Katie had mixed feelings.

They were leaving Ceres. As much as the *Dawn Threader*, Ceres had been Katie's home. Not one she'd liked much, but still home. The place she knew. The place she had understood after a fashion. The place she was now leaving and wasn't going to see again for years, if ever.

The dining room and lounge of *The Solar Star* was a beautiful space. Clean and bright, it was capable of masquerading as any number of things it wasn't.

A metaphor for much of life, Katie couldn't help thinking. She'd thought she'd understood Ceres well enough. As well as she understood the maintenance routines and safety protocols on the *Dawn Threader*.

She'd been wrong. Her lack of understanding had almost cost her her life a couple of times. Almost cost her her chance of going to the Academy several more times. Now that she had time to think back on it, she was appalled.

There had to be a lesson or lessons to be learned. She'd thought there was one right of thinking about things. One reality, that once you understood it, you could manipulate at will. Only it turned out everybody had their own reality that they only partly shared with others.

The lovely, pleasant space she was now sitting in while watching Ceres dwindle in size was a good illustration of that fact.

Most of the *Solar Star*'s passengers were earth-born bureaucrats of some stripe, and their families. They'd call the sides of the lounge walls, a ceiling, and a floor. Not port side, starboard side, aft, forward, top, and bottom side like a spacer would. Certainly not the bulkheads, deckhead, and deck labels that an old-time sailor, of the sort Katie so liked to read about, would have used.

For the lives they lived, each point of view made sense.

As did taking the illusion the "wall-sized" screens on those sides projected at face value did. The screens could and would project cityscapes and great natural views from Earth, but right now they were projecting the illusion of being in an observation lounge in a spaceship steadily pulling away from Ceres.

Not entirely inaccurate.

Not if you were willing to overlook the minor facts that *The Solar Star* had no large transparent viewports in its hull and that the whole lounge was spinning around the central axis of the ship. This last being necessary to the illusion of there being gravity in space.

The idea that what was illusion and what was true was relative and depended on who you were, and your circumstances was not one Katie was comfortable with. She was well educated enough to know theoretical physicists might disagree with her, but as far as Katie was concerned there was a real world. Not one where everything relative and everything depended on who was observing it and where from.

Only it was glaringly obvious she needed to do more by way of taking different points of view into consideration.

She'd unintentionally hurt the people who loved her the most. Her parents for sure, and she still worried about them, but Calvin too. Maybe Sam also, but mainly she suspected she'd frustrated him with her obtuseness. Not much better.

It would have helped to have better understood even the people neutral towards or hostile to her. She'd wrecked the lives of the crew of the *Sand Piper*. Was that fair? She didn't know. However, she'd not even considered hinting to them they needed to be more careful or putting off making accusations of smuggling until after her return and further investigation. She'd leaped to doing what she was convinced was right without any consideration of all the consequences.

The Commander she'd paid a bit more attention to because she'd realized she needed his endorsement. She wasn't sure, but she suspected she could have done better with him. If nothing else, she might have learned something by trying to understand him better.

If she'd made a better effort to understand Billy and his dad she might have sensed something was up with them much sooner. Even bad people aren't just machines you pull levers on.

So, yeah, it'd worked out. Mostly. It could have gone better.

She was on her way to Earth and the Academy.

It was the first step in a long journey she'd planned out for herself.

It'd been a bigger, much more awkward step than she'd planned on.

Wasn't likely the rest of the steps on the trip were going to be any easier. She needed to learn all the lessons she could.

She also needed to look forward. Much of what she'd known so far wasn't going to apply on Earth or at the Academy.

It was going to be a long journey.

But she was on her way.

If you enjoyed this novel, please leave a review.

To be notified of future releases visit my website at
http://www.napoleonsims.com/publishing

# Appendix A:
# Scout Courier Operations

Scout Couriers are each supposed to have three crews assigned which take turns deploying.

Due to the restricted quarters and lack of sustained gravity each crew gets one day leave for each day of deployment, this is in addition to time spent on "shore" tasks like training, courses, admin, mission planning, debriefings, base duties, and maintenance. Crews spend well less than half of their time deployed and usually less than a third of it. Deployments for scouting range from around a week to three weeks. Courier runs are much more variable running from less than a day to up to over three months if there's a need to make one to an outer system location.

Each crew has five members, two watches consisting of a pilot and tech officer, and a captain (by position the slot normally being filled by a crew member with the rank of senior lieutenant)

Watches are twelve hours on and twelve hours off with two person watches (1 pilot and 1 tech officer), the captain's schedule is floating.

Everybody is required to spend one hour a day in the exercise pods which they do at two standard times a day normally (usually ongoing watch exercises during last hour of off coming watch) due to the hassle that deploying the exercise pods represents.

Eight hours of sleep (in tube) is mandatory. The remaining 180 minutes in the day is split into roughly 45 minute sections. Main meal (dinner; lunch is eaten on watch), personal time, bed prep time (use facilities, wash, change clothes), and after sleep time, morning prep (toiletries, dress, breakfast)

Note: the Captain's routine is a little more flexible he/she floats monitoring the other crew, and taking up any slack their tight schedules don't allow for.

Despite the tight schedule the actual watches tend to be extremely boring particularly for the pilots and it's a constant challenge for the captains to keep crew engaged and alert.

Note this is a much higher manning level and more stringent routine than that followed by civilian ships. Also most Space Force officers are Earth, or at least Mars, born, unlike civilian spacers who tend to be born to spacer or Belt families.

# Appendix B:
# The Sand Piper, a Bird Class Scout Courier

## Crew:

Has a five person crew (captain, two pilots, two sensor/comms/weapons/engineering officers)

Has room for additional two passengers in two sleeping tubes with toilet tube and wash tube.

No grossly fat or even just large people need apply, tubes are too constricting just under meter diameter

Captain gets dedicated toilet & wash, plus, "office" tube.

## Layout:

Approx 22 meters long

3 meter "bridge section" with stations for all 5 crew plus one passenger/supernumerary station.
Bridge is special section (like snake head with transparent nose) ahead of main hull spindle

Main hull spindle is 16 meters long, has the shape of a cylinder with an octagonal cross section,
and has an 8 meter outer diameter and an 2 1/2 meter internal one,

Main hull contains:
3 meter living and utility section, weighted table and bench section can accommodate 4 persons at a time
Main air lock, emergency and EVA gear storage, Meal prep station, beverage prep station, meal storage bin, Access to rail gun interior portion and rail gun ammo storage bin.

Five meter cabin equivalents section. 3 cabin eqv consist of a pair of sleeping tubes, toilet tube, and wash tube, plus some minimal storage for clothing and personal effects, 1 cabin eqv for captain has only one sleeping tube plus an "office" tube.

Two meter exercise pod access and internal air lock section lies aft.

Hull outside of living and cabin sections is bare except for antennas, sensors and maneuvering jets, and two exercise pods on cable containing booms that extend from 4 m to 8 m. Total radius for centrifugal boom is 24 m.

External fuel tanks aft of exercise pod section add two meters to girth of ship there.

Immediately aft of the exercise pod section there is 3 meters of storage for cargo when operating as courier.

Finally there is an airtight door and 3 meters of engineering space, consisting of control panels, accesses to ship's machinery, auxiliary machinery, and storage for spare parts and consumables. This is the last section within the main hull spindle.

Attached to the aft of the spindle are the main engines, consisting of five anti-matter catalyzed fusion engines. They're mounted in a rectangular box like mounting structure with nozzles this takes up another 3 meters.

| | | |
|---|---|---|
| Bridge | 3 m | 3 m |
| Living | 3 m | 6 m |
| Cabins | 5 m | 11 m |
| Ex Pod | 2 m | 13 m |
| Stores | 3 m | 16 m |
| Engineering | 3 m | 19 m |
| Engine | 3 m | 22 m |

Note the gear is located by number of meters aft of bridge and side. Each octagonal side is numbered from 0 to 7 counter clock wise looking forward.

Each side is also named

0 - bottom "notionally the floor" marked with black rubber. Aligned with bridge deck.

1 - starboard lower side

2 - starboard middle side

3 - starboard upper side

4 - top side

5 - port upper side

6 - port middle side

7 - port lower side.

Damage control stations:

#1 - 1 meters aft on side 7, port lower side (fwd utility on port between airlock and bridge)

#2 - 11 meters aft on side 6, port middle side (after part cabins on port)

#3 - 16 meters aft on side 2, stbd middle side (after part cargo on starboard)

## Weapons

Actually weapon, a single axis 12mm railgun mounted below bridge and utility section. Ammo bin and internal parts of mechanism are accessed via a panel in the "bottom" of the utility section.

The rail gun has some limited traversal but basically is hard mounted to point straight ahead. The entire ship must be pointed to aim it.

# Time

Ceres and the Space Force keep the same time. They use the 24 hour clock and Zulu a.k.a. UTC a.k.a. Greenwich Mean Time. Same time as London, England, on Earth with no daylight savings adjustments.

## Special watch system with Katie Present:

| Blue Sensor Watch | LTJG Kevin Wong | 0700 - 1500 |
| --- | --- | --- |
| First Exercise Period | Gregorian, McLeod, Kincaid | 0700 - 0800 |
| Starboard Pilot Watch | LTJG Iris Gregorian | 0800 - 2000 |
| White Sensor Watch | SLT Timothy McLeod | 1500 - 2300 |
| Second Exercise Period | Romanov, Wong, Anderson | 1900 - 2000 |
| Port Pilot Watch | LTJG Samuel Romanov | 2000 - 0800 |
| Red Sensor Watch | Katherine Kincaid | 2300 - 0700 |

Meals are catch as catch can, however, the general pattern was to eat substantially at the beginning and end of watches and to be relieved for a short break mid - watch for lunch or a snack.

The dining table only sits four anyways. Generally the off watch crew would gather for meals around the following times: 0600-0700, 1130-1230, 1600-1700, and 1900-2000.

Meals are pre-prepared as a snack, lunch, breakfast and supper per day. They're warmed up mostly at the meal preparation station which amounts to a glorified zero gee microwave with some add-ons like a spigot for boiling hot water, a waste station for packaging and some condiment and utensil dispensers.

The nearby beverage preparation station is in turn a glorified zero gee coffee boat, though you can get tea, hot chocolate, juice and milk as well.

Individual crew order ear-marked meals prior to deployment to suit their personal tastes.